KANINE PARKER

THE HELMCOTT CHRONICLES
SHADOW'S EDGE

Windstorm Publishing

Copyright © 2024 by Kanine Parker
All rights reserved.

No part of this book may be reproduced or transmitted in any form or by any means, electronic or mechanical, including photocopying, recording, or by any information storage and retrieval system, without written permission from the author.

NOTE: This is a work of fiction. Names, characters, places, and incidents either are the product of the author's imagination or are used fictitiously, and any resemblance to actual persons, living or dead, business establishments, events, or locales is entirely coincidental. The scanning, uploading, and distribution of this book via the internet or via any other means without the permission of the author is illegal and punishable by law. Please purchase only authorized electronic editions, and do not participate in or encourage electronic piracy of copyrighted materials.

Your support of the author's rights is appreciated.

For more information on the author's books, including specials and sales; and for info about signings, appearances, and media, check us out online.

This book is dedicated to

My mom and dad- they taught me what it means
to have worthwhile goals, and how to achieve them.

K. P.

CONTENTS

Chapter 1 .... *1*
Chapter 2 .... *14*
Chapter 3 .... *27*
Chapter 4 .... *35*
Chapter 5 .... *46*
Chapter 6 .... *56*
Chapter 7 .... *71*
Chapter 8 .... *84*
Chapter 9 .... *105*
Chapter 10 .... *123*
Chapter 11 .... *142*
Chapter 12 .... *160*
Chapter 13 .... *183*
Acknowledgements *191*
Meet the Author *193*

Summer, 2076

CHAPTER 1

Annika crouched just in time, avoiding the laser zooming towards her head. This was only one of the many she had just as narrowly avoided. She was perched on a wobbly wooden box inside a steel-lined room; one that she visited often. She eyed one of the sweeping lasers nearing her. The only way to avoid it would be to leap two feet to her right and up seven feet onto a 6-inch-wide beam. She steadied herself, and two seconds later she leapt, clearing the jump and grasping for the metal beam. She dangled precariously for a few frightening seconds, then swung her petite, flexible body onto the beam. The floor was covered in an intricate pattern of lasers and traps, both which were dangerous. Attempting to navigate them would be futile. Eight feet away sat the exit door with a keypad. If only she could reach that door… Annika took a deep breath and, at a painfully slow pace, slid herself along the beam, sweating from the effort. The far corner of her eye noticed something rapidly advancing. Annika flipped herself upside down and released her leg hold on the beam, so she was now hanging. A laser swooped past where she had just been; had she remained there a moment longer, she would be crumpled on the ground. She was now hanging by 8 fingers, her sweaty hands struggling to find traction on the slippery steel beam. To her dismay, she started to slip, unable to keep her feeble grip. She glanced down, looking for an option, and saw a large wooden box beneath her. Unfortunately, there was a laser approaching the box, and landing on it would not end well. The last of her finger strength gave out, and Annika plummeted. She angled herself to land lightly- she did not want to break the box. Landing in a spider-man-like pose, she then flattened herself, pressing closely to the box as speedily and smoothly as possible. Her feet drooped dangerously close to the floor. The laser sailed past her head, missing it by mere inches. Annika let out a shaky breath. When she had requested this level be harder, she wasn't imagining it quite so difficult!

Only a few feet away sat the door. Ohh, that beautiful door. Annika hopped over two lasers and approached the panel. Having no code, she spun and kicked the panel as hard as she could. It erupted into sparks and the door slid open. She had timed it perfectly; the two guards on the other side were struck down in the face by lasers sweeping past, effectively knocking them unconscious. Annika strode out, feeling pleased – Oh! She slammed herself to the wall as an unanticipated guard shot his laser rifle at her. The energy was mostly stopped with her high-tech jumpsuit, only leaving a small graze in the fabric. Harder? Definitely. As the guard came nearer, she shot out her leg and kicked the weapon out of his hand. He stumbled backwards, clutching his hand in pain. She struck again with that wicked leg of hers, catching her attacker square in the chest and knocking him to the ground. She kicked his weapon away and stepped over him. Mid stride, he grabbed her leg, causing her to stumble and fall. As she tried to roll away, the two struggled for only a moment before she caught hold of his hand and wrenched it behind him. The guard howled in pain. A moment later, another stray laser struck him through the empty doorway, knocking him unconscious. Annika released him, then ran off down the hall.

Tired, and a bit bruised, Annika tried to locate the exit. There were so many turns! Breathing heavily, she stopped for a moment to rest. Everything was quiet- and then it wasn't. Annika's ears detected voices- five of them. She was trapped. With guards behind and in front of her, she had nowhere to go; except up. Her eyes flicked to the ceiling. Nothing. Annika changed directions and began jogging back to where she just came from. Her blue eyes frantically scanned the walls and ceiling for exits. Her gaze passed over an irregularity in the wall. A large ventilation shaft was jutting out of it. Annika stared at it in disbelief. How did she miss that?

The approaching voices reminded her she needed to hurry. Reaching up, she pulled on the grate. It easily dislodged and fell towards the floor. In her panic to make sure it didn't make a noise, she thrust her arm out, and the grate tumbled on to it. The noise was muffled, but left the 15-year-old with a painful deep scratch just above where the sleeve of her jumpsuit ended. She carefully picked up the grate and wiped her blood off the floor. Annika hastily boosted herself into the shaft. She hooked her legs into the vent divots and leaned out, seizing the grate and hauling it up. She quietly secured it in place and breathed a sigh of relief when it held firm. She turned to view her surroundings. Her head grazed the top of the shaft. It was dusty and grimy, but her only real concern was infecting her wound. Getting on her hands and knees, Annika quickly crawled through the shaft until she came to another grate. Peering through the slits, she saw two people. The woman held a remote that controlled the giant stopwatch mounted on the wall. It was, at the moment, out of Annika's line of sight. They were the LaserTrainer timekeepers, Ike and Vanessa. She calculated that where they were standing, she could safely kick the grate out without it hitting them. She squeezed into a U-turn, and kicked hard, smiling inwardly at their startled gasps. She lowered herself out of the shaft and dropped down. "Stop." Annika called out as she turned to face them. Vanessa hit the stop button, and both she and Ike gawked at the time it showed. It made Annika nervous until she saw the clock too. The clock read 12:52 minutes. Annika tried not to groan. *That's a great score.* She inwardly scolded herself. *You're too much of an over achiever. That's now probably their new fastest time.* She was correct. "H-how did you do that so fast!" Ike spluttered. Vanessa instantly agreed. "We added a whole new defense layer! More lasers, more guards, a hidden exit. How are you so fast? That should have been hard, even for you!" They genuinely wanted an answer. Annika's only response was "Hard? Nah. Try to up your game next time." She gave her signature smirk and walked towards the door, making sure her wrist wasn't revealing her injury. It had stopped bleeding, and didn't hurt very much anymore. She left the building without another word; she had somewhere to be.

Once outside, Annika breathed a sigh of relief in the crisp evening air. She relished a good challenge; however, she was not a fan of looking weak. She suffered too much on the inside to look weak on the outside. Annika checked her wristwatch. If she was to arrive to her destination on time, she had to hurry. She broke into a jog down the alleyway. That was where the laser training was located, so it was partially hidden. The low-key business enjoyed training the local teens in laser parkour. Annika loved jogging. She went just the right pace to see the scenery but not get chilly. Glancing at her watch, she realized her meeting was in eight minutes, and at this pace it would take fifteen to get there. Annika broke into a run, enjoying the feel of her waist length red hair streaming behind her. She was very agile, and had worked hard to become a good athlete. This was one of those times where it paid off. After running for a while, she was stopped by an unanticipated thing. Traffic. Annika restlessly looked at her watch again. She had three minutes, and she would not make it on time if she had to wait for cars. Perhaps, she decided, it was time to do her favorite thing in the whole world. Annika climbed up the steel ladder on the side of her local department store. The rungs were rusty and old. She stepped lightly on them, hoping the rungs wouldn't break. The top of the building was about 33 feet tall. A fall could be fatal, but Annika wasn't afraid. She approached the edge of the building and observed her destination. Her location was four buildings over, and this route would get her there on time. Annika estimated there was an eighteen-foot gap between them all, and she knew the last building had a ladder that would deposit her only eight feet away from her destination. Annika backed up for a running start. She hoped there were people below her. Twice she had gotten a color picture of her jumping a gap between buildings in the newspaper. She wasn't sure who took them, but they were awesome to see. Annika sprinted for the edge, building up speed, and leapt. There was a split second she was suspended in midair, then was hurtling down on the other side. Annika rolled out of the jump and sprinted again, enjoying the thrill of the midair suspense. She cleared the jumps in a matter of seconds, then slid down the ladder on the last building. She breathlessly jogged to the front of her destination and looked at her watch once more, watching it tick to 6:30 on the dot. Annika smiled, and pushed open the door to El Grande Restaurante, the best Mexican restaurant in town.

As Annika stepped inside, the smells of delicious food wafted over her, making her stomach grumble hungrily after her earlier exertion. While moving to her regular table, she became aware of being watched, as a dirty, red-haired girl in a semi-expensive restaurant stuck out. There was a man and a teenage girl sitting at her normal table, laughing about a joke that had been made. The man noticed her approach and looked up. "Annika." He greeted her. She walked over and took an empty seat. "You're right on time." He said with a smile. Annika grinned back. "Come on, Dad. This table has been our meeting place for five months now. Have I ever been late?" "No, you haven't." He laughed. "I already ordered. It should be here soon." Annika thanked him and turned towards the girl. "Hi, Ivy!" She greeted her friend. "Hi!" Ivy answered. "You'll *never* guess what happened in laser training today!" Ivy blurted it with so much enthusiasm she looked like she would explode. Her brown eyes were twinkling with excitement, and her long brown bangs fluttered about her face as she spoke. "You actually passed?" Annika guessed. "Nope! I completely FAILED!" Annika laughed in disbelief. "How?" Ivy began what sounded like a well-rehearsed story. "The second I walked in, I realized I'd forgotten something in the lobby. When I turned around to bang on the door, a laser got my legs, and it activated a bunch of alarms! I'm lucky I was wearing pants." Annika listened with wide eyes. Ivy eagerly continued. "The alarms were blaring and flashing, and when they didn't shut off, I just ran the rest of the way to the door on the other side." Annika gaped at her friend, unable to hide her surprise. *Who does that? It goes against the entire point of laser training!* Annika thought. "I kicked the door panel to break it using that special move you taught me, but I think I did it wrong because I bruised my foot. It still hurts. But it worked! The door slid open and I rushed out, but I was caught by 8 guards! I don't know what happened. There used to be two!" She complained. Annika stifled back laughter. It was obvious the alarms had summoned them. Ivy misinterpreted the muffled laugh as a sympathetic noise and became more dramatic. "They hauled me down a hallway with a bunch of turns. Every time I tried to escape another one caught me. I went limp and decided to stay limp until they released their tight hold, and it worked! I wrenched free and bolted back where I came from. I heard them yelling something, but I ignored them. I came back to the laser room and found a giant ventilation shaft. Somehow, I missed it, but I'm sure you saw it immediately. I reached up and pulled the cover grate off. It toppled onto me. Did you know the edges are sharp? I pulled myself into the shaft and I crawled and crawled and crawled! I was moving really fast with my eyes closed because of the cobwebs. I ended up crashing into the other side, and what do you know; the other grate was loose too! There's nothing like the sensation of crawling super fast, crashing your nose into a sharp grate, and then falling 6 feet onto your already pained face. I ended up with a bloody nose." Ivy lightly touched her nose. Annika realized it was a bit swollen looking. "Oh my gosh, Ivy. That's rough!" She sympathized. Ivy grinned. "You want to hear the rest?" Annika nodded, unable to help herself. "There I was, lying flat on my face yelling 'Stop the time! Stop the time!' Ike and Vanessa helped me stand up, and were like 'you already lost' and I was like 'I know.' then I walked out and met your dad here. My time was 4:23 minutes." Ivy finished with a smile, leaning proudly back in her chair, tipping it back. "No, don't!" Annika cried out, but it was too late. Ivy crashed backwards with a startled yelp. The table behind her toppled backwards, sending many chairs all over the place. Ivy smacked the back of her head on one of the chairs, her body splayed over the seats. Groaning, she picked herself up and tried to pick the table up. Everyone was staring at her while she grunted and strained. Embarrassed, Ivy tried harder, but it was all in vain. Annika, used to these types of things happening, got up and went over to her friend, easily turning the table right way up and putting the chairs into their places. The girls cleaned up the silverware on the ground and put everything into place before returning to their seats. In an attempt to distract them from her incident, Ivy called out "Hey, Rachel and Matthew are here!" Two blonde teenagers had just entered the restaurant, and Ivy waved to them as they approached. Annika pulled out two chairs for them when they got closer. "Hi Annika, Ivy." Rachel greeted, taking a seat next to Annika and flipping her hair out of her face. Matthew took the last chair next to Rachel. "Hello." They replied cheerfully back. "Guess what happened in laser training today?" Ivy eagerly said. "What?" Rachel asked, knowing it would be hilarious no matter what. Ivy began a retell of her story, now that she had new ears to tell it to. Seeing they were distracted, Mr. Helmcott beckoned his daughter closer. "Let's talk." He whispered quietly in Greek. Greek was their special language they used to talk privately, only learning it to annoy Annika's sister Amelia when all she talked about was how excited she was for college. Annika answered in Greek, letting her friends' voices fade away into the background. "About what?" "How was laser practice today?" He questioned. "Fun." "Was it hard?" Annika scoffed at the thought. "No." He studied her face. "You're bluffing." She stared back calmly. "Why do you say that?" He smiled. "I watched you on the cameras. You sweat quite a lot." She froze. "That's not true." His smile turned smug. "I don't know how you held onto that steel beam. It was quite a save." "How could you possibly know about that?" She demanded angrily. He spread his hands outward. "On the cameras." He repeated. "There aren't any." She protested. Her father smirked. "Multiple angles. Makes for a very interesting show every time. Meaning I've seen all your previous levels as well." Annika gritted her teeth in frustration. "I specified no cameras." Her father frowned at his daughter. "Do you really think I would let you go in there without some way to monitor you?" He pointed out. Annika sighed. "It's not dangerous!" She argued. "You know the lasers will knock you unconscious if they hit your skin. How else could you have taken down those guards? It was pure luck Ivy wasn't hit by a stray laser!" "Is all of Ivy's story true?" Annika asked skeptically. "100%." Her dad confirmed. "But you would've fallen a long way had that laser gotten you." He continued. "It absolutely *is* dangerous." She held her arms out for him to see. "The only bare skin I have is my hands and my head!" "What are you trying to prove?" He replied pointedly, leaning back in his chair. Annika didn't know. She heard

Ivy and Rachel in the background, laughing about whatever joke had been told. Matthew was still silent, but was smiling. Annika decided to change the subject, but her dad wasn't finished. "Why do you tell your friends there is no challenge when there is? I understand you're really good at it- you've never hit a laser in any of the 100+ level's you've done. But some **are** hard for you. You relish a good challenge, Annika. So why do you just smirk or laugh and say 'Challenge? Nah.' I mean it! Your friends think so highly of you, but nobody's perfect." "The levels were easy." Annika admitted. "The first 80 or so were no challenge at all for me. Ivy, Rachel, and Matthew would tell stories of close calls, or setting the alarms off, and when they asked me, I told them the truth. There wasn't any challenge. It impressed them. Ivy enjoys bragging to the other laser trainers about how I've never touched a single laser. Their looks of admiration made me feel-" She hesitated, searching for the right word. "Special. Then they got harder. There was more thrill, more intensity. I just kept saying the same thing. I felt if my record fell, people would think less of me." Her dad patted her hand with a knowing smile. "You sound just like me when I was your age." He chuckled. "But that's a story that can wait for another time. Annika, when you speak of your challenges good naturedly, they seem more impressive. Look at Ivy! Don't you notice how excitedly she tells her tale? How she acts like everything that went wrong is the most awesome thing in the world? Matthew and Rachel don't move on until they pass the level. Ivy usually tries the same level as you. She's like, 'how did you pass? I failed in three seconds!' You're right- your friends are impressed with you. But they would be more impressed if you talked like Ivy." "Incessantly?" Annika guessed. Her dad laughed. "She does do that." He agreed. "But no. Ivy laughs it off. She loves to tell of her latest fails keeping up with you. She enjoys the attention, and you, Rachel, and Matthew enjoy the stories." "She wouldn't if they were real." Annika pointed out. He sighed. "Annika, you're missing the point. You don't have to be perfect. Right now, if you happen to fail, people will wonder how the mighty Annika went from champion to average overnight. But, if you open up about your struggles and triumphs, your friends will admire your tenacity more than just your skills. We all know you're tough on the outside, but you're human on the inside. Sometimes I think your thick shell started when your mom died." He added quietly. Annika's face tightened with remorse. "Maybe it did. Because then people don't think something's wrong in my perfect life. Nobody asks or wonders where my mom is when I keep them busy. It wasn't fair for eleven-year-old me to leave on an oversea field trip and come back to find Amelia had already left for college and mom was dead." This was not supposed to come out in public, especially with her friends so close. No, she did not want them to know about this. She couldn't live with their sympathetic looks or attempts to protect her. Annika struggled to compose herself before her friends noticed, but it was too late; out of the corner of her eye she saw Matthew watching her worriedly. He didn't know what they were saying, but she looked upset, so it had to be something personal. Well, if someone had to notice, at least it was Matthew. She could rely on the fact he wouldn't tell anyone. Annika slightly shook her head at him, and he turned back and asked Ivy a question to keep her talking. Annika faced her dad again, and realized he had watched the exchange. "You chose good friends." Her father said quietly. "Don't lose them or say things you don't mean that will lose their trust in you. Good friends are hard to get." Annika nodded. "I know." "Food's here!" Ivy cried out. Annika and her dad looked up to see a waiter carrying plates of steaming food. He set the food on the table, apologizing about the long wait. Mr. Helmcott paid the bill, and the waiter left. Annika's stomach flared with a sudden growl of hunger, causing everyone at her table to stare at her in surprise. She gave a sheepish grin and dug in. The aroma cheered her up. There was nothing like eating Mexican food to raise spirits. Ivy and Rachel started up a lively conversation with lots of laughter, which increased when Ivy tried to say something with her mouth full and her food fell into her cup. Annika mostly listened while shoveling her enchiladas into her mouth, eventually zoning out like she usually did. *I am so lucky.* Annika thought to herself, gazing around the table. Yes, some parts of her life sucked, but she was so blessed. Three great friends, a great dad, a great life. She wasn't poor, hungry, lonely, or bullied. Her father worked hard to provide for her, and she got to do many things most people never did. How many other people got to jump rooftops or do laser training? Not a lot. Someone nudged her shoulder, taking her out of her semi-trance. "Hmm?" Annika asked, a bit startled. "I asked what you thought about my achievement." Rachel laughed. "Oh." Annika blushed. "I wasn't listening. Sorry." Rachel smiled in understanding. "That's alright. I passed level 20 in laser training!" Annika brightened. "That's awesome! Great job." "Thanks. I had a close call and nearly set the alarms off." Rachel nudged Matthew. "Tell them how you did." She urged. Matthew shook his head. "Can I?" Rachel prompted hopefully. He shrugged, so Rachel took it as a yes. "He passed level 32 today." She began, and applause rang out. Matthew dipped his head respectfully but said nothing, though his raised eyebrow at their enthusiasm was comical. Rachel told their group of how he expertly dodged the moving lasers by practically dancing through them. Mr. Helmcott, Ivy, and Annika stared at him in surprise. "Matthew? Dancing? Now that I wish I'd seen." Annika teased. "It was epic! The way he maneuvered around them, while dodging the higher ones was incredible!" Rachel cried. "It wasn't that awesome." Matthew muttered, embarrassed by his friends' enthusiastic painting. Rachel chose to ignore his comment and went on telling extravagantly how he beat it. Matthew leaned back in his chair, locked eyes with Annika, and did the universal sign for crazy behind Rachel's back. Annika giggled. Rachel heard it and turned towards Annika. "What? It's true." She said, confused. Rachel was referring to the story she was telling, but to Annika it seemed like she was confirming his silent accusation. Annika shook her head, holding back the laughter that tried to escape. "Oh, nothing. Please continue." Rachel gave her a suspicious look, but turned back to face Ivy and Mr. Helmcott and started up where she left off. Once again, Matthew leaned back slightly, made sure Annika was looking, and rolled his eyes. Annika laughed again, and Rachel whirled around to glare at her. Matthew and Annika shot up rigidly and avoided looking at each other. Rachel focused on Annika, a slight frown on her face. "What is so funny?" She demanded. "Hmm?" Annika asked, feigning ignorance, and fidgeting with her hair. Rachel refused to give up so easily this time. "Why do you keep laughing?" Annika tried to think of a reason that wouldn't expose Matthew. "Um." Was all she managed. Rachel sighed. "You weren't even paying attention." She complained. "Yes I was!" Annika cried out in defense. Rachel narrowed her eyes. "Ok then. What was I specifically talking about before you interrupted me?" She challenged. Annika couldn't think of anything. She noticed Ivy trying to mouth something, but even with squinting it did not make sense. "Fried potatoes... on a submarine?" She guessed. Rachel, Matthew, and her dad gave her weird looks. Ivy chose to drop her head onto the table with a loud THUNK and immediately jerked it up, rubbing her head in pain. After having gotten over their initial surprise, Rachel sighed, Matthew did his best to keep a smile off his face, and her dad smirked. Annika sighed as well. "You're right. I wasn't paying attention. Sorry." She admitted, inwardly wondering why she didn't say so in the beginning. "Don't say sorry to me! Say sorry to Matthew." Rachel insisted. Annika did her best to keep a smile off her face as she turned to Matthew. Rachel had made this too easy. "Sorry Matthew." He was in much better control of his emotions this time, and gave one slow, silent nod of acceptance. "He doesn't even care." Annika threw out. "Yes, he does." Rachel protested, turning to face him. "Do you?" She asked hopefully. Matthew shook his head no. Rachel looked sad; then Ivy burst out laughing. Then Mr. Helmcott joined in. Finally, Rachel gave way, and the four of them were laughing. Matthew grinned, but didn't make a sound. It went as laughter goes; one calms down, looks at the others' faces, and cracks up again. When they finally all calmed down, leaving only smiles, Rachel turned to Annika again. "I'd like to finish. Will you please listen?" "Aye Aye." Annika saluted her friend. She really was going to listen; until she realized Matthew was trying to get her attention again. She leaned back to see what he wanted. "Sorry." He mouthed. Annika smiled and shook her head, indicating it didn't matter. She switched her focus back to Rachel, who was finishing up. "And down went the last two guards! Then he took their keys, unlocked the door, and stopped the time. It was only 16:31 minutes!" Annika reflected to her own time. If she was 96 levels ahead of him, and *still* got a better time, that had to mean something. Besides, the SIA wouldn't have hired her at 13 if her skills weren't exceptional. *You push too hard*. Part of her brain said. *I don't try hard enough!* The other part argued. "Hey Annika." Ivy said. "Yeah?" "We've all talked about our laser training today, except you." The comment drew the attention of the others. Annika automatically began to say the same reply she always gave, but stopped when she realized her dad was giving her a meaningful glance. *"Let them in."* His eyes seemed to say. "Uh." The one-word response made her friends lean in closer in anticipation. "You didn't... fail, did you?" Ivy whispered worriedly. "What?" Annika was surprised. How could that even cross Ivy's mind? *That just proves what your dad said*. A traitorous part of her own mind whispered. Annika had to admit he was right. "Of course not. But..." Their eyes widened. Annika struggled to get the next words out. Her mind was flashing terrifying scenes of her friends abandoning her. Her dad noticed and spoke up for her. "She *might* have had a close call." He piped up helpfully, knowing what was going through their minds. Annika? Not having an easy session? What! He was right. Their jaws dropped. "How close?" Rachel asked. Mr. Helmcott held his thumb and pointer finger about a centimeter apart, a near accurate representation of how close it had been. "What did she do?" Matthew asked. "She was laying on one of the ceiling beams and had to roll off sideways while holding on so she didn't fall." Her dad answered proudly. Annika's friends were agonizingly quiet as they tried to imagine what it looked like. "How did you even get up there?" Ivy asked, remembering how high up it was. "I... just jumped." Annika replied, becoming amazed with her day's feats. Rachel turned to Ivy. "Can you describe what the room looked like?" She asked hopefully. Ivy thought back to the room. Her memory wasn't as good as Matthew's, but she could remember it well and began to describe the room's layout. Annika tuned out, uninterested, but was pulled back to reality only a few minutes later. "Wha'?" Annika asked again. They smiled. "Your dad said he has something for us." Rachel helpfully updated her. Mr. Helmcott reached into a tote bag by his feet and pulled out two large white envelopes. There was no return address on either of them. One was addressed to Rachel Ravenstone, and the other to Annika Helmcott. "What are they?" A baffled Annika asked, taking the one addressed to her. He shrugged. "I don't know. They came in the mail this morning. Mrs. Ravenstone brought yours over, Rachel, and asked me to give it to you since she knew you were eating with us tonight." "Wow!" Rachel cried, completely ignoring him as she read the letter inside the envelope Mr. Helmcott had given her. "I was invited to be on *Survival Race!* That popular game show we love to watch!" Annika felt a bit betrayed. "You opened it already?" Rachel grinned. "What, did you think I was going to wait for you?" She laughed. "Yes." Annika indignantly replied. "Open yours." Rachel prompted. Annika didn't need to be asked again. She slid her finger under the flap and eased it open. There was a piece of white paper nestled inside. Annika tugged it out, unfolded it, and began to read. "Well?" Rachel asked expectantly. Annika grinned at her friend. "We're going to be on TV tomorrow morning." She announced to the table. They cheered. Since it was getting late, they all filed out of the restaurant and into Mr. Helmcott's Cybertruck to go home, talking about what they thought it would be like being on the famous game show.

CHAPTER 2

Rachel woke up feeling energized and excited, but it took her a moment to remember why. It wasn't her birthday. Or anyone's birthday, for that matter. She stood in the middle of her room and turned in a slow circle, in hopes to find a clue as to why she woke up so excited. Sure enough, a large white envelope sat on her nightstand. *I'm going to be on Survival Race!* She remembered. Rachel quickly dressed and barreled down the stairs to start breakfast for her family. It would be a long car drive, and she needed to have her chores done before Mr. Helmcott and Annika came to pick her up. She paused at the bottom of the stairs, which looked into the kitchen. Her mom, dad, and twin sisters Isabelle and Madeline were already seated around the table eating Rachel's favorite breakfast: Waffles with fruit. Her mom heard her and looked up. "Morning, Honey." She smiled. "Surprised?" Her mom asked her. Rachel was. Her parents hated getting up early. "Yeah." She replied, entering the kitchen and taking the empty seat. Her mom served her a pile of waffles, poured maple syrup on them, and pushed them towards her daughter. Rachel picked up her fork, scooped some berries onto her plate, and dug in. She grunted with pleasure, making her mom, Jessica, smile in satisfaction. "I'm glad you like them." Jessica told her daughter. Rachel finished swallowing a mouthful to respond. "These are amazing! Thank you so much. I really appreciate you guys making these so I didn't have to." She said appreciatively. "Are you really gonna be on TV?" 9-year-old Maddie asked her older sister with wide eyes. "Mmhmm." Rachel nodded, her mouth full. "I don't think it's live though. It might not be aired for a couple of weeks to a month." "How will we last so long without you?" Jessica joked good naturedly. "We'll keep an eye out for it." Rachel's dad promised. "We'll make sure we record the whole thing." Rachel smiled gratefully at her family. "Thanks." She checked the clock. "I'd better hurry with my chores. Mr. Helmcott will be here soon." Her mom stopped her. "Don't bother. We'll take care of it." Rachel was hesitant to agree. "Alright. Thank you." She relented. "I'm going to pack a car bag. Can you please let me know when they arrive?" "We will!" The twins called, running to the window. Rachel bounded up the stairs to her room and pulled her closet doors open. She selected her favorite bag and slipped two card games into it. After one more scan to make sure there wasn't anything else in there she wanted, she shut the doors and moved to her bed. Making sure no one was peeking through the doorway, she pulled a secret candy stash from under her bed and added it to her bag. She placed a small pillow on top to hide it, and put a notebook on top for extra security, then added her hairbrush just in case. Rachel surveyed her room one last time. Was she missing anything? "They're here!" Isabelle yelled. *Too late.* Rachel decided, snatching her phone from her nightstand. She jammed it into her bag and raced down the stairs. Mr. Helmcott's Cybertruck was just outside their house, and Annika was waving from an open door. Isabelle and Maddie were shouting hi and waving to her. Rachel hugged her family, and her mom gave her a lunch sack. "In case you get hungry." Jessica informed her. "I don't know how long I'll be gone." She warned. Her parents dismissed it. "That doesn't matter." Her father assured her. "Go now, or you'll be late!" Rachel raced out the door to where one of her best friends was waiting.

*****

Annika checked her watch. It was 9:50 a.m. It was a ten-minute drive to Rachel's house, and a three hour drive to the *Survival Race!* studio. They were expected there at 1 p.m. Her dad was sitting in the back seat on his phone. Annika had decided she and Rachel would sit up front, and her dad was all too happy to sit in the back. He had declared he wanted to nap on the way. "Thanks for taking us." Annika told him. "Do you seriously think I would miss an opportunity to see the legendary *Survival Race!* studio? Never!" Her father had declared. The car pulled to a stop outside Rachel's house. Annika input new directions into the cars autopilot, and opened the door for Rachel. She heard one of the twins yell "They're here!" and Rachel came racing out, gave her family hugs, and climbed in the car. Annika rolled down the window, and the girls waved goodbye as the car sped them away.

Rachel rolled up the window. "Is your dad here?" She asked. Annika nodded. "Back there." She replied with a jerk of her head. Her dad called up, "I can hear you." They giggled. "I'm really nervous." Rachel told her friend, bouncing in her seat. "By the way, I love this car. It's so sleek!" Annika grinned. "It's my dad's Tesla Cybertruck. It's one of the originals, which means it was made in the 2020's. It's a really rare, limited-edition car, since they stopped making them during the war, but afterwards they made the Model 1.2 Cybertruck. I think the newest model is the Model 14, but I may be mistaken. I'm not that into cars." Rachel looked interested. "Which war?" "World War III. It was like, 50 years ago, or something." "Oh yeah. I think I learned about that in fourth grade. Wasn't that the 'final war that brought everlasting peace and rid the world of evil,' or something like that?" Rachel asked. "Pretty much, but that's the war that also devastated our planet, leaving some cities in ruins and separate from others. Anyway, all the Cybertrucks before the war had autodrive, like this one, but the newer models have other features. I don't really know what." Annika agreed. "Hey, did you bring anything to distract us?" She asked. Rachel nodded and rummaged through her bag. "Card games, music, and-oh!" She paused and stared at an object in her bag. "What is it?" Annika asked, trying to get a better look. "The twin's Silver Falcon CamDisc. It's the one they got for Christmas. She's their favorite superhero." Rachel answered, pulling it out and handing it to Annika. "What's a CamDisc?" Annika asked, her eyebrow raised. "It's like a portable movie, but on a thin Disc like the ones they used before the War. It just goes in your car, and holo-projects so it can be seen. They're super expensive. Isabelle must have slipped it in my bag while Maddie was hugging me." Rachel explained. "How sweet." Annika giggled, turning the disc over in her hands. "Want to put it in? It might entertain us." She suggested. "Sure." Rachel decided. "Why not? I haven't seen this one." She slid the disk into the drive, and the girls settled back to listen.

Ten minutes into the movie, Rachel had pulled out a deck of cards and the friends played game after game after game, ranging from go-fish to full-on Rummy. When the movie finally ended an hour and a half later, the girls were tired of playing cards, and Annika realized her dad was snoring in the back. She rummaged through the bag she had brought and pulled out two pairs of wireless earbuds and her phone. Annika put a pair of earbuds in her ears and handed the other pair to Rachel. She unlocked her phone and pulled up her 'relax' playlist. Her plan was to lay back and relax like her dad, but Rachel was jostling around too much. Annika opened her eyes, ready to scold Rachel, but found her digging through a GIANT container of candy. Rachel grinned, took out a handful of chocolates, and gave them to Annika. Annika's eyes widened in delight. Rachel knew chocolate was her weakness. After checking to make sure her dad was still asleep in the back, Annika tore the wrapper off the candy and put it in her mouth. The blissful taste as chocolate layers melted away was sometimes better then rooftop jumping. You just couldn't beat chocolate, especially when it was one of your best friends offering it. Annika popped a third piece in her mouth and leaned over to see what else was in the jug. A quick glance at her friend revealed her either fast asleep, or peacefully unaware of her surroundings as she listened to the calm song now playing through the earbuds. Annika quietly rifled through the big jar to see what else there was. Caramels were good. Peppermints were good. Annika spotted numerous other candies that didn't even come close to chocolate before she spotted the most perfect sweet ever made. A peppermint-caramel chocolate bar sat near the bottom of the jug. Its wrapping made it look like it came from a Christmas candy sale. She slowly, carefully eased it out, making sure the other candies didn't rustle around and give her away. The candy bar was almost out; then a hand tightly clasped around her wrist. Annika shrieked, shocked, but resisted the urge to punch, knowing it had to be either her dad or Rachel.

It was Rachel; she had a gangster face on. "Yer tryin' to steal me treats. Watcha gotta say for yerself?" "Uh..." Was all Annika could think to say. She wasn't used to being caught, but it was apparent that Rachel had been waiting for her to try to steal something. Rachel laughed and released her wrist. "You can have it." Rachel told Annika, settling back into her serene position. "Really?" Annika asked, surprised. "Yeah. I have, like, three others." On impulse, Annika peered into the jug again. "Did I scare you?" Rachel asked hopefully. "I shrieked like a little girl!" Annika answered. "I thought you were sleeping!" Rachel smiled. "My acting skills are improving!" She announced with satisfaction. Annika tore open the new chocolate and broke off three joined pieces, holding them out to Rachel. "Here; my debt for failing my heist." She joked. Rachel eagerly extended her hand to accept the treat, but a different hand got there first and yanked the pieces out of Annika's. "Thank you." Dan Helmcott announced, cramming the pieces into his mouth. "Consider it payment for waking me up with a scream." The girls stared in dismay. "Dad..." Annika moaned. By that time Rachel had already found two more. She pulled the partial bar out of Annika's hand and handed it to Mr. Helmcott, much to his delight. Then, the new ones went to Annika and herself. Nobody wasted time ripping them open. "I want these for Christmas." Dan declared. "Where did you get these?" He asked Rachel. She gave him a secretive smile. "My uncle made them. He works at a candy factory and he let me help design them. He's my supplier for the jug." "Hank Lilywade?" Annika asked. Rachel gave an affirmative nod. "He was the first person in my family to be on television, and I'll be second." Rachel told them proudly. Annika felt a rush of happiness for her friend. It wasn't Annika's first time; she had been both in the newspaper and on TV. But for Rachel, this was a big deal. Her family wasn't as well-known as the Helmcott's- now she could finally bring them some recognition. "Oh!" Rachel gasped, almost dropping her chocolate in her frantic rummage through her bag. "What?" The Helmcott's asked, worried. Rachel pulled a silver notebook out of her bag with a sigh of relief. "I want to plan out what we're going to do while we're there. I don't want to mess up." She told them. Annika couldn't believe she was serious. *I suppose it's natural to want to be prepared her first time on TV.* Annika thought to herself. "I'll help you." Annika decided, as she finished her chocolate. She searched her own bag for two pens and gave one to Rachel. "Don't mind me. I'm just going to play HoverCraft for a while." Dan called out, grabbing a sneaky extra handful of chocolate as he retreated to the back seats. Although Rachel was bent over her notebook, scribbling like mad, she called out, "You could have asked for those chocolates instead of stealing them, you know." Dan reddened slightly. How had she seen that? It was almost like she had eyes on the back of her head. "Sorry." He muttered, deciding that he had lost his appetite for the pilfered goodies. He set them aside and pulled out his phone for a little bit of pleasure playing, feeling like he deserved it after having to suffer through that CamDisc for an hour.

It was nearly an hour later before Rachel was satisfied with their work. Annika secretly believed they were preparing it just for the sake of Rachel's peace of mind, but it helped take her mind off the long drive. Everyone was extremely relieved when the Cybertruck finally pulled into a parking space in front of the *Survival Race!* studio. The girls quickly checked each other out. Rachel was wearing her favorite shirt- a deep blue ¾ sleeve top and glittery black stretchy pants, complete with her silver sandals. Annika was wearing her pale red shirt. It was her favorite. She loved how sometimes the lighting made it look red, and sometimes it made it look white. She had light grey stretchy pants and her red and black tennis shoes that she saved for special occasions. The girls brushed their long hair, then took turns braiding each other's hair and checking the mirror for chocolate smears. An important day required good-looking, respectable people. Observing them from the back, Dan reflected sadly how much his daughter reminded him of his wife who had been lost in a car accident four years earlier. Annika had the same fiery red hair and determined expression. And the energy. After the girls were satisfied, the trio exited the car and stretched. The studio was massive and extended back far past their sight. Its sterling steel shell glimmered in the sunshine. There were double doors in the entrance, between two marble pillars holding up the stone roof that protracted partially over the sidewalk to provide shade from the hot sun. A thick chain fence stretched high into the sky. It extended far beyond her sight; Annika assumed the fence kept people off the many acres that were used for the *Survival Race!* show. Numerous signs warned that the fence was electric. Just standing there, blinking against the sunlight, and gazing upon the studio was enough to satisfy Annika. It was hard to believe she not only got to go inside, but also got to be on the legendary show! Of the many things Annika had seen and the places she'd been, she decided this was the coolest yet. A pang of regret twinged inside of her, and Annika found herself wishing her mom could be here to see this. She allowed herself to feel sad for only a moment; then pushed it away and straightened her posture. Her mom wouldn't want her to be feeling gloomy on a day like today. "Ready to go in?" Dan asked after a moment. Annika impulsively checked her watch. They were 92 seconds early. "In a little bit." She replied. They looked a bit confused, but Dan quickly interpreted what she meant. "You are so punctual." He laughed. "Do you usually wait before entering the restaurant?" Annika shook her head. "Most of the time I hardly get there." She confessed. "What time do you usually leave the LaserTrainer?" "About 6:15." Her father looked amazed but said nothing else on the subject. "Annika." He said suddenly, pulling a small object out of his pocket. "Come over here." He beckoned her over to the side of the car, out of Rachel's sight. "I want you to have this." He told her, opening his fist to reveal a gorgeous raindrop-shaped sapphire fixed to a simple black ponytail. "It's beautiful!" Annika breathed, gingerly taking it from her father. "It used to be your mothers, before she died." Dan explained. "It was her good-luck charm. I was going to give it to Amelia, but I think you should have it instead. I know you're not into jewelry, but it won't hamper anything you do." Touched at his thoughtfulness, Annika pulled her regular ponytail out of her hair and used the new one to resecure her braid, admiring the glinting jewel. It was the first possession of her mother's that she had received, and it was perfect. "I'm going to wear it all the time." Annika promised, hugging her dad tightly. "Thank you." They walked back around the car, where Annika noticed Rachel gazing about her with a dazed expression. "What's on your mind?" Annika asked her. "This place is so beautiful! The show always shows amazing things inside, but it never shows anything on the outside. At least, not of the complex!" Rachel responded. Annika nodded, realizing Rachel wanted in that moment to look and not talk. They waited for another ten seconds, soaking in the landscape, before they went in. Annika waited until her watch said nine seconds left before starting for the door. "Come on. I don't want to be late." She called back. Reluctantly, they followed.

Annika strode towards the door confidently, her bag swinging on her arm as she admired the intricate detail carved into the marble as she passed. It truly was a work of art; it made Annika wonder who had designed it. She pushed on the doors, expecting them to swing open. The doors resisted. Annika stepped back, surprised, and realized a 'Please Pull' sign hung next to the doors. Embarrassed, Annika pulled the doors open and stepped into the chilled studio where dreams came true.

Cathy Brisson believed in opportunities. When wisely used, they could turn into success. Cathy had created *Survival Race!* a gameshow for teens, to give them opportunities that they wouldn't find elsewhere. She had similar studios all over the world. This month, four very special girls were invited to participate. *This is going to be one of our best shows yet.* Cathy thought, coming out of her office to greet the new contestants. She had no idea just how crazy it would get. Cathy peered around the corner and found the four girls talking already. Smiling, she pulled up the sleeve of her shirt to get one more glance at the names penned on her forearm. *Rebecca. Bethany. Eliza. Annika.* Got it. She signaled the camera to begin recording and stepped out into the open. "Hello, girls!" She announced with a smile.

Annika, Dan, and Rachel hurried out of the hot sun, crowding inside the doorway. Two girls around their age sat on chairs to the left, talking to each other. When one of them noticed they had entered, her hand went to her ears, and she tugged her earrings off before dropping them into a dark blue backpack. She did it so quickly that no one noticed. A small round coffee table between them held a platter of cookies. Two chairs opposite them sat empty. The only decorations were hundreds of small frames hung along the right wall, each with a little gold plaque beneath it. When she squinted, Rachel could tell each frame held a picture of a smiling teenager. The room looked exactly like it did on TV. Rachel suspected she wouldn't be getting a behind-the-scenes peek like she had hoped. "I think it's time for me to leave." Dan Helmcott ventured, wondering if they were already recording. "I'll send the car..." He trailed off. "How long will you girls be gone?" "I'll just text you." Annika told him. He agreed, gave them each a hug, and left. Rachel glanced about her uncertainly. What were they supposed to do? Annika took lead and headed towards the girls that were seated, Rachel following close behind. The two broke off their conversation and waved them over. "Hi! I'm Bethany." One of the girls greeted as they sat down. Bethany had shoulder length wavy blond hair. Her shining dark blue eyes matched her tank top, and the pale green shorts accompanied perfectly. Rachel felt a bit envious at how well they went together. "I'm Eliza." Introduced the other girl, her long black hair falling forward as she shook their hands. "I'm Rachel, and this is Annika." Rachel responded, already feeling as if she belonged with these friendly girls. "Do you know how this works? Has it started already? Do we get a behind the scenes? Or did you already get one! How did you two get invited on? Do you know each other outside of this? How old are you guys? We're fifteen. Did you get any special instructions? OMG Bethany, I LOVE your outfit!! Where did you get it? When do we start? Will our phones be confiscated? Have you gotten to meet Cathy yet? I KNEW we should have come in early, but Annika insisted on being punctual. Still, its gorgeous outside, isn't it? This is so amazing!!" Here Rachel paused to take a breath. The others stared at her in surprise. Rachel waited for answers, but received none. "I have never heard you talk like that." Annika finally said, seeming to be having trouble finding the words. Rachel grinned and opened her mouth to respond, but the voice that rang out was not her own. "Hello girls!" It announced. The four new friends turned face-to-face with Cathy Brisson, the famous creator and director of *Survival Race! This is happening.* Rachel thought, her heart hammering in her chest. *I really hope I'm not dreaming.*

Out of the corner of her eye, Rachel noticed a blinking red dot. They were recording. She willed her hand to stay away from her hair. It practically itched for her to check it; a nervous habit she tried and failed to get rid of. Annika slightly nudged her. "Hi." She managed with a weak smile. Using her peripheral vision, Rachel watched how the others behaved. All of them seemed calm and relaxed. Rachel tried to relax as well, hoping to seem more natural. As if acting on its own will, her hand gravitated upwards again. She gritted her teeth in frustration. Now was not the time for a silly habit to be acting up! Rachel realized they were giving her subtle strange looks. Feeling a hand grasp hers, Rachel realized Annika was giving comfort. It was surprising; Annika had given up holding hands after her mom had died. Deciding to give in now meant a lot. Rachel sent a grateful glance to Annika, being careful not to reveal too much. Annika wasn't aware her closest friends knew her biggest secret. Rachel didn't know what Annika assumed about their ignorance of her never-present mother. They simply never talked about Mrs. Helmcott. She never had a problem if they talked about all the fun things they did with their moms. Rachel guessed Annika didn't want her friends trying to protect and hide her. Rachel was pulled out of her thoughts by another nudge from Annika. Cathy had asked for their names. "My name is Eliza Charminger." "I'm Bethany Meyers." "Annika Helmcott." "My name is Rachel Ravenstone." She said proudly. "All right!" Cathy said, her voice sounding a bit off as she studied Rachel. "Who wants to go first in the personal interviews?" The four girls looked uncertainly at each other. None of them really wanted to be first. "I'll go." Bethany finally volunteered. "If that's okay wi-" She was cut off by the others hurried agreement. Cathy raised an eyebrow at their enthusiasm but only led Bethany away. The three waved her off and sat back down. The camera's blinked off. Rachel let go of Annika's hand. "Thank you. I-" Annika waved her explanation away. "You're my friend. That's what friends do." Annika answered, turning away from Rachel. Rachel knew her well enough to see past her façade. There was a new pain in her eyes, the same that showed up briefly while they were outside. Still, Rachel couldn't help marveling at how well her friend masked it. Anyone who did not know her would never know anything Annika didn't want them to know. "Why did Ms. Brisson give Rachel that look?" Rachel heard Eliza quietly whisper to Annika. *So I wasn't the only one to notice that.* Rachel thought. An assistant walked over before Annika could reply. "Ok girls, here's the plan. When you hear Miss Meyers talking, only quiet whispers are allowed. VERY quiet whispers. When she comes out, one of you will go back for your interview until you all have had a turn. Feel free to eat the cookies, but I'd make sure you check your teeth before coming in for your interview, okay?" They agreed, and she walked away. A few minutes later, they heard Bethany's voice drifting through the wall. "Well, I lead survival expeditions. We usually camp for a week, in a group of 5-15 people. I've been granted special papers that give me legal leadership over groups, meaning I can't get arrested for being 'underage.' I've trekked through ice, sand, snow, forests, jungles, you name it. I traveled a lot as a kid." "Did you hear that?" Rachel whispered. "She does survival- Annika?" Annika was staring across the room at something. Eliza was as well. Rachel followed their gaze. "Cathy isn't holding the interview?" She noticed, confused. Eliza gave her a look. "Cathy never holds the interviews. Haven't you watched the show?" Rachel flushed and didn't answer. Of course she had! Cathy was talking with two others seated close to her. But, on a closer look, Rachel realized they weren't talking; they were signing! "What are they saying?" Rachel quietly asked Annika, feeling a bit nervous when she didn't say anything. Annika's eyes were frantically following every twist of their hands, likely trying to translate fast enough to keep up. "Eliza?" Rachel tried, hoping someone would answer her questions. "I don't know what they're saying." Eliza answered in a hushed voice. "But it seems like a big deal to Annika." Suddenly, Annika's eyes widened and a sharp gasp flew out of her mouth. "What's wrong? Annika?" Rachel tried to get Annika to respond, but her friend was focusing even more intently on the director and assistants that were signing at a crazy pace. That was the moment Bethany came out. "You go." Eliza suggested to Rachel, noticing Bethany approaching as well. "Why me?" "Annika's ignoring both of us. She'd be too distracted to focus on an interview." "Why don't you go?" Rachel countered, feeling a bit desperate. She couldn't just leave, not when Annika was actually shocked or worried about something. It had to be big to get her to gasp like that. Eliza sheepishly opened her mouth and revealed a half-chewed cookie. Rachel fought the urge to gag. "I need to clean it out before I go on." Noting Rachel's look of distress, she added. "You'll do fine. Now hurry! And don't stress; you look great." Rachel sighed, feeling slightly embarrassed Eliza had noticed her bad habit, and started towards Bethany, quickly passing her on the way to the room she had come out of.

"Okay, she's gone." Eliza said, spitting the cookie into the garbage and rinsing her mouth clean with a drink of water. "Now. What's wrong?" Bethany came up and sat down beside them. "Something's wrong?" She asked, concerned, looking between them for clues. "Annika saw Cathy and some assistants signing." Eliza started. "Wait, you read sign language? Like, more than just the alphabet?" Bethany interrupted. Cathy had stopped signing, so Annika turned back to the conversation at hand. Eliza gave Bethany an exasperated look. "Yes, apparently." Bethany had the decency to look sorry, but said nothing. "Anyway, she read what they said and was so shocked she gasped. Before Annika could tell us what had her so surprised, you walked out, so Annika whispered to me to get Rachel to go in next. Trusting her, I shoved a cookie in my mouth and got Rachel to go after you. Now Annika *really* owes me an explanation." Eliza sucked in a large breath and faced Annika. "So talk." Rachel's voice came through the wall, interrupting what Annika was going to say. "I've been taking survival trips for years. Once I got lost in Paris for 18 hours with only $10." "Wait, really? She got lost? How old was she?" Bethany whispered to Annika. Annika stared at her, perplexed. "How often does she get off subject? And how do you know each other anyway?" Annika asked Eliza. Eliza groaned. "Now you're as bad as her! She gets off subject a lot. We know each other from school, but never hung out. That doesn't matter. What was so surprising? **What did you learn?**" Eliza hissed. "Rachel's not supposed to be here." Annika admitted, dropping her face into her hands. "What!" They cried.

CHAPTER 3

"**Y**ou mean you smuggled her on and got caught?" Bethany guessed. "What? No, of course not." Annika gave her a weird look, then continued. "The invitation wasn't supposed to be sent to her; it was meant to go to her cousin." Eliza's eyes widened in surprise. "How did they get that so wrong?" Annika sighed. "It's not as hard as it seems. The reason Rebecca (that's her cousin) has the same last name is because their fathers are brothers. Cathy intended to invite Rebecca Ravenstone, but they misheard her and sent it to Rachel Ravenstone instead. Now it's too late, so they're stuck with the wrong person. Rachel was so excited for this. Once she finds out they didn't actually want *her*," Annika's head drooped. "Are they going to tell her?" Bethany asked. "No. They don't want it to ruin the show. Everyone's just supposed to act like she was actually meant to be here and that it wasn't a mistake. How am I going to tell her?" Annika lamented. "Why would you tell her?" Eliza asked. "If they won't, why would you?" Annika stared at her in shock. "Wouldn't you want to know? Rachels' dream is to be on this show." She answered. Eliza nodded. "Then why would you ruin it for her? All you would achieve would be making it seem like they're bad guys. This way, she still gets her dream, intentional or not. If you tell her, how could she remember this place as a good memory? Telling her could end disastrously!" "But they're not telling her for their own selfish reasons!" Annika argued, fighting to keep her voice low. "How would them telling her change anything? Are they just gonna say 'Hey Rachel, we actually wanted your cousin, but it's too late for that so we're just going to keep you anyway, ok?' I mean really. That would achieve nothing!" Eliza countered. "Rachel at least deserves to know!" Annika fumed. "How would she react to hearing this?" Bethany asked, reminding

Annika she was there. "What?" "You know Rachel best. What would her response be? Would she go out of her way to ruin the show, or try extra hard to win and prove she's just as good as the rest of us?" "She IS just as good as the rest of us!" Annika hissed back, trying to control herself. Had there not been a 'stay quiet' rule, she would have been yelling in frustration. "That's not what I meant." Bethany amended. "I mean, they pick especially talented people for a reason. She might feel a need to show she can be great even without earlier training. If she wins, she might get them to invite not as well-known people onto the show. She can do great things! But they made a mistake. They decided what they're going to do about it and they moved on. Now we know. Since it's none of our business, Eliza and I are going to stay out of it and not say anything. It's YOUR decision to tell her or not. I just suggest thinking out every possible ending before deciding." Bethany popped a cookie in her mouth to signal she was done talking. "Rachel's almost done." Eliza reported after an uncomfortable silence. "Who's going in next?" She added after a pause. "I don't know." Annika admitted with a sigh. Bethany swallowed another cookie to add, "If Eliza goes next, there would be less time for Rachel to talk to you." Annika shook her head. "I'm not going to avoid her. She didn't do anything wrong." Annika sighed. Why did this feel like such a difficult choice? "Here comes Rachel." Bethany warned. The door had opened, and the assistant interviewing them was beckoning again. "I'm going next." Annika decided, rising to stand. "Are you sure?" Eliza asked, concerned. Annika didn't look like she was ready. Annika turned back to face them, and had rearranged her expression from one of frustration and upset to excited with a very small trace of nerves. Annika had mastered expression control only seven months prior. They looked surprised, but Eliza grinned. She understood the amount of control that took. Bethany just looked baffled. "Maybe Rachel will have forgotten about my, uh, *reaction*, when I come back." Annika emphasized. They nodded. "Shouldn't be too hard. She happens to be fascinated with Bethany's outfit!" Eliza chimed in, everyone smiling at the memory. Annika had forgotten about Rachel's nervous rush of questions. She stole a quick glance at her friends face as they passed each other. Rachel was beaming; Annika had never seen her so excited in the six years they had known each other. It made Annika feel hollow inside. Should she really tell her? Rachel was obviously having the time of her life here, and they'd be staying for another 3-4 weeks! Careful to keep her façade up, Annika slipped into the room, telling herself she could wrestle with her problem when this was over. It wasn't fair for this to ruin the entire time for her.

The interviewer, whose name was Jane, settled into a chair, tossed her sandy brown ringlets over her shoulder, and pointed for Annika to sit across from her. She sank into the red chair, shifting until she found a spot on the faded fabric that wasn't too uncomfortable. They weren't the only people in the room; there were several manned cameras hovering at different angles around the room. Seeing as they were still fiddling around with them, Annika took the chance to look around. The sky-blue walls deeply contrasted the chairs they sat on. Two overhead lights shone down, illuminating the only furniture in the room; two red chairs and a small black coffee table. A door sat to her left. It was unlabeled, and to its right was a long, darkened pane of glass she could not see through. Annika was momentarily disoriented. She clearly remembered coming through a door on her *right*. It was still there. She wondered what was on the other side, behind the glass. Jane cleared her throat, bringing Annika's attention to the interview. "So, how this works is I'm going to ask you a question, and you answer as best you can. If you'd like, you can elaborate a bit, or tell a short story. Please don't monologue. The goal is for the viewers to have a little bit of a backstory. You know, to choose who to cheer on? Oh, and start with an introduction." Jane told Annika. Annika felt a bit tense. She'd watched PLENTY of show interviews before. She'd probably just tell a cool story or something. Jane noticed her tenseness, and added, "Don't be afraid." Annika almost snorted at that. Her? Afraid? She jumped twenty-foot rooftop gaps 30 feet off the ground, and she'd be scared over an *interview?* Yeah, right. Choosing to be polite, she only nodded instead, forcing herself to relax. The camera lights blinked on; they were ready. Annika waited for a slight cue nod from Jane, then introduced herself. "Hi. I'm Annika Helmcott." She began with a smile. "Hi Annika. I hear you're a daredevil. What do you do to earn that title?" Jane asked her. Annika grinned. "I like jumping the rooftop gaps." Jane's jaw dropped. "Like, ON the roofs? Jumping from one roof to another?" Annika nodded. "It's fun." Jane's eyes were wide. "But what if you fall?" Annika wasn't sure what to say to that. How could she explain she simply *didn't* fall without sounding like a snooty brat? "I calculate the distance and speed I need to complete the jump, and then I don't overthink it." Jane shook her head in admiration and picked something off the coffee table to show her. "Is this you?" Annika studied the photo. A tall, red headed girl was suspended in the air over a 16-foot building gap. She was in mid leap, and the ground looked to be maybe forty feet away. "Yes." She confirmed, blushing slightly. How had they gotten that? She had to admit it was a spectacular picture. She looked like she was having the time of her life! Then again, she probably had been. Maybe she would ask Jane if she could keep the picture. "This picture was published in the Grangeville News. There was an entire article on Annika Helmcott- legendary daredevil and hero. What exactly does the 'hero' mean?" Jane asked. "My friends and I learned of a religious arson organization. We went in undercover and sabotaged them from the inside-out. Of the 15 members, we captured 14." Annika explained. Jane's eyes widened with disbelief. "That sounds dangerous! What if you had gotten hurt?" Annika shrugged. "There was always the possibility, but someone had to stop them or even more people would be hurt, not just me." She responded. Jane seemed at a loss for words. "Wow. How old did you say you were?" "Fifteen." Annika answered. "Wow." Jane said again. Then she glanced at her palm. "So, what got you started on survival training?" Annika didn't have to think long. "I wanted to be able to survive any situation and be well equipped in knowledge that might save my life. I taught myself to identify plants and animals, safely prepare food and drink, how to track animals..." She paused, trying to remember what else she had forgotten. "Oh! I took martial arts, gymnastics, laser training, and marathon classes.

Survival isn't just the wild; I wanted to be able to survive ANY situation." Annika finished proudly. Jane looked seriously impressed. "What was your most challenging 'survival' time you've had?" Jane asked as her next question. Annika considered telling the story of the 'girls only' hike she had gone on with her mother and older sister when she was nine. At the time, it had been terrifying. She had slipped over a cliffside during the several hour hike to the campsite, dropping about 16 feet into a clump of bushes. Annika had miraculously come out with only a few bad scratches. There was no way to get back up; the cliffside was almost a sheer drop, and the trail she was now on was completely separate from the one the rest of her group still traveled. The only way to get back was to walk the entire way back to the main lodge where they started. She could not even yell, as their guide had cautioned that this place was very susceptible to rockslides. It didn't help that their group was 23 people, so no one would notice she was missing for a few more hours. She also knew that many wild animals made their homes here. That was why groups were so big; lone hikers could get attacked by the animals living here if they were scared or provoked. To make everything worse, it was becoming dark, meaning she couldn't keep hiking back if she wanted a place to sleep and a fire that night. Annika had no choice but to set up camp and spend the night away from her group. It was dangerous to continue alone in the fading light, and she didn't have much experience starting fires and pitching tents, so she would need all the daylight she could get. The first thing she had done was take inventory on everything she had in her backpack. She had pulled out a tent, a sleeping bag, a water bottle, a pack of matches, pajamas, a blanket, two bags of trail mix, and a giant bag of marshmallows that was supposed to be for the big campfire their group was going to have. It took Annika 20 minutes to find both a good campsite and enough kindling for a fire, and 18 matches to get it lit. Annika had left temporarily to get bigger wood, but it took longer than she expected, and came back to a burned-out pile of wood. She was forced to use the rest of her matches just to get the fire going again, and suffered painful burns on her fingertips from her inexperience with matches. After that, Annika made sure never to leave her fire alone; if it went out again, she would have no way to relight it. It was another hour before Annika got the tent up, with her burned fingers making an impossible job even harder. She triple checked it was a good distance from the fire; if it had caught flames, she knew she wouldn't have survived the night. Her poor fingers had started to bleed; the burn blisters had cracked to the point where she was fighting off tears of pain, but she still refused to cry, telling herself over and over that she would get through this semi-nightmare. To her immense relief, she found a container of band-aids in her sleeping bag. She had quickly put them on, grateful that she wasn't dripping blood anymore. She had been worried that the stench of her blood might attract animals. Her stomach was growling at that point, but the food she had wouldn't sustain her for long. Annika located a long stick and used it to roast ¾ of the bag of marshmallows. She was so hungry that she ate each one as soon as it was done, burning her tongue in the process. She had scrambled for her water bottle, downing a bunch to cool her mouth before remembering it had to last her until she got back. Only a third of its contents remained, so she capped it and hid her water in her backpack so she wouldn't be tempted to drink it again. Annika had put her pajamas on, then curled in her tent, trying to stay warm. She recalled feeling like it was the worst night of her life, but after it was over, she truthfully told her mom she would love to do it again. After a fitful sleep, Annika had woken at the crack of dawn the next morning to find her fire had safely burned out. She wrapped up her tent and sleeping bag, put them in her backpack, torn open a bag of trail mix, and began the long hike back. Seven hours of nonstop hiking later, she had collapsed onto the steps of the main lodge, too weary to even go inside. She was found by one of the staff a few minutes later, and brought inside to be properly fed and rested. Her mother and sister arrived a few hours later for a joyous reunion. The story of her incredible journey made the headlines in several local papers. It had been an especially challenging time for her 9-year-old self. But now, looking at Jane, Annika felt that to relate this story would bring up questions and comments she didn't want to respond to. Jane was still waiting for an answer, so Annika replied, "I'd say a lot of my survival challenges have been pretty minor. I think this is going to be my toughest yet!" Annika was purposefully vague, and Jane looked a bit disappointed, but didn't push for details, only replying, "Well then. I look forward to seeing you in action!" The camera's blinked off; the interview was over. Jane stood up, smiling at Annika. "Could you go send Eliza in please? After her interview, I'll show you where you will be sleeping." Jane informed her. Annika nodded and exited the room. She hurried over to the others and told Eliza, "She's ready for you." Eliza thanked her and walked away. Rachel and Bethany were talking about some brand of clothing. Annika smiled inwardly and picked up a dark chocolate cookie with chocolate chunks, biting into the sweet treat as she took a seat. She found it amusing that Rachel was on her dream survival show, and still found someone to discuss fashion with. Suddenly, the cookie turned bitter in her mouth as the memories flooded back. It was obvious that Rachel was elated to be here, to belong here. But when she found out about the mistake they had made... Annika realized with a pang that she didn't know how Rachel would react. Did she really not know her best friend as well as she thought? *It's only going to get harder to tell her the more she sees.* Annika thought. And she was right.

Rachel and Bethany stopped their conversation when Eliza came back. "So what do we get to do now?" Rachel asked eagerly. She really wanted a tour of this massive place. "We can talk and get to know each other for another 10 minutes, then we will be taken on a short tour, get settled in to our new home away from home, then tomorrow we can start training and getting familiar with this place. There's apparently a lot to do, so we won't be racing for a few weeks." Eliza answered, taking the empty seat and picking up a sugar cookie. Rachel's face fell in disappointment. "Why so long until we start?" Bethany queried, taking a cookie for herself as well. "Something about getting cameras ready, and making sure we can do the necessary physical exertion so none of us end up in the hospital, blah, blah, blah. I'm just happy we get to stay for so long. This place is awesome!" As if to prove it, Eliza reached for another sugar cookie and stuffed it into her mouth. Rachel grinned. Then another question came to mind. "Why wouldn't we be physically capable if we were invited onto one of the most challenging physical game shows ever?" She asked Eliza. Bethany snorted with laughter and began choking on her cookie. Eliza started pounding on her back a little too hard, and Bethany twisted away, still coughing. She accepted the cup of water Annika offered, quickly downing it. "Are you ok?" Annika checked. Bethany nodded. "Yes, thank you." She replied gratefully. Annika nodded, and sitting back down, picked up the book she had been reading and once again zoned out of their conversation. "What was so funny?" Rachel hesitantly asked Bethany, who smirked. "Why would being invited onto the 'most challenging physical game show ever' mean you're physically capable of its challenges?" Bethany asked. Rachel seemed confused, so Bethany tried a different approach. "Why were we invited onto this show?" Rachel furrowed her brow. "Because we all do survival training?" Bethany nodded. "That could be." She agreed. "But why us? Lots of people like to challenge themselves in the wild. The gap certainly shrinks because we're teenage girls, and this is a teenage game show, but there's still a ton of people who fall into the description. So, why *us*?" Rachel didn't know. What *did* make the four of them special above others? "Maybe because we do things not very many others do?" She suggested. "Like what?" Bethany asked. "Well." Rachel began. "You lead survival expeditions, I do survival trips and laser training, Eliza does..." She paused, embarrassed. "What do you do?" She asked Eliza. "I've got ingenuity, wits, and good hand-eye coordination." Eliza answered quickly. Rachel found it strange that Eliza would choose to name those over something more physical. They were qualities that many people had. They didn't make you *special*. What had Eliza talked about in her interview anyway? She looked to Bethany and Annika for answers, but Bethany was eating a cookie and staring about the room, and Annika was fully absorbed in her book. Rachel sighed and turned back to Eliza. "Um... Sure. You do, uh, those things, and Annika does..." She paused. "Well, Annika does everything." She finished. Eliza laughed. "Here comes Jane." Annika announced without even glancing up from her book.

CHAPTER 4

It wasn't the first time Rachel had wondered how Annika knew those things. She had long ago given up trying to understand how and why Annika did what she did. "Hi girls!" Jane called out as she walked closer. "Who's ready for a tour?" "Me!" Cried three voices as Bethany, Rachel, and Eliza jumped up. Annika slipped a bookmark into her book, placed it into her bag, and stood up to join the others as she slung her bag over her shoulder. "I am." She replied somewhat belatedly. "Great!" Exclaimed Jane. "Grab your bags and follow me!" Eliza swung a dark blue backpack onto her shoulder, Rachel picked up the bag she had speedily packed that morning, and Bethany had a rolling suitcase. "What could you possibly put into that big thing?" Rachel jokingly asked Bethany, who gave her a weird look before answering. "Clothes, of course, and toiletries. If we're going to be here for a month, we're going to need more than one outfit. Did you plan to wear that for a month?" Rachel immediately felt embarrassed. Why hadn't she thought of that? A quick look at Annika's face said she hadn't considered that either. Then again, you never could tell what Annika was thinking just by looking at her face. Annika had an insane amount of control over her expressions. The four girls followed Jane through a set of double doors, near what Rachel had assumed to be the back of the building. The group walked into a brightly lit hallway flanked with many doors on either side. The light came from skylights in the ceiling, rectangular panes of glass positioned a foot apart all along the ceiling. Jane turned around so she was facing them, and began walking backwards. "Can any of you cook?" She asked. Four hands raised. Jane smiled, and turned back around. "Great to hear. Our contestants oversee their own meals here, so hopefully you girls can put together some healthy meals. One time all four of the participants had no cooking experience, so they were stuck eating boxed and canned food for their entire time here. None of them did very well in the race." Jane chuckled at the memory. "I hope you all are friends by now." Jane added after a pause. Annika and Bethany asked "Why?" at the same time Rachel said "We are." Jane grinned. "Good. Because you four will be sharing a room." "Why?" Bethany asked again. "This complex may seem large, but a lot of the space goes to filming, storage, crew quarters, training spaces..." She trailed off, looking uncomfortable. "And other stuff. Point is, we've got 4 beds, a bathroom, and a kitchen in there, so it will have to do." The four girls were quick to agree it would be perfect; none of them wanted to sound whiny. "Oh, and Bethany?" Jane asked. "Yes?" "You won't need to worry about clothing. We supply training uniforms and bathroom supplies, but if you're more comfortable using your own products, that's fine too." Bethany looked disappointed. "Does that mean I can't wear anything I brought?" "Kinda." Jane replied. "When you're not in the room, I need you to wear the provided uniforms. With such a huge staff, not everyone is going to recognize you, and they may try to kick you out if they think you are trespassing. In your room though, you can wear whatever you want." She added, seeming to suspect Bethany was about to ask 'why' again. Eliza looked amused and opened her mouth to say something, but was cut off by Jane. "Here we are!" She announced as they came to a stop in front of two wide red double doors. Rachel noticed two glass-stained semi-circle windows placed in the door. They were very pretty, but seemed out of place here. Jane pulled open the doors with a flourish. Eliza and Bethany were far enough away that they weren't hit when Jane flung the doors open. Annika quickly stepped back, out of range; that left Rachel as the unlucky receiver of a door to her big toe. Rachel let out a small cry of pain and tried to move her foot, but found she couldn't. Terrified, she glanced down. The door had gotten wedged onto her sandal; she couldn't get it off. Her toe was starting to turn red. "Isn't it incredible?" Jane asked as she strode into the room. Annika, Bethany, and Eliza were close behind. Nobody had noticed Rachel's problem. The three girls were already touching things, letting out 'whoa' as they asked Jane how everything worked. Rachel's eyes were beginning to tear up from the pain as she knelt and tried to tug her shoe out from under the thick door, but it was hopeless. She stood back up, frustration building up inside of her. Jane turned around and noticed Rachel still standing in the doorway. "Come on, Rachel. What are you still doing over there?" Jane called out with a laugh before turning back to Eliza, who stood over a complicated machine. Rachel felt a bit of anger towards Jane. How had she not realized Rachel was stuck? Gritting her teeth, Rachel jerked her foot back, finally releasing it. She stiffened as a sharp pain shot up her leg, and she nervously bent down to check on her toe. It didn't look too good, but the pain was fading. Relieved, Rachel straightened and walked into the room. There was no need to make a fuss about it, she decided. There was no way she was letting a tiny incident ruin her entire time. Determined, Rachel stopped in front of a strange-looking contraption. "This one's my personal favorite." A voice behind Rachel told her. Rachel jumped and wheeled around. Jane stood there, smiling. "Would you like me to show you how to operate it?" "Uh, yeah. Yes please." Rachel answered. Jane quickly showed her how to use the complex machine, which involved pulling straps connected to heavy weights while bicycle pedaling weights on the bottom at the same time. By the time Rachel got the hang of it, her arms and legs were sore from the effort it had taken to use it. Jane led her around, demonstrating the different ways to use each machine. "Well!" Jane finally said, clapping her hands to get everyone's attention. "Time to move on!" The five of them filed out of the room. Jane led them through more hallways and turns before coming to yet another set of red double doors. Rachel had been watching carefully to ensure she didn't get trapped again. Jane pushed them open; Rachel was surprised. Why did some doors push open but others pulled open? There was no chance to ask Jane, because their tour guide was already outside. "Welcome to the training grounds!" Jane yelled to them. She waited until her four charges drew closer before continuing. "This is my favorite place here." Jane gestured at the huge lawn. A long, wide track went far past Rachel's vision. It was the exact picture of a marathon track. Rachel started to ask Jane how long it was, but Bethany beat her to it. "Jane, how long is that red track? And why does it curve like that?" Curve? Rachel looked closer, shielding her eyes from the sun. Bethany was right. The track went a ways, then doubled back. It twisted and turned, but never overlapped. "That's our high-tech racing track." Jane was interrupted by Bethany asking, "What's so high-tech about it?" Jane took a deep breath. "I was getting to that before you interjected." Jane informed her. "Oh. Sorry." Bethany replied. But to Rachel, she didn't look very sorry. The problem was Bethany didn't seem to notice her rude behavior. Then she shook herself. What was she doing, thinking about the competition when she was supposed to be listening? Jane had just started speaking. "The track has a special timer. You input how many laps you want to run into the panel next to the start line. Once the racers are lined up, they step on a pressure panel that counts down from 10. The track goes one mile each lap; that's why it twists and turns. There wouldn't be enough space for a straight track. Once you pass the finish line, the timer above your track stops. When everyone has finished, it announces which lane won. There's five lanes, so I'll be able to race you too. You could also race yourself, to try to better your time." Annika looked delighted. "Can we try it now?" She begged. "No. We need to complete the tour before night. Come on!" Annika looked crestfallen, but hurried to keep up with Jane. Jane proceeded to show them a woodsy racing track. It was almost exactly like the one she had just showed them, but it was covered with sticks, rocks, low-hanging branches, and wildlife. Jane explained it was to give them more of a feel traveling in the forest. The thing that interested Rachel most was an obstacle course. It was constructed of several natural things; vines to swing on, log walls to climb over, branches to duck under, and logs crossing large pools of water. The fence around it went far into the distance. Pointing to the water, she asked, "What happens if you fall in?" "You swim across or pull yourself back up." Jane replied. "Besides, in this heat, who wouldn't mind a nice cold dunk, hmm?" She had a point there, Rachel realized. Maybe she- "But you're NOT supposed to fall in. We have a swimming pool for that." "There's a swimming pool!?" Eliza cried. Jane nodded. "It's pretty big. We have it so you can work on strengthening those muscles as well." "Will we be swimming in the competition?" Annika asked. Rachel wanted to smack herself.

Everyone else was asking such great questions! Jane winked at Annika. "That depends." "On what?" Bethany asked again. "What path you take." "I don't understand. I thought it was a straight path." Eliza said. Jane laughed. "Oh, not at all! No, your racing territory is about 90 miles long and 4 miles wide. Odds are, someone will get their directions mixed up and start heading the wrong way. It's quite funny when a contestant bursts through the trees just to find themselves right back at start. Funny, but sad." She saw their faces and cracked up. All four of them had their jaws open in surprise and horror on their faces. "Wait, seriously?" Bethany clarified. Jane nodded. "How much land does Ms. Brisson own?" Annika asked. "Hundreds of thousands of acres, but your racing territory is technically considered state land. After World War III, Cathy bought out almost all bundles of mountainous land she could get her hands on, but when that proved to be not enough, she made a contract with the state to secure more of the national forests land." Was Jane's reply. "Now, any more questions?" No one spoke, so she clapped her hands. "Great! Let's-" Bethany cut her off again. "Wait! Sorry, um, what are those tents for?" She asked apologetically, pointing to a row of large red tents. Jane didn't seem bothered by the interruption this time. "Those are our training tents. I'll be teaching you first aid, how to prepare Already Made Meals, knot tying, etc. Alright, now let's go." She led them out of the training grounds and down more hallways until they came to yet another set of red double doors. "What's with all the red doors?" Rachel asked. The question had been hounding her for a while. "Great question! The red doors are the rooms you four are allowed to enter." Jane answered. Rachel grinned. She had finally contributed a good question. "What's behind the other doors?" Bethany queried. "Equipment, staff quarters, and such. I can show you, but we don't want kids getting into fragile things." At the word 'kids' Annika let out a small scoff. She wasn't a kid. Jane halted besides a plain black door and bent down by the sensor panel, allowing it to read her retina. The door's locking mechanism clicked, allowing Jane to push the door open. As it opened, lights inside flickered to life. "See? Just equipment." "What type of equipment?" Eliza asked as she peered inside. Jane walked in and lifted a sheet off a large, old-fashioned camera. "This is one of the cameras we used to use. Its hover mechanism is currently broken, so that's why it's in here. They aren't manufactured anymore, so if another one breaks we can use it as spare parts." She replaced the sheet, and joined them back in the hall, pulling the door shut until it clicked, locking again. The lights died away again as the door sealed. "I wasn't really supposed to show you that, but I don't want you girls getting curious and getting into things you're not allowed to. As your proctor while you are here, anything bad you do gets thrown onto me. Not all that long ago, two contestants were sneaking about where they weren't supposed to be. They broke several hundred dollars of equipment and got kicked out of the competition. **I** got in trouble. I don't want that to happen again, since some things here could seriously hurt or even kill you if it is used incorrectly. That's why there are off limits places. The red doors were designed so it is clear where you are allowed to be. Do you understand?" She finished. All four girls nodded solemnly. Rachel knew she would definitely be staying away from places she couldn't go. She would *not* jeopardize her stay here. Jane looked relieved. "Good. Shall we continue?" They nodded. She led them back to the red doors they had passed and pulled them open. With a squeak, Rachel jumped back, but the doors didn't swing open enough to hit anyone. At Annika's questioning look, she gave an embarrassed shrug. Eliza whooped. Annika turned her head sharply and ran in, Rachel close behind. Eliza stood at the edge of a ginormous pool. Looking down, Rachel realized she could not see the bottom, even though the water was crystal clear. Rachel walked along the edge, trying to see if there was a shallower spot. She didn't like the idea of plunging into water with no way to get out. Rachel found a ladder underneath the diving boards that extended far into the water, but stopped at about 10 feet down. Did the water look deeper in this particular spot? "It's deeper under the diving boards." Jane called out. Rachel sighed. She liked swimming, and was definitely a good swimmer, but it was likely she would drown before getting anywhere in here. Jane was showing the others some racing platforms. Rachel made a mental note to stay far away from this room. Then something else occurred to her. This place was a maze. How would they find all the red doors if they were so scattered? "Hey Jane." Rachel called as she backed away from the water. She wasn't as clumsy as Ivy, but she wouldn't take any chances of falling in. "Yes?" "How do we find the doors we want without getting lost?" "There's maps in your welcome packets. But I wouldn't worry too much. You'll have this place memorized within a week!" Jane answered. Rachel doubted that, but the vote of confidence was nice. "Welcome packets?" Bethany repeated. "Yup." "Well, let's go!" Bethany beelined for the door they had entered through, Rachel close behind. Jane and Annika followed, but Eliza lingered behind. "Maybe I'll just stay here." Eliza suggested. Jane laughed. "You can come back first thing tomorrow morning." She promised, leading Rachel and Bethany out the door. Annika went back and murmured something to Eliza that Rachel found inaudible. Whatever she had said, it made Eliza smile and follow Annika out of the room. Rachel felt a bit hurt, and not from the throbbing pain in her toe. It seemed like Annika had been ignoring Rachel after the interviews. Now she was having secret conversations with a girl she met five hours ago! Rachel sighed. Maybe she could talk to Annika tonight, just the two of them, all about today, just like the old times. They could even pull out her candy stash again! Of course, Annika could have other friends if she wanted. It was just that it had been the four of them for so long; Annika, Ivy, Matthew, and her. It had been Annika who had brought them together. Ivy had been Annika's first friend. Rachel had still been in Paris when Annika moved down from Green Bay, Wisconsin. Rachel had come back as a nine-year-old little girl, hearing about the 'new girl that didn't go to school.' Annika had introduced herself three weeks later, inviting Rachel to hang out with her and Ivy. A year later, Matthew had moved down from Barnstable, Massachusetts, and Annika befriended him as well. Soon all four were inseparable, and had been together for the last six years. Annika was always friendly to everyone; they all were, but it was truly just the four of them. It was weird not having Ivy and Matthew here with them. Rachel was suddenly reminded of her phone in her bag. Maybe she could take some pictures to send to them! Before she could ask Jane, they were stopped in front of more double red doors. Jane pulled them open, holding the heavy door so they could get in. "Your personal room!" She declared, following them in. Rachel's eyes widened, trying to take it all in. The room was pink. The floor, the walls, and the ceiling were light pink. Two small grey couches faced each other with a small, round, black coffee table in the center. A fluffy, dark grey carpet covered the whole living room floor. A TV was mounted on the wall behind one of the couches. Off to the right was a large gap in the wall where Rachel could see a small kitchen. The kitchen walls were a pale blue, with a small black stove, a black microwave, and black cupboards. The cream tiled floor had a square table and four chairs, once again all black. It looked very homey. "Feel free to explore." Jane urged. Rachel wanted a better look at the kitchen. Behind her, she saw Annika retying her shoe, and Eliza checking the drawers on the coffee table. Bethany had disappeared. Drifting into the kitchen, Rachel noticed a tall black refrigerator she hadn't seen before. It had magnets of cute baby animals on it. Upon opening the fridge, she found fresh fruits, vegetables, milk, eggs, butter, condiments, and jellies, among other things. She opened the cupboards next and stared at the flours, sugar, cereals, beans, canned goods, hotdog and burger buns, and other grains. Only one of the cupboards held dishes. Twelve identical white plates, twelve identical white bowls, and four sets of three cups, some blue, some black, some grey, and some white. She also found a stack of black washcloths. After she was satisfied there was nothing more to be found in the kitchen/dining room, she walked back out to locate the others. Jane was in their living room, talking to Eliza, who looked up as Rachel passed and told her, "We got stuck with the bottom bunks, but I'm sure if you want the top Annika would trade with you." *Wait, they'd already claimed bunks?* Rachel thought in disbelief. Eliza pointed to a grey door. Nodding her thanks, Rachel opened the door and stepped inside. Bethany was again missing, but Annika lay on the top bunk on the left, reading a book. Hearing Rachel come in, she put down her book, which Rachel realized was a booklet created for the *Survival Race!* contestants to read. Grinning, Annika called out, "If you want top bunk, I'll switch you." Relieved Annika wasn't ignoring her anymore, she replied, "Nah, I'd rather have the bottom. Thanks, though. What are you reading?" Annika held the booklet up. "It's a booklet about this place. It was included in the welcome packet. It has a backstory, rules, a map, et cetera. Yours is on your bed, beneath me." Annika informed her. "Huh. Do you know where Bethany is?" Rachel asked, trying to process all the information she had been given. "In the bathroom, trying on her new uniform." "Uniform?" Rachel echoed. Annika laughed. "See for yourself." She told her, and returned to reading. Rachel surveyed the room. Its cream-colored walls were quite a welcome change from the pink in the living room. Two bunk beds were along the back wall of the room, each with blue sheets, thick blue and white blankets, and a blue pillow. A soft grey rug was in the middle of the floor. On both sides of the room were wardrobes; Rachel assumed one was for her and Annika and the other was for Bethany and Eliza. On the same wall with the door she had come through was a bookshelf filled with books and games. On the left wall was another door that Rachel suspected was the bathroom. Approaching her new bed, Rachel noticed a large, sealed package resting on the pillow. Tearing it open, she dumped the contents out and surveyed them. There was a booklet exactly like Annika's, two smaller wrapped packages, a pile of already stamped envelopes accompanied with paper and pencils, a *Survival Race!* tee shirt, a *Survival Race!* mug, and a bag of toiletries with a large, glittery R on the front. Rachel grinned. Souvenirs! She eyed the largest of the small packages. THAT must be the uniform. She ripped it open and pulled a bright red jumpsuit from the bag with the words *Survival Race!* emblazoned on the back. It was the same color of Annika's hair, and looked like something Rachel would love wearing. Annika preferred jumpsuits over normal clothes anytime she was laser training, rooftop jumping, or practicing her martial arts. They didn't get in the way of whatever she happened to be doing at the time. Rachel was surprised Annika wasn't already wearing it. Or was she? Rachel poked her head out from under the bunk. Annika was still wearing the outfit she put on this morning, but the shoes were different! Rachel looked back to the smallest package and peered inside. A shiny pair of brand-new tennis shoes were nestled inside, the same shade of red as their uniforms. Relieved, Rachel hurriedly slipped them on. She didn't want anyone noticing her injured toe. If she made a fuss about it, they might decide she couldn't race. Rachel stood up to test them, walking back and forth along the carpet. They had to be the comfiest shoes she had ever worn. Suddenly, the bathroom door swung open. Bethany stood there, grinning ear to ear. The uniform she had put on looked awesome. It fit perfectly, and paired with the shoes... Rachel never imagined that she would one day get to wear a *Survival Race!* uniform. They looked so much better in real life than on TV! After complimenting Bethany, who left to go show Eliza and Jane, Rachel stepped into the bathroom. The peach walls had a sweet, calming effect. The room smelled like grapefruit, and the tiles were solid beneath her feet. Along the wall was a row of four sinks, and across from them were four stalls. At the end of the bathroom were two showers, each with sliding doors that locked from the inside. Hearing loud voices in the living room, Rachel left the bathroom to investigate. Eliza, Annika, and Bethany were trying to negotiate who would make dinner. Jane stood leaning in the doorway, looking amused. Finally, Eliza declared, "Fine! I'll do dishes." Rachel decided to input before it started again. "Who's going to make dessert?" Annika and Bethany eyed each other. "I will." Bethany decided, since Annika made no attempt to claim the job. "Great!" Rachel replied. "Annika's on dinner, Bethany's on dessert, and I'll set and clear the table while Eliza does dishes." Rachel clarified. "But tomorrow, we should come up with a rotation schedule for these types of things." She added. The others agreed, and Jane gave Rachel a thumbs up when no one was looking. Rachel felt proud at the silent compliment. "Well, if you girls are all figured out, I'll be going. I'll be back at seven a.m. tomorrow." Jane announced. "Seven!" All four cried out at the same time. "That's way too early." "I planned on getting up way earlier!" "Can't I sleep in?" "Am I allowed to go out sooner on my own?" It was hard to understand who was saying what, so Jane held up her hands for silence. "**I** was thinking that at 7 a.m. tomorrow I would come by to wake you all up. Then, I'd be back at 7:40 so we could start the day. If you really choose to sleep in, I won't stop you, but if you want to be ready in a few weeks I would suggest getting up at seven with me." Jane informed them. There was silence while they thought, then Eliza said, "I'm hungry." The others agreed, and Annika headed into the kitchen. The rest started to follow, but Rachel changed directions and raced after Jane, hoping to ask her one last question, but she was already gone. Disappointed, Rachel headed back inside. She set the table using the bowls and four different colored cups. After setting out the spoons, Rachel went into the living room and proceeded to cream Eliza in several games of go fish before Annika announced dinner was done. The four sat down, and Annika ladled big scoops of chili into each bowl. They finished the delicious meal quickly, everyone going back for seconds. After they all felt so full they could burst, Eliza cleared the table and Bethany brought out a lemon pie she had made. Everyone was served large slices, and the pie disappeared just as fast as the chili had, leaving almost no leftovers to put away. Eliza washed and dried the dishes; then they all got into their supplied pajamas from the wardrobe. Rachel felt so tired she was sure she'd fall asleep instantly. Before she drifted off, she heard Annika ask if anyone minded if she read for a little bit. No one answered; they were all fast asleep. An hour later, Annika finally shut off her light and fell deep asleep.

CHAPTER 5

Annika rolled over, blinking blearily in the sunlight that filled the room she now shared with Rachel, Bethany, and Eliza. Yawning, she sat up and stretched, letting the previous day's memories flood back. She grinned, suddenly wide awake. What time was it? She looked around the room, wondering where she had put the watch she almost never took off. Annika silently climbed down her bunk's ladder onto the plush carpet below. Walking over to her new wardrobe, she pulled open the doors, noticing her watch on her wrist as she did so. Oh. She must have forgotten to take it off last night. Well, no harm done. Shrugging, Annika pulled out the new uniform she had gotten in her welcome packet, a pair of red socks, and her new tennis shoes. She quickly changed and brushed her teeth in the bathroom, then went back into the bedroom area, pulled her hairbrush out of her bag, and began the tedious job of brushing her waist-length hair. Even though it took ten minutes every morning and evening to brush it, she valued her hair too much to cut it. Once it was tangle free, she pulled it into a braid and secured it with her new ponytail. It was so pretty, and it hadn't bothered her at all yesterday. To think that this used to be Mom's... It was a tiny connection that Annika knew she would hold onto forever. After making her bed, she checked her watch. The time was 6:48 a.m. Annika surveyed the room one last time to make sure she hadn't forgotten anything. Now reaffirmed she had not missed anything, she turned for the doorway and froze part way. Had she just seen *eyes* looking at her? Turning back towards the beds, she found Eliza watching her, still looking partly asleep. Annika raised an eyebrow in her direction. How long had Eliza been watching her? It was slightly creepy; Annika silently scolded herself for not noticing earlier. Eliza rolled out of bed, yawning, and crossed the room to her wardrobe, pulling out a swimsuit and shorts, then disappeared into the bathroom. Annika left the bedroom and entered the living room. It was still hard to believe they would be living here for several weeks. Deciding she wasn't really hungry yet, Annika clicked the TV on, turned the sound down super low, and watched the most recent *Survival Race!* episode that had aired. It always began with a private intro from Cathy Brisson. The cameras then followed her into where they had been sitting yesterday, and she called out her signature "Hi girls!" The cameras showed the four contestants jump up at the sound, there were introductions... It was so weird watching those four contestants, and knowing everything else the cameras didn't show. Annika briefly wondered how bad Rachel's nervousness would show. Poor Rachel; she loved acting and performing, but without a script or knowing what was going to happen combined with her worry of screwing up caused her to fret more than enjoy. Annika knew that sometime soon she would have to tell Rachel the truth she had discovered yesterday. Rachel would be angry if she found out on her own and found out Annika already knew. All Annika wanted was for them both to enjoy this opportunity, not to spend the next month being ghosted by an angry best friend. Eliza exited the bedroom, coming into the living room and sitting down besides Annika. Annika moved to pause the show, but Eliza stopped her. "That's my cousin." She told Annika in a low whisper, pointing to one of the girls on the screen. Annika leaned closer to study her. The cousin had jet black hair and sparkling green eyes; her oval face looked identical to Eliza's. They looked so eerily similar, apart from the eyes; it was like they were twins. "She looks a lot like you." Annika commented. Eliza nodded. "Our moms are identical twins, so our differences come only from our dads. People are always saying we look like sisters." Eliza explained. The show cut to a commercial, so Annika turned it off. "Are many of your family members on the show?" Annika asked, wondering how both cousins were invited on. Eliza shrugged. "I think there were a couple of aunts, and some removed cousin. I'm not really sure." Annika was impressed. Technically, only well-known family names were invited on. They didn't invite random people, but carefully selected four teens every two months for each *Survival Race!* studio location. What had the Charminger's done to receive such fame? She was about to ask, but a quiet knock sounded on the door, making the girls jump in surprise. Annika shot up and flew to the door, swinging it open before another knock could sound on the wood. Jane stood there, a surprised expression on her face, hand poised to knock again. She quickly recovered from her shock and greeted them with a smile. "Good morning! I'm glad to see you two awake. Did you sleep well?" The girls nodded. "Great! If you don't mind, could you go wake the others up?" There was a yawn from behind them. Bethany stood in the bedroom doorway, blinking sleepily. "Good morning, Jane." She said, padding over to join them. "Is it seven already?" "It sure is!" Jane replied brightly. "Is Rachel awake?" Bethany nodded. "She's getting changed." Jane looked happy at the news. "I'll be back in 40 minutes to take you wherever you want to start today." "No need." Annika interrupted. "I memorized the map last night." Jane looked surprised again, but quickly recovered. "Great! If you ever need me, just ask a staff for my whereabouts, ok?" With a smile, Jane darted down the hall, disappearing out of sight. The three girls stared at each other for a moment; then Annika laughed and headed towards the kitchen to start breakfast. Eliza followed her, setting the table while Annika made French toast and oatmeal. 15 minutes later, Rachel and Bethany joined them at the table, and they devoured the entire meal. While Rachel washed dishes, Bethany and Eliza made 8 sandwiches for lunch. They also packed an orange for each of them. Annika smiled, glad they were all getting along so well. She partially wondered why the *Survival Race!* managers would encourage friendship and bonding if after a month the four friends would be competing for fame and money. Perhaps so there would be no sore losers? At last, they were ready to go. Annika was itching to race the track they had seen yesterday, and she knew Eliza would instantly head for the pool. The four roommates exited their "house" to find commotion in the halls. There were people everywhere. All along the hallway were people pushing equipment, shouting, laughing, talking, slamming doors, making phone calls, running; the noise was endless. The four stood there, shocked at the sight. Bethany turned around and went back into their house, shutting the door behind her, and came back out. "Our room is soundproof!" She yelled to them. "I can't hear any of it from in there!" People were starting to notice them, many calling out greetings and waving. They waved back, and Annika stepped into the busy hallway. "Stay close, and I'll get us wherever we want to go. I memorized the map last night." She called back. Eyes wide, they followed her into the traffic, pushing against the flow of people. Annika led them through twists and turns, repeatedly looking back to make sure she hadn't lost anyone. They finally came to a set of red double doors, and she pushed them open. Crowding inside the pool room, they were grateful to get a bit of peace inside the soundproofed room. They weren't alone; two women were talking, standing at the far edge of the massive pool. They noticed the girls and cut off their conversation, walking over to greet their newest contestants. "Hello girls! I'm Avery, and this is Nellie. We're your swimming instructors while you're here." The taller one introduced. She had short, sandy blonde hair that came to her chin, and was wearing a skin-tight tank top and shorts. Annika noticed her feet were bare. Nellie had her thick, dark brown hair piled into a neat bun on top of her head, and was wearing the same outfit Avery was. "So, who's going to be swimming this morning?" Nellie asked hopefully. "I am." Eliza declared, pulling off her T-shirt to reveal the bathing suit underneath. "Anyone else?" Avery tried. "Sure." Bethany agreed. "But I don't have any swim clothes." "Easily taken care of." Avery promised, motioning for Bethany to follow her to the row of life jackets and sealed bags of swimsuits along the wall. Noticing Nellie was looking at her, Annika quickly said, "Oh, no thanks. I was going to run the track today. Maybe tomorrow?" "Me too." Rachel agreed, giving the pool a nervous look. "Some other time?" She asked, backing out of the room. Annika gave the swimming instructors an apologetic look, but they were already busy. Nellie gestured at a sensor panel on the wall and the ceiling split open, the roof pulling back on either side to let the cool morning air and sunshine in. Annika gaped for a moment, shocked at how awesome this place was. With a wild whoop, Eliza sprinted for the edge of the water and flipped into a dive, quickly disappearing into the depths. She resurfaced seconds later and stroked to the side, and hauled herself out. Nellie applauded her, hurrying over. "That was amazing! Where did you learn to do that?" Annika didn't hear the reply as she left the room and joined Rachel in the hall. "Where do you want to go?" She called to Rachel, trying to be heard over all the noise. Rachel said something, but it was lost in the noise. "What?" "I said, I wanted to try the obstacle course!" Rachel yelled again. Oh. With a nod, Annika pushed back into the traffic and led Rachel to more doors, then pushed them open. Annika took a deep breath in the fresh, open air outside. The bright warm sun shone on the field that occupied the tracks and obstacle course. The tents were still in shade. Rachel started towards the tents while Annika was surveying the tracks from afar, and when she looked around Rachel was entering one of the tents. Surprised, Annika jogged after her. "Rachel!" She called out. There were sounds of rustling; then her best friend poked her head out. "Yeah?" Rachel asked quizzically, waiting for Annika to draw closer before pulling her head back inside. Annika stuck her head inside. Rachel had a mini fridge open and was rearranging its contents. "What are you doing?" "Putting our lunches away so they don't spoil." Rachel answered, sticking the bag holding their food inside the fridge and exiting the tent. "Good idea. That never occurred to me." Annika admitted. "I'm gonna go run the track. Have fun on the obstacle course!" She called, heading for the track. "You too!" Rachel called back, turning away towards the course. Annika approached the gleaming red track and stepped on the #1 lane. Ten seconds later, a booming countdown began. "3, 2, 1, GO!" Annika took off, sprinting down the track, her eyes tracking every twist. Inhaling deeply, she couldn't help marveling at how large this *Survival Race!* studio was. It took THOUSANDS of acres for the actual race land alone! Annika could not wait for the competition in a few weeks. She felt confident that even without training she could beat the others, but she definitely would be taking advantage of all the things here that were available. She would never be here again, and she wasn't going to skip anything. Annika relaxed and increased her speed, her feet pounding on the track as she pushed herself to go faster. It felt as if she had only been running for a couple minutes when she crossed the finish line. She slowed to a walk, breathing hard. The same loud voice declared, "The winner is Lane #1, with a time of 6 minutes!"

Rachel surveyed the woody course. Its obstacles looked like they could give her splinters. She frowned. There had to be *some* sort of protection for her hands. She walked back to the tents, hoping there was something they provided to avoid injuries. She peeked her head inside the first tent; it was full of medical supplies, which did not make her feel better. It took a bit of searching in the third tent to find a bin labeled **Gloves for Obstacle Course**. Rachel smiled. She appreciated people who labeled things so they were easy to find. She opened the bin, reached inside, and pulled out-granola bars? She scowled. Was this somebody's idea of a joke? She found a bin labeled **Granola Bars** and opened it. Inside sat thick gloves with a nice grip. They looked perfect for the obstacle course. She moved to switch them to their correct bins, then paused. What if someone had intentionally put them that way? She checked some of the other bins, but everything matched its label. She hesitated again, then left them where they were, taking a pair of gloves and leaving the rest in the **Granola Bars** bin. Whether it was on purpose or a mistake, it wasn't her job to fix it, and she didn't want to get in trouble. She pulled the gloves on and backed out of the tent. She wanted to finish the course before lunch. When she got back to the course, she noticed a sign that said, "Please do not attempt obstacle course without the special gloves we provide. Thank you." Rachel laughed, then eyed the first pile of logs that started the course. It reached 30 feet into the air, and had several feet and handholds to help her scale it. Rachel reached up and grabbed a log, then put her foot on another. She pulled herself up, grabbing another log to continue her climb. She reached the top in a matter of minutes, and sat on the top to catch her breath. Rachel gazed over the side. Five feet away was another log wall, and another after that. She turned to climb down the side, but stopped, an idea forming in her mind. Instead of scaling all the walls, which sounded tiresome, couldn't she just jump to the next wall? It wasn't that far away. Besides, Annika did it all the time. Rachel stood up, trying not to wobble as she balanced on the logs. Concentrating on the wall, she jumped and pushed off the logs with all her might. Rachel soared over the wall; then realized she had gone too far. With a small shriek, she twisted in midair, trying to change her momentum. She was going to fall! With a midair lunge, she curled her fingers around a log, gripping it as hard as she could and turning her face away from the logs as her body smashed into them. Pain rippled through her, and Rachel struggled to keep her hold on the log. If she fell from this height, she would definitely end up with broken bones. Shakily, Rachel hauled herself to the top of the log wall and lay there, trembling as she tried to calm down. Only after her heartbeat was slowed to its regular pace did she sit up and inspect her wounds. Many scratches covered her arms and legs; few actually bled, but they were long and painful. Rachel winced when she noticed a tear in her shorts. Jane would not be happy if she found out Rachel had damaged their property. She lay back down. How could she have possibly thought that jumping to the next wall would be a good idea? She could have broken her neck if she had fallen! It was Rachel's first near-death experience, and she never wanted another. She hadn't come here to shortcut; she was here to get better. Ashamed, she looked back to the start of the course. Should she just go out and be done? Rachel had managed to injure herself both yesterday AND today! What if that was a sign she didn't belong here? Heart heavy, Rachel turned to climb down the side, but once again stopped herself. What was she doing? She wasn't a quitter! Yes, she messed up. It certainly wouldn't happen again. Rachel was determined to finish this course-the right way. In a matter of minutes, she had scaled the walls. Muscles burning, Rachel flopped on the ground and studied her next obstacle. Several vines hung over a pool of water. She grabbed one and gave it a good tug; it stayed strong. She placed her gloves in a metal box and pressed the button on top, and the box moved on its metal track over to the other side, where it waited for her to take them out. Rachel laughed at their smart-yet old- way to keep gloves dry. She looped a vine around her hand, took a running start, and jumped, wrapping herself around the vine.

When she was close enough to the next one, she released her vine and grabbed the next, easily and successfully crossing the water. Rachel dropped to the ground, breathless and exhilarated. That was so awesome! She was slightly tempted to do it again, but decided against it, since she didn't want to be in here all day. Rachel lost track of passing time as she zoomed through obstacle after obstacle. The course seemed never-ending. She got to a particularly hard part, balancing on a skinny branch as she tried to cross a large pool of water. Rachel was two-thirds of the way across, her bare feet gripping the bark as she inched along. She had tied her shoes around her neck to give her a better grip; the gloves were in the box and were waiting for her to collect them. "Rachel! There you are!" At the sound of Bethany's voice, Rachel startled and slipped, letting out a small shriek before she plunged into the icy cold water. Her feet found ground almost instantly in the shallow six-feet-deep water, and she pushed off, propelling herself to the surface. Rachel broke through the water, spluttering as she treaded water. Suddenly, Rachel realized she couldn't feel the weight of her shoes around her neck anymore. Alarmed, she turned, looking for her shoes. They were floating away from her, somehow balancing on the soles. She stroked over to them and put her shoes on the log. Miraculously, both her shoes and socks were dry. Relieved, she turned and glared at Bethany. She stood by the fence separating them, looking extremely contrite. "Sorry! I didn't mean to startle you." She apologized. Since Bethany truly did look sorry, Rachel let go of her frustration with a sigh. "It's fine." "I've been looking for you." Bethany told her. "Why?" Rachel asked, surprised. "The rest of us have been in the exercise room for the past two hours. We kept waiting for you to join us, but when you didn't, we went to find you. When I discovered your food was still in the tent, I realized you either hadn't finished the course, or had gotten hurt. I've been walking along this fence for over fifteen minutes trying to find you! Oh, I brought your food." Bethany informed Rachel. Suddenly, as if a switch had been flipped, Rachel felt famished. How long had it been since she last ate? "Sorry, I've been stuck in this course all day. There's no exit!" Rachel apologized. Bethany raised an eyebrow. "That sounds like a bad design flaw." Bethany backed up from the fence, then tossed the wrapped sandwiches, orange, and water bottle over with one wild toss before jogging off. Rachel scrambled along the bank to catch them as her food came soaring over the fence. The water bottle clunked immediately to the grass, but the sandwiches overshot, and Rachel scrabbled wildly to stop them from splashing into the water, managing to bat them out of the air towards the grass, and plunging into the water again. The orange smacked the water a second later. When Rachel had resurfaced again, she sent another glare Bethany's direction, but she wasn't there anymore. Grumbling to herself, Rachel grabbed her orange and waded out of the water again, then sat down on the bank to eat. Rachel finished her sandwiches, ate her orange, and brushed off the crumbs as she stood up. There was no way she'd be able to balance on a slippery log with wet feet, so she dove back into the water, quickly stroking to the log where she had placed her shoes. Floating on her back, Rachel placed her shoes on her stomach and backstroked to the other end of the water. She had successfully kept her shoes dry. She placed them on the ground and reached up to pull herself out, but a hand grabbed hers and helped her up. Bethany stood there smiling smugly. "How did you get in?" Rachel asked in shock. Bethany gestured vaguely behind her. "There was a sliding door. I just pulled it open and walked in." Bethany led Rachel over to a part of the fence and tugged on one of the links. Part of the fence rattled backwards, leaving a doorway out of the course. "So, will you come hang out with us now?" Bethany asked. Rachel shook her head. "No, thanks. I'm going to keep tackling these obstacles. I'll meet you all in our room around 7 p.m. Thanks for helping me find a way out of here." She replied. Bethany looked disappointed, but said, "Sure. See you in five hours." And walked out of the gap in the fence, pulling it shut behind her and jogging away without another look back. Rachel sighed and turned back to the course. If she wanted to get through most of it by nightfall, she would have to hurry. Thankful she was almost dry from the hot afternoon sun, Rachel put her socks and shoes back on, took one last drink from the water bottle Bethany had brought her, and swung herself into the branches of a nearby tree that would get her high enough to jump on a vine close by.

It was dark when Rachel opened the door that led inside the *Survival Race!* studio. The halls were empty, and dimly lit with moonlight streaming in from the skylights. The shadows seemed creepy. Rachel sped up her pace, wanting to get back to Annika and the others. Suddenly, she stopped, as she realized she had no idea how to get back. Annika had led them all to their destinations; it had been too crowded for Rachel to focus on anything other than keeping Annika in sight. Rachel wandered the halls for 30 minutes, stopping at every red door before finally opening the door to their living room. She heard laughter and voices coming from the kitchen, and the smell of something delicious filled the 'house.' Bethany spotted her and waved hello. Rachel waved back, then joined them at the table after a quick shower. Someone had made sub sandwiches. Rachel's was crammed with turkey, cheese, lettuce, avocado, and tomato. "Why were you so late?" Bethany asked Rachel. "I got lost on the way back. Thanks for making dinner." She replied. After finishing dinner, the four girls played an ancient board game called Sorry that Annika had brought; her grandfather had taught her to play it before he died, and though it was from before the War, it was much more fun than playing HoverCraft, which was her dad's favorite game. The next day was almost just as exhausting for Rachel. They ate a hurried breakfast, packed sandwiches and pears for lunch, and split up. Rachel spent the entire day going through the last half of the course, and reunited with the others at 7 p.m. Before bedtime, she scrawled a hasty letter to her family and gave it to Jane to mail. Jane promised they would receive it within 2-3 days. Rachel also asked if they were allowed to take pictures. "Yes, but only of this room, and nothing is allowed to be posted anywhere online." Jane confirmed. "Just take them with your phone." After Jane left, Rachel climbed into bed and fell instantly asleep.

CHAPTER 6

Matthew gave a small sigh as he added another book to his ever-growing pile of books he'd read since Annika and Rachel had left. It was day four of them being gone, and he'd had no one to hang out with; Ivy was always too busy running errands or babysitting her siblings to even text him. Her parents had taken advantage of half their group being gone, having Ivy complete the chores they had been stuck doing while she ran around with her friends. Mr. and Mrs. Taryn had decided it was time for Ivy to start paying them back for all the times she was gone. Ivy had agreed without complaint, but Matthew believed he would die from boredom if he was alone the entire month. A soft knock sounded at his door, and his dad, Ben, poked his head in. "Sulking again?" Ben teasingly asked his son. "I'm not sulking." Matthew replied, moving over so his dad could sit beside him on the bed. Ben eyed the tower of books beside the bed. "You sure?" When Matthew didn't answer, his dad said, "If you want something to do, you could always go see if the Taryn's could use some help. You could say you're looking for something to occupy yourself with." Still, Matthew said nothing, so Ben got up and walked to the door. "Just an idea." He muttered before closing the door behind him. Matthew flopped backwards on his bed and stared at the ceiling. It wasn't a bad idea, but what could he possibly do to help the Taryn's? He got up and put on his jacket and shoes. At the very least, he could go for a walk. Matthew opened his door and started down the hallway, but froze as his ears picked up his parent's voices from the living room. "I'm glad Matthew has friends here. Back in Massachusetts, he grew up completely friendless! Before he met those girls, all he ever did was read." Ben said. "Yes, but I do wish he had some guy friends to hang out with. It doesn't seem right for a 16-year-old boy to have only female friends." Matthew's mother, Caroline, said. Matthew rolled his eyes and left the house, closing the door softly behind him. What did it matter whether his best friends were boys or girls? All the boys at school thought he was a weak loser because he liked computers and reading instead of playing high school sports. How could chasing a ball around a field or being tackled by beefy teens be more fun than dodging lasers and racing Annika across a large meadow? Matthew crossed the street and began walking on the sidewalk. He might as well go to town, get himself a snack and some flowers for mom. He reached into his jean pocket and pulled out several small gold coins stamped with ones. "Well, maybe not the flowers." He mused aloud with a smile. He entered town 25 minutes later, and headed towards GrocersMart, the best grocery store around for miles. Matthew made his way to the candy and chocolate aisle, deciding he wanted something sweet. He was browsing the selection when he heard a commotion a few aisles over. "I want that one!" "No, I hate that one!" "Let's do the strawberry one!" "Ew, I hate strawberries! You cannot do that one!" "Do my favorite, do my favorite!" Several kids were squabbling. Frowning, Matthew left his aisle and found where the fighting was coming from. Seven young kids, all under the age of ten, were fighting over which cereal to buy. In the middle of them was a teenage girl trying to separate three of the kids that were trying to hit each other. Upon spotting Matthew, one of the children cried, "Look, its him!" All fighting ceased instantly, and Ivy looked up in surprise. "Matthew!" She greeted. He dropped his gaze to her seven siblings, who were trying their best to look like good little kids. "Need some help?" He asked sympathetically. "No... Well, sure." She agreed with a half-smile. "Thank you." Ivy handed Matthew a long list of items she needed to get. Only a few had been crossed off. He looked at the list, memorized it, then handed it back. "If you get the bottom five, I'll get everything else." He offered. Ivy agreed and tossed two random boxes of cereal in her cart when no one was looking. She pushed the cart away, making sure her siblings were still following her. Matthew grabbed a cart for himself, then consulted his memory for the first item: eggs. It was one of those times having an enhanced memory came in handy. While it wasn't quite a 'photographic' memory, Matthew had found that even at a young age he could remember events, faces, and tiny details with startling clarity. It didn't matter how long ago something had occurred; it was like a crystal-clear snapshot in his mind that never went away. In most instances, like today, it was a blessing. Other times, it felt like a curse, especially when he couldn't forget things he'd rather not remember. Matthew had always referred to it as a photographic memory for the sake of simplicity, since in the end, that's what it was. For the next 20 minutes he was busy, moving about the store adding Ivy's groceries to his cart. Occasionally he heard Ivy's patient voice over her siblings, explaining why they couldn't get a pound of candy or a certain type of fruit. Two elderly women Matthew recognized as Annika's neighbors moved out of his way as he entered the bread aisle, and he almost froze when he heard them mention Annika's name. Pretending to check the ingredients on a loaf of bread, he listened intently to their conversation, deciding he could feel guilty later. "Did you hear? Annika Helmcott is one of the next contestants for *Survival Race!*" "Really? Her parents must be so proud!" "Well, I'm sure her dad is, but her mom..." "Oh yeah. Didn't Louisa Helmcott die in a car accident?" "That's what they say, but I don't believe it for even a second." "Why not?" "Because. Two days before she died, a black car with no license plate pulled up outside their house while I was pruning my roses. Five men got out and knocked on the Helmcott's door. I made sure they didn't see me; I did not like the look of those men. Minutes later, Louisa was being escorted into the car and they drove off. Two days later she dies in a car crash. But, get this- there was no funeral, and the body they carted away looked nothing like Louisa. I've known Louisa for many years, and I happened to be walking by when the crash occurred. It wasn't Louisa, but all the doctors said it was! Her husband claimed they had a private funeral, but I don't believe that either. I mean, his daughters weren't even home! Amelia was at college, and little Annika was on a homeschoolers field trip. Every time I tried to talk to Dan about his wife, he would get this pained expression and say he didn't want to talk about it. Can't imagine what he told his daughters when they came home. After Annika got home, she didn't exit her house for almost two months after that. Well, that was years ago. I just wish I knew where Louisa is, if it wasn't her in the crash. Who actually died? And, why did they lie about it?" The other woman was thoughtful, then said, "I don't know, but if they've kept it a secret this long, I doubt we'll ever find out. What breed of roses were you pruning?" They changed the topic to gardening, and moved out of range. Matthew couldn't stop running the women's words through his mind. He, Ivy, and Rachel hadn't known a lot. A few days after Annika had disappeared into her house in grief, 12-year-old Matthew had gone to the Helmcott's house, asking where she was. Rachel had gotten a fish and wanted Annika to come over and see it, but wasn't allowed to leave her house. Mr. Helmcott had quietly explained to Matthew that Annika's mother had died in a car crash, and that Annika might be absent for a while. Two months later, when Annika finally came over, the fish was dead. Annika told them she'd been sick, which was true, but never talked about her mother. Matthew had told Ivy and Rachel what had happened, so they always carefully avoided the subject. But, after watching Rachel hug her own mother, Annika seemed determined not to let the absence of her own mother bother her. She never outwardly had a problem being around her friends' mothers again, much to her friend's relief. But if Annika's neighbor was right, and the woman in the crash wasn't Mrs. Helmcott, then why had Mr. Helmcott told Matthew she was dead? Why would he have kept up that pretense for four years? Why did he lie to his daughters? And where was Mrs. Helmcott if she hadn't died in the crash? Where had those men taken her? And if all or most of the woman's story was true, how much of it did Annika or Amelia know? The whole thing didn't make sense, and Matthew realized he wanted to know what had actually happened. Here was a mystery from four years ago, something exciting to brighten up his summer. He located Ivy and her siblings in the checkout lane. After she'd paid for everything they'd collected, he helped her carry the bags to her car. "First 8 to get buckled get a Hershey bar!" Ivy called, winking at Matthew as she held up an 8-pack of small Hershey chocolates. Yelling gleefully, her siblings raced to get buckled, leaving Ivy and

Matthew alone. "Ivy, listen. I overheard two women talking about Mrs. Helmcott." Her brow furrowed in confusion. "Mrs. Helmcott- Annika's mom?" He nodded. "They think she's still alive." Now Ivy looked really confused. "You told us Mr. Helmcott said she died in a car crash." "That is what he told me." Matthew agreed. "But the woman thinks the crash was faked." Ivy's eyes widened. "Then what happened to her?" She asked. "The neighbor said she saw five men take Mrs. Helmcott away in an unlicensed car. Two days later Mrs. Helmcott died in the crash. She also said there wasn't a funeral. She thinks the crash was staged. I want to find out what actually happened." Ivy looked a bit worried, but said, "Okay, but I probably won't be much help while I'm in charge of these guys." She gestured towards her car, where shouts of "Done!" and "We want chocolate!" could be heard. They said goodbye, and Matthew walked quickly home, and went straight to his bedroom. He turned on his computer and pulled up the search engine. He wanted answers, and with his hacking skills he was sure he could find them.

A knock on his door brought Matthew back to the present. It had been a few days since he had heard the elderly women talking about Mrs. Helmcott. Matthew had hardly left his room in the time since, searching the internet for any mention of Louisa Helmcott. He had found pictures taken from the crash, and confirmed the woman was not Louisa. Comparing the online picture to the one in his mind, he could tell the faces were different, and Mrs. Helmcott's hair was much darker than in the photos. Most of the doctors and EMT's who arrived at the crash were retired, dead, or non-contactable. Only a Dr. Bryce MacHaven was still working. When a knock sounded at the door, Matthew quickly shut off his computer, and went to answer the door. His mother stood there, holding a bowl of soup. Glancing at the clock, Matthew realized he had again forgotten to come down for dinner. Sheepishly, he accepted the food and sat down at his desk to eat. "I hope you haven't been on the computer this entire time." Caroline said, running her eyes over his room. "It's not healthy for you. What have you been doing this past week? I hardly see you anymore!"

That's because you're always working. Matthew thought, but said, "Sorry. Do you know a doctor named Bryce MacHaven?" He asked her. Caroline looked surprised. "I've heard that name somewhere. Why?" Her son hesitated. "I wanted to ask him some questions." Caroline looked delighted. "So you're thinking about being a doctor after all? Wait here, I'll see if I can find his phone number." She rushed away. Matthew ate while she was gone. Minutes later, his breathless mom appeared in the doorway again. "Tomorrow morning, at nine a.m. in his office." Matthew smiled. "Thanks, mom. This means a lot to me." She smiled back. "Your father and I were just about to start a game. Want to join us?" "Sure." He agreed, picking up his empty bowl and following her to the kitchen. It was least he could do, considering she'd unknowingly done him a huge favor.

The next morning came quickly, and Matthew was on the road at 8 in the morning. It was a long walk to Dr. MacHaven's office. He reached the hospital that the doctor worked at around 8:50, and pushed the doors open. The smell hit him first, making him want to gag on the metallic stench of blood and antiseptic. It was busy and crowded, and noisy. When he got to the front desk, he told the lady sitting there, "I'm looking for Dr. MacHaven's office." "Take the elevator to the second floor, take two rights, his door is on the left. You can't miss it." He nodded his thanks and stepped away, then found an empty elevator and rode it to the second floor. Following the receptionist's instructions, he located a sturdy wood door with a gold name plate reading "Dr. Bryce MacHaven" nailed to the door. Matthew knocked gently on the door, suddenly wondering if he was early. Or late. "Enter!" Called a cheerful voice. Matthew twisted the knob and opened the door. A tall, dark-haired man stood by a mini-fridge, filling a cup with juice. His features were chiseled, and he had a small stubble growing on his chin. When he smiled, dimples appeared. "Welcome! You must be Matthew Carimella?" The doctor greeted. Matthew nodded. "Come in, come in. Would you like something to drink? Juice, perhaps?" "Sure, thank you." Matthew replied, entering the room and closing the door behind him. Dr. MacHaven handed him a cup of orange juice and seated himself behind the desk, gesturing for Matthew to take a seat on one of the chairs in the office. "So! I hear you have some questions for me." "Yes. Do you recognize the name Louisa Helmcott?" Matthew asked, jumping right in to the whole reason he was there. Dr. MacHaven frowned and sipped his drink. "No, I can't say I do." "You proclaimed her dead in a car crash four years ago." Matthew prompted. Dr. MacHaven frowned again. "Maybe I do remember that. Was she someone you knew?" "Yes." Matthew gave no further explanation. "Where was she buried?" He asked. "I believe she was cremated. But when your mother called, she made it sound as if you were interested in being a doctor. Surely you didn't come all this way to talk about a dead person?" Dr. MacHaven asked, seeming a bit suspicious. "Actually, I did. I was looking at some of the pictures taken at the crash, and I don't think the woman in that crash was Louisa Helmcott. Could you have mistaken her with someone else?" Matthew questioned, locking eyes with the doctor. Dr. MacHaven's face hardened, and his tone changed. No longer cheery and loud, it was cold and angry. "I knew Louisa Helmcott. She was my friend for many years. You dare to suggest that you, being roughly 11 or 12 when the crash occurred, knew her better than I, who was on the site where the crash occurred? Yes, I am positive it was Louisa. There is no doubt in my mind that she died four years ago. I also think you should leave right now, and stop looking for ghosts that aren't there." Dr. MacHaven stood up, so Matthew walked out, leaving his untouched juice on the table. He was positive he could remember Mrs. Helmcott better than the doctor, thanks to his photographic memory, but dared not reveal that to Dr. MacHaven. Something about him was off, something weird. He left the hospital and returned home. Dr. MacHaven seemed convinced she was long gone, but it just couldn't be true. Besides, why would he first say he didn't recognize the name Louisa Helmcott, then later claim he was a good friend and remembered her better than Matthew? Perhaps the only lead he had now was... Mr. Helmcott. If Mrs. Helmcott really hadn't died, then did her husband know where she was? But... should he ask? If she was alive, then why would Mr. Helmcott lie to his daughters, and to the entire world? Louisa

Helmcott was well-known. Her death was big news. What would have made him keep up the lie for four years? It made no sense. It might be better not to tell Mr. Helmcott yet. But should he tell anyone what he learned? Ugh, there were too many questions. He could always update Ivy, he supposed. "Matthew, dinner's done!" His mom called. When he entered the kitchen, he wanted to laugh at the pleased expression his mom wore, like she hadn't actually expected him to come. "Mom? Can I go over to the Taryn's house after dinner?" "As long as they're okay with it. Hey, how did the interview go?" She answered. "What interview?" Matthew's dad asked as he dished three bowls up of his delicious mac-and-cheese. "Matthew interviewed Dr. MacHaven today." Caroline said. "Oh yeah? Why?" Ben inquired, surprised. Matthew shrugged. "Wanted to find out a bit more about what he does." His dad raised an eyebrow. "I thought you weren't interested in being a doctor like your mom." "I'm not." Matthew replied, and began to eat. His mother looked extremely disappointed, but said nothing. Matthew wasn't able to get to the Taryn's house until 8:40 p.m. Mr. and Mrs. Taryn's car was gone, but Ivy's car was still parked in the driveway, and the kitchen light was on, casting a silhouette on the closed blinds. Ivy was home. Since Mr. and Mrs. Taryn had given permission for Matthew, Rachel, and Annika to visit even if they weren't home, Matthew did not feel too uncomfortable knocking softly on their door. A moment later, he heard the quiet hiss of the electronic locking system releasing, and the door swung open. Ivy stood there, her long bangs tucked behind her ears, clutching a dirty rag in her left hand. She looked surprised to see him. "Matthew! What are you doing here?" She asked, keeping her voice low. "I wanted to update you on what I learned about Mrs. Helmcott. I thought it would be better to wait until your siblings were in bed." Ivy smiled. "Good idea. I just got them to sleep about 20 minutes ago. Do you want to come in?" She added, remembering her manners. When Matthew nodded, she led him to the kitchen. Matthew relocked the door behind him. Rather than sitting down at the table, Ivy crouched down by one of the walls and began scrubbing it with her rag. Looking around, Matthew realized the walls were covered in bits of dried food. Ivy was in the middle of cleaning pieces of dried mashed potatoes off the wall. "What happened?" He asked, squatting down beside her. "Carrie decided to start a food fight, since mom and dad went on a 'well-deserved' date night. It got *way* out of hand. I had to make sure they all got baths before I put them to bed." She rolled her eyes. "You know how 3-year-olds are. As soon as the parents are gone, they cause as much trouble as possible. In this case, it happened to be a VERY messy food fight." Matthew gave a soft laugh. He couldn't help it. Something about the way Ivy described it made him wish he'd been there. Ivy stopped her scrubbing and turned to face him, surprise etched onto her face. "Matthew!" "What?" He asked, wondering what he'd done. "I don't think I've ever heard you laugh before." She told him, an unreadable emotion on her face. Matthew thought about that. "Probably not." He agreed. "Why don't you ever laugh?" She asked in confusion. He took a moment before responding. "Because usually when you and Rachel and Annika laugh, you laugh loudly. So rather than trying to force a laugh that's loud enough to be heard, I just smile, since I don't like being loud anyway. Besides, I like hearing you guys laugh." Ivy had nothing to say to that, so she returned to her task of cleaning the walls. "Can I help?" Matthew asked. Ivy looked up. "You don't have to." She assured him. "I want to." Matthew stood up and walked over to the kitchen sink. Finding a rag in it, he rinsed it and brought it back to where Ivy was and began to clean the wall alongside her. The two friends worked in companionable silence for a while before Matthew remembered why he came over in the first place. "I've been researching Louisa Helmcott." Matthew reminded Ivy. She listened intently while Matthew explained what he had learned on the internet, and about his weird conversation with Dr. MacHaven. When he had finished relating everything, Ivy pondered what he said before replying. "Dr. MacHaven sounds like he was trying to hide something. He obviously didn't like you asking questions about a supposed closed case. If Mrs. Helmcott's death was faked, he was definitely a part of it, and he doesn't want anyone to find out about his involvement; it could mean the end of his career. The next step seems to be finding out where Mrs. Helmcott has been all this time. Maybe you should talk to Mr.

Helmcott, tell him what you know and find out what he knows. Other than the men that took her away, he was the last person to come in contact with her before she disappeared. He likely knows details no one else does. Mr. Helmcott might be our last best chance to find out what happened. That's what I think, anyway." She finished. Matthew stared at his friend, on the borderline of shock. "What?" It was her turn to ask. "When did you get so smart?" He asked her. Ivy held his gaze as she replied, "I've always been smart, Matthew. I've just always let you and Annika handle the heavy thinking for our group." Suddenly, Matthew realized what she was hinting at. Ivy was far too nice to admit it, but she was tired of just being the groups morale. She wanted to do something more than just making them laugh. "I'm sorry." And the smile she gave him told Matthew he was forgiven. They moved around the kitchen for another hour, cleaning and trading stories from before they had met Annika. When at last the Taryn's large kitchen was sparkling clean, Matthew headed for the door, tired and ready to go home. Ivy met him on the front porch and thanked him for his help. As he started down the stairs, she called to him, "You know, I don't think I've ever heard you talk as much as you did tonight." He paused and turned back to face her. "It's easy to talk when your company is a good listener." He told her. Smiling, he bade her goodnight and headed home, letting himself into his house past 10 p.m. It was dark and silent, so he retreated to his bedroom and fell fast asleep.

* * * * *

Ding! Ding! Ding! Ding! Ding Ding! Ding! Riiiiiing! Matthew's phone rang early the next morning. He grabbed it angrily. He had been woken up by constant text pings, and now whoever it was, was calling him! Did they not realize it was not even eight in the morning? "Hello?" He answered crossly. "Hi Matthew! Good morning! Have you been receiving our texts? Annika and Rachel are on our group text!" It was Ivy. Oh. "Uh, thanks. Be right there." He answered, regretting his harsh tone of voice earlier. "Ok. Bye!" Ivy chirped, hanging up. Fully awake now, Matthew opened his messages, typed a quick "hi" so they knew he was there, and scrolled up to the top of the days' messages to see what he had missed.

Today

Annika: Hey guys!

Rachel: Hi!

Annika: Ivy? Matthew?

Rachel: Hello hello hello?

Annika: Guys, wake up!

Ivy: Annika! Rachel! It's so good to hear from you!

Rachel: Ivy!

Annika: Miss us?

Ivy: Yes! Are you having fun there?

Annika: Yeah! We've been training most of the time

Ivy: *You* need to train? :)

Rachel: No, I'm probably the only one of us four who is going to need training.

Ivy: Oh, who are your competitors?

Rachel: Their names are Bethany Meyers and Eliza Charminger. They're super nice.

Annika: They're really good, too

66 | SHADOW'S EDGE

Ivy: Worried they'll beat you? :)

Annika: Nah.

Rachel: Liar.

Annika: Who, me?

Rachel: Yes you! I saw the look on your face when Eliza beat you in the swimming contest.

Annika: Pssh. That was nothing.

Rachel: Suuure

Ivy: Haha :)

Annika: Where's Matthew?

Ivy: I don't know

Rachel: Is he getting our messages?

Ivy: Hold on, I'll call him

Matthew: Hi

Rachel: Matthew! What took so long?

Rachel: Matthew?

Rachel: Hello?

Matthew: Hi, sorry, was catching up

Annika: How have you been?

Matthew: Good

Rachel: Been keeping busy?

Ivy: I have! Mom and dad have me on sibling watch 24/7, to

"make up" for all the times I've been gone

Annika: Ouch. How long have we been gone?

Matthew: Today is your ninth day there

Annika: Oh wow

Rachel: Has it really been that long? Time passes fast here

Ivy: Oh no! They forgot us already!

Annika: We didn't forget you...

Ivy: That hurts

Matthew: When will you be back?

Annika: A few weeks. We get 2 more weeks of training, and then the race spans a week.

Rachel: Did my family get the letter I sent them?

Ivy: Yes, they did! They already mailed one back. You should get it soon. They also sent a surprise.

Rachel: What is it?

Ivy: Not telling

Rachel: Come on, please?

Ivy: Hmm, nah

Rachel: :(

Matthew: Who do you think is going to win?

Annika: Me

Rachel: I don't know. After seeing how good Eliza and Bethany and Annika are, I'm not sure I belong with this group. They're too good!

Ivy: Don't be ridiculous! The letter had your name on it; of course you belong there! Right, Annika?

Matthew: I'm with Ivy

Rachel: Thanks, guys. :)

Ivy: Annika?

Annika: Sorry, what?

Ivy: Never mind

Annika: Uh oh, Jane's here

Ivy: Who's Jane?

Rachel: Bye!

Ivy: Bye?

Matthew stared at the messages long after his friends had left their phones. It seemed like Annika and Rachel were enjoying themselves, which was good. But Ivy's "They forgot us" comment seemed to hit a little too close to home. They wouldn't be back for another few weeks, and who knew what- Ding! Matthew snapped his attention back to his phone, and clicked on the new message. It was from an Unknown ID. Its short, to the point text made Matthew's blood run cold.

Unknown: If you want answers about what really happened to Louisa Helmcott, meet me at Shadow Park midnight tonight. Bring a trusted adult with you. Do not be late.

Shakily, he typed back,

Matthew: Who are you?

He never got a response.

CHAPTER 7

Matthew stood in front of the Helmcott's house, trying to muster up the courage to knock. He wasn't quite sure why he was afraid to talk to Mr. Helmcott, but he only had 12 hours until the meeting with the mystery person, and there was no way Mr. Helmcott would accompany him without knowing why. He raised his fist and tapped three short knocks on the door, giving an involuntary wince at the disruptive noise. It took Dan a minute to answer the door, and he opened it to find Matthew pacing nervously. "Matthew!" He said, surprised. "Hi, Mr. Helmcott." He took a deep breath. "I need to confess." Dan raised his eyebrows, studied Matthew for a moment, then opened his door wider, saying, "Well then, come on in." As Matthew stepped over the threshold, the first thing he noticed was the chill. It was late July, so it made sense to keep your house air-conditioned, but this was an actual chill, making Matthew zip up his sweater, hoping to keep out some of the cold. That explained why Dan was wearing such a thick sweater. Dan led Matthew into his living room, motioning for Matthew to sit on the soft grey couch across from him, and clearing a stack of mystery novels off the table so they could see each other. Then Dan spoke. "You said you came here to confess?" Matthew nodded, then admitted, "I've been looking into Mrs. Helmcott's death, and I don't think it was actually her in the crash." Several emotions flashed across Dan's face before settling on one- confusion. "Why have you been researching Louisa's death?" Matthew told him everything, from the conversation he'd heard in the grocery store, to the days of searching the internet and comparing pictures, his visit with Dr. MacHaven, the conversation with Ivy, and finally showed Dan the mysterious text he'd gotten. "Mr. Helmcott, I know this wasn't any of my business-" "You're right about that." Dan stood up abruptly.

"It *is* none of your business." "But I came to you because I trust you. Do you really think your wife died four years ago in that crash?" Matthew persisted. Dan sat back down, and after a moment replied, "You don't know the full story." "Then tell me. Please." Matthew begged. It was a long time before Dan spoke again, and when he did it was in a voice so low Matthew had to strain to hear him. "It was such a normal day, the day they took Louisa away. I was making lunch for us when I heard a pounding on the door. I went to answer it, and found five SIA men standing there." "The Secret Intelligence Agency?" Matthew asked incredulously. "I thought only Annika worked for them." Dan shook his head. "Louisa had also been working for the SIA, but I never knew much more than that, since she didn't want me to be involved and I didn't want to be involved anyway. They said they were here to talk to Louisa, and shoved past me. They demanded to know where Louisa was, and when I said I didn't know, they searched the house, finally finding her in our bunker." At that, Matthew's eyes widened. The Helmcott's had a bunker? Dan continued with his story, not seeming to realize what he'd just told Matthew. "She was screaming and thrashing, trying to break free, so one of the agents pulled out a gun and pointed it at me. Louisa stopped fighting instantly." Dan shuddered at the memory. "When I asked what was going on, they calmly informed me that Louisa had been committing terrible crimes against the SIA for a while, and that they had finally captured her and were taking her in for questioning and punishment. When I asked for how long, they said indefinitely. The entire time they were explaining this, Louisa stayed neutral; her head was down, her shoulders sagged. She looked defeated, and that scared me more than the gun still aimed at me. In one last desperate attempt to stop them from taking her away from me, I told them Louisa was a too well-known figure in our community, and that she couldn't just disappear. It turns out they'd thought of that already, and told me that they were going to stage her death. I looked at Louisa, silently begging her to help me, and then she raised her head and said, "Just let me talk to him one last time, and then I'll go without a fight." I was shocked, but they agreed, and gave us a semi-respectful distance to talk. Before I could get a word out, she was speed talking, her eyes pleading me to listen. She said, 'Please, Dan, don't tell the girls I'm still alive. Especially not Annika. She'll try to find me, and I don't want her to get hurt. I know I'm guilty, to them, and I knew they would catch up to me eventually. Please support the story when they stage my death. For me. Do it for me, Dan. Promise me.' And she held my gaze with the same intense eyes Annika has until I promised. But even though I had promised Louisa, I was also depending on another promise from the SIA. They promised they would never bother my family again, and never hurt or capture anyone else. Then, I watched as they herded Louisa to the door and locked her in their car. I watched as they drove her away. I went along with the story two days later, when she 'died' in a car accident. It broke my heart, lying to Amelia and Annika, watching their faces crumple when I told them they would never see their mother again. It made me feel sick, every time the neighbors tried to offer their sympathy, and I just wanted to shout that she wasn't actually gone, but I didn't. All these years, I've kept my last promise to my wife in mind, every time I lied I remembered her words, begging me to play along. And, eventually, I started to believe she really is dead. You see, Matthew, even if she didn't die in the car accident, who knows if she survived the SIA's 'questioning', or what she's gone through? It's been four years, and four years is a very long time." Dan stared at Matthew; his look resigned. It was obvious Dan had been thinking about that every day for the past four years, and it pained Matthew to see the middle-aged man looking so lost, so he held up his phone again. "Maybe we can find out." Dan stared at the dark screen for a long while before finally nodding. "Fine. We'll go and meet this mysterious person and hear what they have to say. But you're going to need a good excuse as to why you're leaving the house at midnight if you want your parents to let you go." He told Matthew, who smiled in response. "You and I are going stargazing. There happens to be a rare meteor shower you wanted to see, and you asked me to come with you, since you thought I might be interested." Matthew pointedly informed him. A smile broke across Dan's face. "Sounds fun."

That night after dinner, Matthew told his parents that Mr. Helmcott had invited him to view a rare meteor shower that night, around midnight. His father called Dan to confirm, while his mother reminded Matthew to wear a thick sweater. As he started down the hall to his room, he heard his mother tell his dad, "Well, at least astronomer is a respectful career." Matthew rolled his eyes and shut his door.

It was 11:48 p.m. when Mr. Helmcott knocked on the Carimella's door. Matthew, who had been reading on the couch, sprang up and opened the door. Dan stood there, a surprised expression on his face, hand poised in midair to knock again. He quickly recovered from his shock and greeted Matthew with a smile, though it looked tight and nervous. "Ready to go?" Matthew nodded and joined the older man on the porch. "Do you know the way to Shadow Park?" Matthew asked quietly. Dan nodded. "Louisa and I used to bring Annika and Amelia there all the time when they were little." The two men walked silently through the brisk, chilly night, Dan leading Matthew through the dark, empty streets. They arrived at the park 10 minutes later, cautiously entering the fenced playground area. Dan switched on a flashlight and swung its beam around the park. There was no one there; and then there was. "I'm glad you're here." They jumped and spun towards the sound. The flashlight's beam fell upon a row of trees, but there was no one. Who had spoken? The voice came again, but this time it sounded irritable. "Turn that off and come over here." Dan flicked the light off, and a shadowy figure emerged from the trees, dimly lit from the light of the moon. Matthew and Dan moved towards the figure, and Matthew noticed that Dan had a small bulge in the shape of a gun under his sweater. Matthew suddenly realized how happy he was to have an adult with him. He would not have enjoyed coming out here alone. They drew to a stop in front of the figure, and were finally able to see him clearly. The mysterious texter was a young man, looking to be in his early twenties. His brown hair hung in jagged bangs over his forehead, and his green eyes sparkled in the moonlight. He didn't look like the type of person who sent teenagers texts telling them to meet at midnight in a park. Smiling at Matthew, the stranger said, "I'm glad you were able to make it. Hopefully you were smart enough to use the meteor shower as cover?" Matthew nodded, caught off guard. This guy had thought of everything! Dan held out his hand to shake, and said "I'm Dan Helmcott." The stranger shook the offered hand and smiled. "I was hoping you would come." Matthew extended his hand as well. "I'm Matthew." Then he realized the man probably already knew that, if he was reaching out. He shook his hand. "Kevin." Matthew noted that he didn't offer a last name. Dan cut straight to the chase. "What do you know about Louisa?" "She's being held in a labor camp." Kevin answered immediately. "What?" Matthew whispered in disbelief. "Two days before she 'died,' she sent out a distress signal, saying she had been caught. A few days later, we retrieved a message from the SIA informing us that Louisa Helmcott had been given a life sentence to work in one of their labor camps. We tried everything to barter her back, but there was no way the SIA was giving up their prize. Louisa had been a massive thorn in their organization for a long time, and I bet they were fighting to be first in line to interrogate all the secrets out of her. Oh, sorry." Kevin stopped when he realized Dan didn't look good. The stress of finding out there was a good chance his wife was alive, but in a labor camp, and being painfully interrogated was too much. While Dan was taking a moment to recover and sort through his thoughts, a light flashed overhead. Emerging from under the trees, Matthew and Kevin watched the bright meteor shower soar overhead, and Dan joined them. The show seemed to stretch for hours, yet it was only a couple minutes long from start to finish. "Wow." Matthew breathed. "I didn't know the sky could do that." Kevin smiled. "Space may be the biggest mystery in the galaxy. I doubt we'll ever learn all there is to know about our night sky. But the meteor shower was not the main reason we met tonight." He told Matthew, turning to face Mr. Helmcott. Dan nodded, ready to start asking questions. "Louisa worked for the SIA. Why are you implying she was their greatest enemy?" Dan asked. "She did work for the SIA." Kevin replied. "Until she realized how evil they were and left to join us at the National Investigation Bureau." Now Dan looked skeptical. "Louisa never told me she joined the NIB.

Besides, the whole reason we fought World War III fifty years ago was to exterminate all the evil people who were destroying our people and our planet. Evil doesn't just spring back up after fifty years!" Kevin sighed. "I wish I could agree with you, but it's just not how it turned out. Louisa became one of our best agents, effortlessly destroying plans and supplies the SIA was counting on. She left them scrambling to catch up. Then, on one mission where she and a few other agents oversaw getting rid of a bunch of explosives, one of our agents made an error and was seriously injured. When the SIA captured him, he spilled a lot of important information, including who was on the sabotage mission with him. The SIA put the facts together and captured Louisa. It was one of our worst recorded missions; we lost two agents, only sabotaged 20% of the explosives, and had to change a lot of locations and passwords, since we couldn't be sure of what our agent had told the SIA." And then Kevin's voice grew cold as he told the next part of the story. "Then, two years after Louisa was captured, her youngest daughter joined the SIA and caused us absolute destruction. At only 13 years old, she was capturing our agents, obliterating bases and ruining valuable information, and generally undoing **EVERYTHING** that Louisa had done. I expect the SIA got quite a laugh at having Annika unknowingly undo everything her mother had worked to achieve, all the while thinking she was following in her mother's footsteps." Matthew stared at Kevin in dismay. If what he was saying was true, then this information would tear Annika apart. She had once told Matthew the only reason she joined the government was to honor her mother's memory and continue her work. She would be horrified to find out that all this time she'd been undoing her mother's work, and that she was working for the organization that took her mother as prisoner! How do you even begin to tell someone that? Dan looked equally shaken. "If I had known, I never would have let her..." Kevin shrugged, and his mild manner returned. "Thankfully, she hasn't done anything for a while now. As long as she stays away from Elle..." "Elle?" Matthew asked curiously. Kevin looked hesitant, then said, "Elle Thompson, a friend of ours. She's working on something extremely important and her work must not be disturbed or destroyed by Annika." "Don't worry, she's on the game show *Survival Race!* right now. She won't accept a mission while she's there." Dan quickly assured Kevin. He looked impressed. "*Survival Race!* Nice." Then Matthew had a question. "How do you benefit from telling us all of this?" Kevin sucked in a breath before answering. "We want you to join us on a mission to break into a mansion." At their shocked looks, he quickly added, "Look, we don't usually involve outsiders, but everything was lining up too perfectly to ignore. We have to act fast, and there isn't enough time to train others to do what you two already excel at." "We are NOT joining the NIB." Dan jumped in, shooting Matthew a look that said 'don't argue.' Kevin put his hands up in mock surrender. "You don't have to. But you want your wife back, and we want our agent back. Why not work together to make that happen?" "Break into a mansion?" Matthew asked incredulously. "The mansion belongs to the SIA director, Leo Makrus. We have reason to believe there are computer files in there telling where the labor camps are located, and who's in them. The reason we want you two to join us on this mission is because you, Mr. Helmcott, are exceptionally good at picking locks, and you, Matthew, are an expert with computers. Then there would be me, of course, and a fourth for backup, probably another NIB agent..." Kevin trailed off. "Ivy." Matthew said instantly, without thinking. "Pardon?" Kevin asked uncertainly. "She's my friend. I want her to come." Kevin gave him a look. "This is a top-secret operation. We can't just invite anyone." "Ivy isn't anyone. Besides, she already knows everything." Matthew insisted, purposely neglecting to mention that Ivy knew nothing of this meeting- yet. Kevin looked horrified. "Everything? Did I not tell you this was a *secret* meeting when I texted you?" "No, you didn't. You just left creepy instructions to meet you in a park at midnight!" Matthew retorted. "Yeah, and you noticed I told you to bring a trusted adult? It's because I'm not some creepy guy trying to kidnap you. We just want your help. At least with him here you have someone to vouch for you that I never harmed you." Kevin reminded him. Matthew had nothing to say to that, so he asked instead, "Can she come?" Kevin heaved a sigh. "I'll discuss it with my boss. But we get **ONE** chance at retrieving the information. We can't fail." "When do we get to go?" Matthew asked eagerly. "Go where?" Kevin asked. "On the mission!" Matthew clarified. "Not for several weeks." Kevin answered. "Weeks?" Dan repeated. "But Louisa..." Kevin shook his head. "If she has been able to last this long, a few more weeks won't hurt her. To carry out a 'heist' this big, it will require careful planning and timing. If we execute this perfectly, we can have Louisa- and everyone else that was captured- back within two months." Matthew glanced at Dan, wondering what he would think of that timeline. He fully expected to see impatience on the older man's face, but found instead a new fire blazing in his eyes. His wife was still alive, and he would stop at nothing to get her back.

The next morning over breakfast, Matthew asked his parents if Mr. Helmcott could stay with them while Annika was at the *Survival Race!* studio. "He's probably pretty lonely, being in that big house all by himself, and the meteor shower last night was really cool. Maybe we could keep each other company while you guys are at work?" He suggested. After a bit of discussion his parents agreed, and Dan moved into the guest room that very day. Over the course of several weeks, they worked on their plans, disguising the mansion's layout and guard count with star charts and figures. Kevin had Matthew design a special code on a flashdrive, insisting that it would come in handy. At night, when they went out to view certain star clusters or nebulas, they secretly met with Kevin, exchanging information, having the flashdrive swap hands as both Matthew and some of the NIB worked on creating the code, and adjusting the heist timeline. Matthew also visited Ivy often, filling her in on the new plan each time an important part got changed. One night during dinner, he was so focused on finalizing the last details of their heist that would take place tomorrow, he wasn't paying attention when his mother announced that the Ravenstone twins had stopped by earlier that day, and dropped off a recording of the latest *Survival Race!* episode; the one with Rachel and Annika. They'd also dropped copies off at the Taryn and Helmcott households. When his mother asked if they wanted to watch it tonight, Matthew and Dan distractedly answered no, and that they were planning on going to bed early tonight so they would be well rested for the field trip tomorrow. "Oh yeah." Matthew's dad said, leaning forward. "Where did you say this 'field trip' was?" "There is a valuable art collection a rich man owns, and he's letting people view it for the first- and only- time tomorrow. Matthew and Ivy really wanted to go see it, so I said I'd take them, since you two will be working, and Ivy's parents will need to watch their children while Ivy's gone. At least with me there, no one will have to worry about them getting lost." Dan answered. "Are they old enough?" Caroline asked. Dan nodded. "Only people 15 and older can go in, so they'll be ok." That seemed to satisfy them, but Matthew could tell his mom was a bit suspicious, because when she thought Matthew was out of hearing range she told her husband, "First doctor, then astronomer, and now art collector. Why does he keep changing his mind?"

The day of the heist came quickly enough, and Matthew found he was on edge. Dan looked just as jittery. They hurried through their breakfast, then climbed into Dan's Cybertruck and drove to the Taryn's house. Ivy met them at the door, her brown eyes twinkling with excitement and nerves. She took the seat beside Matthew, and as soon as she was buckled Dan drove off again; they still had to pick up one more person. "I've never done anything like this before." Ivy confided to Matthew. "It feels like it should be wrong. We're going to break into a person's home and steal something!" Matthew nodded. Part of him felt the same way, but a bigger part of him knew it was the only way. "We're only taking information. Besides, people are being invited in. We're just taking a different door." He said, feeling like he was reassuring himself just as much as her. They stopped in front of Shadow Park, and a moment later Kevin joined them, taking the front seat next to Dan. He held a large backpack, and Matthew knew what was inside. Rope. Lots of it. There were apparently lots of air circulation shafts, and rafters, and that was how they were going to move around undetected. They drove in a tense silence, everyone going over their part in their minds until they finally arrived at the mansion. There were

SO MANY PEOPLE. A lot of the people that milled towards the entrance looked like artists and historians, and Matthew noticed that many license plates originated from other states. This seemed to be an event no one wanted to miss, and Matthew supposed that could be a good thing. With all the guards busy trying to keep the crowd of about 120 under control, maybe they wouldn't notice a few stragglers going in the wrong direction. Dan parked his car on a semi-hidden street and they all got out. Kevin held the large backpack tightly; it was the only sign he was nervous too. His face was a portrait of calm and certainty, and it didn't change as they walked to the rear of the building. Soon, a tall, decoratively twisted gate came into view. The silver iron rusted in some places, but still held strong, despite the obvious age. When they reached the towering gate, Dan surveyed the lock. It needed an 8-digit pin, and they had one try to get it right, or else alarms would start blaring in the mansion. Rather than attempting at a code, Dan pulled a crowbar out of his tool bag and began carefully prying up the edge of the panel. Instead of fully popping off, it remained attached by several wires that Dan dared not pull, since they could be the wires that activated the alarm inside. He was forced to work around them, hesitantly pulling and switching the wires that kept the gate locked. Several tense minutes later, the lock clicked open. They all breathed a sigh of relief and Kevin flashed Dan a strained smile, who didn't return it. There was still one more lock to disable, and it would be even harder. The four silently slipped through the gate and made their way through the empty courtyard. Ivy was unusually quiet the whole time, and when Matthew cast a glance at her, he realized her face was pale and her breath was coming faster. This was the most scared Ivy had ever been, and she knew why. They were breaking into the home of a man who had kept Annika's mother prisoner for four years, and possibly countless other people for even longer. He would not hesitate to capture them as well, and Ivy desperately didn't want to spend the rest of her life in a labor camp, away from her family and friends. Matthew instantly regretted asking Kevin a month ago if Ivy could come instead of another NIB agent. He hadn't considered how difficult it would be for her. Matthew knew that if she got hurt in any way, it would be his fault, only his fault, for dragging her into something she probably wasn't ready for. He took her hand and gave it a gentle squeeze, wanting to do something, anything, to alleviate her terror. She glanced up at him, an expression of surprise and gratitude in her eyes, and clutched it tightly. Up ahead, Dan was fiddling with a complex lock, looking more stressed for every minute that passed where it didn't open. Finally, it unlocked, and Dan's face showed a tremendous amount of relief-and then it faded into a worried frown. "What?" Kevin whispered worriedly. "I've got to be here to keep it open." "What?" Kevin repeated in shock. Dan set his jaw. "I won't be able to open the door on the other side. It needs to stay open if this is how we're going to get back out." "Prop it open." Kevin suggested. Dan shook his head. "It's too heavy. Besides, it times out. I'll need to re-enter the sequence every ten minutes or so. You'll have to go on without me." "But we need you! What if there's other locks?" Kevin asked, his voice rising a little. Matthew swallowed hard. "Use the plasma torch in my tool bag. It'll do the same job." Before Kevin could open his mouth to protest, Dan said, "Go! We can't quit now!" Kevin looked torn, but nodded and accepted the plasma torch and put it in his backpack. He gestured for Matthew and Ivy to enter the building. Before Kevin went in after them, Dan stopped him. "They are your responsibility now." "I will protect them with my life." Kevin promised solemnly. Dan nodded, and Kevin followed them into the mansion.

Matthew shivered as he stepped into the cold building. The hot, harsh light of the sun was immediately counteracted by the chill and the shadows that inhibited the hallway they were standing in. It had a sense of horror to it; a long, dark hallway, cobwebs hanging in the corners, faintly lit with small round lights, extending farther than Matthew could see. At least he knew the door wasn't going to close on them. Ivy shivered beside him. "Why is it so creepy down here?" She whispered in a barely audible tone. Matthew didn't know. "Maybe they don't come down here anymore." "Why?" That was a good question. Why did they stop coming down this hallway? Was there something down here? None of their intel on this place had hinted at anything. Kevin pulled a complex paper map out of his backpack, and studied it closely before pointing to a place on the map that had been circled. Matthew and Ivy moved closer so they could see what he was pointing at. "This is where we are." He traced a line with his finger up to a room near the top of the map. "This is where we need to be." Then, he looked up and pointed to their right. "We can go that way, up the stairs and onto the second floor, but there's a much higher chance of running into guards. Or, we can go left, which is a longer hallway, and we'll need to go through some doors before we find the stairs to the second floor. But, there will be less guards there. What do you two think?" Kevin asked. At first, they said nothing, carefully weighing the options in their minds. Then Ivy said, "We should go to the left. If the guards catch us, mission over. We can't risk it." "But there is also a bigger risk that we will get lost." Kevin warned her. Ivy shrugged. "Matthew's photographic memory won't let that happen." Kevin did not look surprised by this information. "Can you do it? Can your mind memorize our path from here on forward?" He asked Matthew seriously. Matthew nodded, though he wished he weren't the one with the responsibility. If he messed up... He pushed the thought away. He wouldn't mess up. He *couldn't* mess up. "Ok. Left it is." Kevin took point, cautiously checking the walls, ceiling, and floor for traps or tripwires. There were none. Matthew walked alongside him in silence, occasionally glancing back at Ivy. She didn't look as scared anymore. Instead, she was studying their surroundings with a look of interest, like she was trying to memorize everything too. She stopped at a bunch of cobwebs, and beckoned Matthew over. "Look at this." She said quietly. "This web is huge. They all are. No one's come down here for a long time." She was right. But why had people stopped coming down here? Suddenly Ivy's head went up. "Where's Kevin?" He was twenty feet ahead of them, walking at a brisk pace, not seeming to notice they had fallen behind. They rushed to catch up. Kevin led them down the winding hallway, taking so many twists and turns that Matthew was afraid he would forget their way back. They walked past many doors; how did Kevin know if any of them led up or not? Finally, they came to a stop, in front of a door that looked exactly like all the other ones they'd already passed. "This is it." Kevin said confidently. Matthew was skeptical, but followed Kevin through the door. Immediately upon entering, Ivy crinkled her nose. "What is that *smell?*" Matthew sniffed the air, curious as to what she was talking about, and instantly regretted it. An overwhelming stench of rotting food and mold filled the sour, stale air of the room. There was no source to the smell; there was nothing in the room at all. There were only three doors; the one they had entered with, and two doors side-by-side across from them. "One of these doors leads to the second-floor stairs." Kevin told them. "And where does the other one go to?" Ivy asked nervously. Kevin shrugged. "No idea." He put his hand on the doorknob of the door on the right, then paused and turned to face them. "If it is the right door, I'll come back to get you two." He waited until they nodded, then pulled the door open and stepped inside, clicking it shut behind him. Matthew and Ivy waited quietly for him to come back, but Matthew started pacing ten seconds after he'd left. Then he noticed something on the ground next to the doors. He stooped to pick it up, and turned it over in his hand. It was a rusted lock. It looked like it had been sitting there for ages. He was still staring at it when Kevin burst into the room, slamming the door shut behind him and panting heavily. It would have been comical if his face hadn't been as pale as an albino's. "What's wrong?" Matthew asked, alarmed. "Something died in there." Kevin answered hoarsely. Ivy threw up.

CHAPTER 8

"**D**ied?" Matthew confirmed, feeling like he wanted to puke too. That explained the smell, at least. Kevin nodded. "At first, all I saw were bones, and scattered animal remains. Then I went a bit farther, just to confirm there were no doors in that room, and stumbled upon a large animal corpse. Judging by the amount of flesh that had decayed, I'd say it's been there for a long time." Well, that explained the rusted lock. Beside him, Ivy threw up again before standing unsteadily and wiping her mouth with her sleeve. Kevin glanced at her. "Sorry." He apologized. Kevin dug through his backpack and pulled out a granola bar and offered it to her. "Maybe later." She groaned, waving it away. "I guess it's the door on the left, then?" Matthew said, trying not to look at the fresh piles of Ivy's breakfast. He wanted to get away from the smell, which was now adding Ivy's puke to the mix. Kevin nodded, and threw open the door on the left. Matthew hurried through. "What about my...?" Ivy gestured to the piles on the ground. "Leave them." Kevin answered without a backwards glance. "No one's gonna come down here and find them anyway." Ivy nodded, and they left the room, quickly shutting the door behind them so the smell wouldn't follow. The new hallway they entered quickly brought them to the base of wide stone steps that ascended to a pair of thick, plain wooden doors. Kevin took the stairs two at a time, his quiet steps leaving gentle echoes as he went. Up at the top, he silently cracked open one of the doors, holding it open just enough to peek an eye through. To his dismay, Kevin saw several small groups of people milling around, and they didn't look like they'd be leaving anytime soon. Kevin waited until he was sure no one was facing the door, then started to push it open wider. Matthew quickly grabbed his wrist. "What are you doing?" He hissed. "There's no way to sneak past that many people, and I'm not keen on going back the way we came. So, we'll just blend in until we can get away." Kevin hissed back. Someone suddenly turned towards their door, and they froze. "What's in there?" She asked one of her friends. "The bathrooms, I think." The friend replied. The girls moved away, and Kevin and Matthew shared a sigh of relief. "So, we good?" Kevin asked Matthew. He nodded. Kevin again waited until no one was looking, then quickly pushed the door open and snuck through, Ivy and Matthew close behind. He smoothly shut the door behind them and moved away from it, towards a piece of art hanging on the wall. The trio stood in front of it for a moment, feeling suddenly exposed. It felt like any moment someone would point and shout, "Look! I found the imposters!" It took all of Matthew's willpower not to flinch every time someone's gaze passed over him. "All right, can everyone gather over here please?" A man's voice boomed from the doorway. He looked pleasant enough, with his shaved head and cheery smile. It didn't stop Kevin's hand from making a fist though. That man worked for the enemy; it was all the justification Kevin would've needed to punch his lights out. But he didn't. There would be plenty of other chances to beat up the people who had imprisoned Louisa and everyone else. The crowd moved towards the man, whose nametag read "Andrew." Kevin, Matthew, and Ivy stayed near the back, semi-hiding behind the others. "I am going to be showing you all some of the treasures the owner, Leo Makrus, has collected over the years." Andrew addressed them. The small crowd was starting to murmur with excitement. Andrew turned and led them out of the room, leading them through the white marble hallways until they reached a large open archway. Inside were glass boxes resting on marble pillars, the contents varying with each room they visited. They saw jewels and silks, animal furs and ancient-looking dishes, famous paintings and a huge whale skeleton, old Egyptian scrolls, crystal statues, and crumbling yellow books with illegible covers. Ivy was amazed at the sheer beauty and history she saw inside every case. And to think there was more in this humongous place! It was almost enough to make her forget the rotting animal corpse Kevin had found.

Almost- but not quite. She got so caught up, she didn't realize Matthew and Kevin were no longer with her until a shoe hit her in the back. She bent down, surprised, and picked up a grey sneaker that had Velcro instead of shoelaces. Annika wore the same style. Behind her, Kevin and Matthew were partially hidden behind a wall, silently high-fiving each other. Kevin was missing a shoe. They beckoned to her when they realized they had her attention. With a final, longing glance behind her at the tour group, she followed Matthew and Kevin, feeling guilty for wanting to stay when Annika's mother's life was on the line. When she got to them, Kevin held out his hand expectantly. Ivy gave him a confused look, then remembered she was still holding his shoe, and sheepishly handed it over. "Can your mind find that room we saw on the map, the one with the entry into the hidden ceiling shafts?" Kevin asked Matthew as he slipped his shoe back on. Matthew nodded. "Sure." He said with considerably more confidence than he actually had, doing his best to ignore the look Ivy was giving him. She saw right through his fake bravado, but at least Kevin didn't. Or, if he did, he didn't let on. Matthew wound his way through the quiet hallways, oftentimes closing his eyes to rely on the map in his memory. Finally, when he was sure he had led them to the right room as marked on the map, he walked confidently forward- and crashed into a door. "Ow." He moaned, ignoring Ivy's snickers from behind him. His eyes open this time, he grabbed the doorknob and pulled it open, and the three crowded inside. To their surprise, the only things inside were two leather couches, cracked with age, a painting of a flowery meadow, and a small glass side table covered with dust. They looked around, confused. "Why is it so dusty in here? And where's the ceiling entrance?" Ivy asked, bewildered. Kevin shrugged. "My guess is this place is so big, Makrus probably doesn't ever come near here. There's no reason to clean it if he's never in here, so it gets abandoned. As for the entrance, I guess we'll just have to look for it." Matthew pried apart the cushions on the couch and looked under it, Kevin lifted the painting and looked for a hidden entrance, and Ivy inspected the table and the ceiling. "You know," Matthew said suddenly. "I think we could have walked through the front door along with everyone else, and still not have been caught." "I was thinking the same thing." Kevin admitted. "Maybe we shouldn't tell Mr. Helmcott that." Ivy suggested slyly. "After all, he did such a good job with those gates..." "Absolutely." Matthew agreed instantly. "There'll be no need to mention it." Kevin chuckled. "Sounds good." They grinned at each other. Then Kevin turned serious. "Are you *sure* that this is the right room?" He asked Matthew. "Yes." Matthew lied. He actually wasn't sure at all. "Because we've searched the entire room. There's nothing here." "Guys?" Ivy interrupted suddenly. She was crouched in front of a large ventilation grate. Kevin stared at it for a moment, thinking. "Ivy, you're a genius." He declared, racing over to her and starting to pry the grate away from the wall. "I am? Right. I knew that." She beamed. Kevin laid the grate on the ground and peered inside. "Perfect." He breathed, and started to climb in. "Follow me!" He called as he disappeared inside. Ivy and Matthew exchanged amused glances, and Ivy crawled in after Kevin. Inside the narrow steel chute was a steel ladder fixed to the wall. Kevin was scaling it at super speed, quickly moving up like his life depended on it. Ivy climbed up after him, grasping the rungs tightly as she climbed, and tried not to think about how high up they were going. She could hear Matthew beneath her. After an endless assent, the shaft stopped going up and flattened into two shafts, one on the left and one on the right. Kevin sat in the one on the left, patiently waiting for her and Matthew. The shaft was so wide, she and Kevin could sit side-by-side. When Matthew arrived, Kevin addressed them in a hushed voice. "Right now, we're right above floor four. We're going to have to climb down on our ropes, travel for a ways, then retie our ropes in a different section, climb up, and travel through the rafters till we get to a spot where we can enter the fifth floor. There we will locate Makrus's office and use the flashdrive Matthew coded to hack into Makrus's computer and steal the file containing the prison building layouts and personnel lists." Kevin informed them. "You guys good with the plan?" They nodded. "Good. Let's go." And with that, he turned his back on them and began crawling away, his backpack brushing against the ceiling as he went along. Matthew and Ivy quickly followed. It seemed like they had been crawling forever in silence. Kevin had warned them that too much noise would echo through the ventilation shafts and give away their position, so it was slow going, especially since Kevin kept turning back to glare at Ivy every time she put her hand or knee down a little too loudly. She was so concentrated on being quiet, she jumped when Matthew suddenly froze and whispered, "What was that sound?" "What sound?" She whispered back, glancing at Kevin in confusion. She had been absolutely silent! But Kevin had stilled too. "Oh no." He gasped suddenly. "Go! Go! Go!" He cried in a strangled voice. He took off in front of them, racing away from them as fast as he could on his hands and knees. Matthew scrambled after him, quickly leaving Ivy behind. "Hey! Wait up!" She cried, tripping over her hands in her efforts to keep up. Abruptly, she heard something. It was like a cross between a giant fan whirling, and the gusts of 100 mile per hour wind. It howled, and buzzed, and shook her to her core. Then she realized the floor was vibrating beneath her. Her calls were lost in the noise, but suddenly it got worse. An icy chill swept through the shaft, freezing the metal beneath her. It stung her hands, her cheeks. It was miserable; and it was inescapable. From out of nowhere, Matthew was beside her again, shouting incomprehensibly and nudging her down the shaft. He led her to a t-turn, where Kevin was waiting. There, huddled against the wall, all they had to fight was the chill as the air rushed past them. At last, the noise died down and the shaft warmed a bit as the last of the freezing air faded into the distance. Kevin looked grim. "I should have remembered there was a chance of the air conditioning turning on. In a massive place like this, and in the middle of summer..." Ivy was shaken. "That was probably the worst thing in my life I have ever experienced." She mumbled. "Do you think anyone heard us being so loud?" Matthew asked worriedly. Kevin hesitated before answering. "There's no way to know. But we do need to keep moving." Ivy and Matthew nodded in agreement. They set off crawling, once again taking great care to be quiet. Up ahead, Kevin finally stopped. When Ivy got closer, she saw him wrestling to get another grate off the floor, whispering to Matthew as he worked. "The shaft ends here. We will be going down, walking a ways, and using the rafters to get us to floor 5 instead. Does that work for you?" Matthew nodded. Ivy leaned against the wall tiredly, watching Kevin work as he lifted the grate from the floor, removed a long coil of rope from his backpack, and tied it to a thick wooden support beam about a foot beneath the ventilation shaft. He gave it a good strong tug, then motioned for Ivy to climb down. "Me? First?" He nodded. Ivy bit her lip, then wiped her hands on her pants before grasping the rope and lowering herself through the hole. She swallowed hard as she looked down. She was at least 40 feet above the floor. It would not be fun to drop from that height. She inched down the rope slowly, taking her time as she went down one hand after the other. It felt like hours had passed before she finally touched the floor, and dropped the rest of the way. She glanced up expectantly. Kevin was giving her a thumbs up. A second later, Matthew was descending, and came down beside her in considerably less time than it had taken her. Kevin was next. He removed something from his backpack and poured a liquid carefully over the wood, soaking it completely a foot on either side of the rope. He came down the rope partially, and moved the grate into place above him before resuming his climb down. Matthew frowned. "Are we just going to leave the rope here?" He mused aloud. Ivy shrugged. A minute later, they got their answer. As soon as Kevin got to the ground, he pulled the plasma torch from his backpack and lit the rope on fire. Matthew and Ivy stared in shock as the flame disintegrated the rope as it climbed, before sizzling out at the top. The liquid Kevin had poured on the wood stopped it from catching fire. Despite the faint smell of something burning, there was no evidence anyone had come from the ceiling. Ivy was impressed; Matthew was not. "How could you be sure the water would stop the wood from burning?" He challenged Kevin, who stayed calm as he put the plasma torch away. "Because I practiced at the NIB headquarters." He answered. "You don't seriously think I would attempt that, potentially endangering you guys, without being sure that it would work. Besides, that wasn't water. It was a special flame retardant we created." Matthew, chastised, said nothing. Kevin's face softened. "I promised Mr. Helmcott I would protect you two. I fully intend to keep that promise- no matter what." They nodded. "Come on. I don't want to stay here any longer than necessary." They broke into a jog, their light footsteps making almost no noise as they moved. But then their footsteps got louder. Kevin looked back at Ivy and Matthew. He had told them to stay quiet! They weren't moving. Both had frozen several yards behind him; but the footsteps were still coming. A female's voice echoed down the hall. "We won't be going much farther than this, folks, since this floor is almost entirely dedicated to Mr. Makrus's private collection, which is not for public viewing. But, if you'll just follow me, I can show you all a few more exhibits before I take you all back down..." Kevin and Matthew exchanged panicked looks. The three of them took off sprinting, using the noises of the oncoming tour group to mask the sound of their thumping sneakers against the marble floors. Kevin led them through wild twists and turns, seeming to have no idea where he was or where he was going. Matthew followed, using his memorized map of the mansion to keep track of where they were. At one corner, Matthew took a different turn than Kevin and Ivy, then had to run back and pull them in his direction. Kevin gladly followed him, relieved that at least Matthew had had the sense to keep track of where they were. Only when the groups shuffling and talking faded away to silence did they slow their pace and look around them. "Do you know where we are?" Kevin asked hopefully. Matthew nodded. "I *think* that we're right underneath the support beams you said we needed to find." He answered. "Well, that was lucky. At least something's going our way." Ivy panted, seemingly oblivious to the fact that Matthew had led them to here on purpose. "Kevin? If a tour group came up here anyway, why did we have to travel through the vents? Couldn't we have just taken a tour group all the way here and then split off?" Ivy asked. Kevin shook his head. "Only one of the group leaders came up here, and she said herself she probably shouldn't have. There was no way to guarantee us getting this far if we stayed with a tour group." He explained. Ivy nodded thoughtfully. "I guess that makes sense." "So, what are we going to do now?" Matthew asked Kevin, curious to see how he planned to get up there. Kevin opened his backpack again and pulled out three- grappling hooks? Matthew watched, astonished, as Kevin swung it in his hand, gaining momentum, then let it fly. The hook coiled perfectly around one of the wooden beams, then caught the rope and hung tightly. Kevin gave it a tug; it stayed firm. He grinned. "Wasn't sure if I would be able to pull that off." He told them matter-of-factly. He pulled another from his bag and quickly attached it to another beam close by, then pulled a third out of his bag. His first throw missed, and the hook clanged to the floor. Matthew winced. Kevin threw it again, but it got lodged into the wood of another beam. Finally, he got it to latch around a beam, and gave it a strong tug to make sure it stayed. "Kevin? Why are these ceilings so high? The first three floors had much shorter ceilings than floors four and five." Ivy asked irritably. "There used to be 8 floors instead of five. We don't know why he took them out, but we think it may have been there was too much space for one person." Kevin answered. "Ah." Ivy sighed. "Alright, let's go." Kevin wrapped his hands around the rope on the right and began climbing. Ivy looked at her hands, which were still stinging from the first climb down. Now they had to climb up? There was no way she would make it. She kept her thoughts to herself as she grabbed the middle rope and began her way up. Matthew took the rope on her left. "Use your feet to bring the bottom of the rope with you." Kevin called down softly. His order perplexed Ivy. Grab the end of the rope with her *feet*? Besides her, Matthew had secured the end of the rope with his feet and was mainly using his knees to climb. Ivy was hardly making it up the rope as it was. There was no way she would be able to pull off that trick as well. She was only about 10 feet off the floor when the sound of voices came again. But this time, they didn't sound like a tour group. They sounded like security. She glanced up at Matthew and Kevin, who were *much* higher than her. They hadn't heard anything. Ivy had only a moments decision. The guards were coming this way, and she would absolutely be spotted. If she got spotted, so would Matthew and Kevin. Since she couldn't make it up in time, she would have to do everything she could to distract them. She took a deep breath, and began climbing back down the rope.

Matthew was almost to the top. He and Kevin were only about 12 feet away from the rafter their grapple hook was cinched on. Matthew looked down, wondering where Ivy was, and almost fell in surprise. Ivy was climbing *down*! Why was she doing that? "Kevin? What is she doing?" Matthew hissed. Kevin looked down; his jaw dropped. "What is she thinking? I'm going down after her." "No." Matthew said suddenly. "I think I hear people." "How many?" Kevin asked in surprise. The NIB's file on Matthew had included he had really good hearing, but this was crazy. They were 50 feet off the floor! How could Matthew hear people from that height, especially since they weren't even in sight yet? "Two." Matthew decided. "And they're coming this way. They're going to see Ivy!" Kevin nodded. "I think that's what she's counting on." He whispered quietly. He could now hear people's voices. Matthew had been right- there were two of them. Beneath them, Ivy suddenly dropped to the floor, landing on her ankle. "Ow!" She yelped. "Did you hear that?" One of the nearing voices asked suddenly. "Yeah." The other replied. The footsteps were running now; they were going to find Ivy any second. Kevin frantically began reeling up the rope Ivy had been on moments before, hoping he could have it high enough that when the guards rounded the corner, all they would see was Ivy, and not ropes dangling from the ceiling. The two guards rounded the corner and stopped in surprise. "A girl?" The first asked, bewildered. The second was a quicker thinker. "What is she doing up here?" Ivy's head shot up, from where she was cradling her ankle. "Oh, thank goodness you found me!" She cried. "I was afraid no one would find me here!" The two guards moved closer, cautiously. "What are you doing here?" "Oh, I was part of a tour group, but I had to use the bathroom, and I think I got lost. When I was running, trying to find my group again, I tripped. I think I sprained my ankle." She was talking fast, and Matthew was barely able to keep up as she fed them lie after lie. One of the men crouched down beside her and inspected her ankle. Matthew was too high up to see what he saw, but it must've been bad, because he said. "Looks like it hurts." Ivy was quick to play it up. "Oh, it does! I haven't been able to walk. I am so lucky you found me! Can you please help me get back to my group? It would mean a lot if you could." The guard looked at his friend, who shrugged. "Why not?" "Oh thank you!" Ivy gushed. He helped her stand, and Matthew could tell the wince on her face was real. He watched helplessly as the guards took her away, Ivy limping and leaning on one of the guards. She never stopped her speed talking, chatting about random things as they led her away. If it was intended to distract them, it worked, for the guard following behind her was rubbing his forehead as if it hurt from her nonstop chatter. "What's going to happen to her?" Matthew whispered hoarsely after he was sure the guards were gone. Kevin didn't know. "Hopefully they will just put her in a group and leave her alone." He hesitated. "We need to keep going. Ivy just sacrificed herself to make sure we could finish our mission. We *can't* fail." Matthew nodded in agreement, though he was still shaken. First Mr. Helmcott had been left behind. Now Ivy! Matthew could only hope she could take care of herself. Above him, Kevin had climbed onto one of the rafters and was sitting on it. He carefully removed the grappling hooks he and Ivy had climbed on and placed them back in his backpack. Matthew climbed up next to him and cautiously sat on one of the rafters. Kevin disconnected his grapple hook and put it away. Looking down, Matthew had a terrifying vision of falling. His hands instinctively clenched tighter around the wood. Kevin seemed oblivious to the danger, for he was climbing across the beams like he was on top of monkey bars at the park. Except this time, the stakes were much higher. Literally. Matthew followed at a much slower pace, painstakingly planning every footstep and hand placement. A loud crack sounded through the still air, and Matthew froze, terrified. He glanced up ahead of him, where Kevin was sitting on a beam. He had the plasma torch in his hand and was burning away some wood. Kevin noticed Matthew watching him and gave a wink. All of a sudden, a thick, square piece of wood crashed into Kevin's lap, making him oof in surprise. Kevin set aside the wood, but continued to aim the plasma torch above him. A series of more loud cracks ensured. Kevin beckoned hurriedly to Matthew, who was nearing. "Get ready to catch it." Kevin whispered. Matthew braced himself, and a second later a huge chunk of marble crashed down, almost toppling Matthew off his perch on the wooden beam. Kevin quickly shut off the plasma torch, put it back in his bag, and relieved Matthew of the heavy marble. Matthew peered up through the new hole above them. It was an empty hallway, fancily decorated with animal skins and heads. That disgusted Matthew. He didn't think he would ever understand why people wanted to decorate their houses with dead carcasses and heads, especially those of animals. On Kevin's urging, Matthew carefully stood up on the wooden beam, placed his hands on the floor above him, and hoisted himself up onto the floor. Kevin passed the marble up to him, then the wood; Matthew placed them both on the floor beside him. Kevin came up next; or tried to. His backpack was too large to fit with him, so he took it off and passed it up to Matthew. Finally, Kevin heaved himself through the hole beside Matthew. "A hallway? Ugh. We are *way* to conspicuous here." He complained. "How are we going to hide the hole?" Matthew asked, concerned. Kevin snorted. "Let's leave it here, so Makrus will fall in it." "Seriously?" Matthew asked in surprise. Kevin rolled his eyes. "I wish. No, we're going use a special NIB glue solution to keep it in place. Here, hold this." He handed Matthew the piece of wood, then removed a long white tube with no label from his backpack. After popping the cap off, he carefully squeezed the goopy white mess around the perimeter of the wood. Matthew lowered the wood back into its place. Thirty seconds later, Kevin stood up and jumped on the wood they had just put in place. Matthew stifled a yell, fully expecting to see the wood break out from under Kevin and send him plummeting to the ground far below. It didn't budge. Kevin laughed at the expression on Matthew's face. "It's a quick drying glue." He explained. "Can you hold the marble?" Matthew picked up the heavy square of marble and held it steady as Kevin carefully squeezed the glue onto it. When he was done, Matthew lowered it onto the wood and waited. Thirty seconds later, Kevin inspected the new seal. "Perfect." He stood up and put his backpack back on. "Now we need to find Makrus's office. Do you know where that's located?" Kevin asked Matthew. Matthew consulted his memory again, and gestured to the right. "It's somewhere in that general direction, but the map didn't say exactly *where* it was." He answered. A bit of disappointment flickered on Kevin's face, but it was quickly replaced with determination. "All right. Can you fight?" Matthew blinked. "What?" "Can you fight?" Kevin repeated in exasperation. "Uh, yeah. I mean, kind of. What type of fighting?" He asked in alarm. "Good ol' hand to hand." Kevin answered cheerfully, walking away. Matthew raced to catch up to him. "Why would we be fighting? The whole point of a heist is to *not get found*, right?" Kevin nodded. "Sure. But this floor is likely going to have the most guards, and we won't be able to avoid them all. My plan is to knock out whoever gets in our way, then wipe their short-term memories with a serum the NIB is loaning me. So, if you can fight too, then I don't have to worry about watching your back as well as mine." Matthew didn't know what to say to that. He'd had some fighting experience when he was doing the laser training, but he hadn't attempted a level since Rachel and Annika had left. It didn't seem as appealing without Rachel there to annoyingly exaggerate his victories. So it was safe to say he was probably a bit rusty- not that he would tell Kevin that. "Do you know which rooms are facing the outside?" Kevin asked, bringing Matthew out of his thoughts. "Uh, what?" Kevin sighed, looking annoyed. "We know his office has a window. That means it is on the outer edges of this ridiculous place. How many rooms on this floor have a window facing out?" Kevin clarified slowly, as if Matthew was a child who couldn't understand simple instructions. Matthew gave him the stink eye before answering. "Six." "Can you lead us to them?" "Yes." "What are you waiting for? We don't have all day." Matthew scowled. Kevin was acting exactly like he'd always imagined an older brother would; which was nice in some ways, and super annoying in other ways. Still, he closed his eyes and located the closest window room with his mind map. Matthew led Kevin down more animal-lined hallways, closing his eyes both to focus on where he was going, and to shut out the images of glassy eyes staring at him from all the heads mounted to the walls. Matthew found the door and, eyes still closed, reached out to open the door, determined not to forget it was there this time. The second he pushed the door open, he was shoved roughly aside by

Kevin, and a series of *thwoop's* occurred. "Wrong room." Kevin informed him when he stood up, rubbing the shoulder that had crashed into the marble floor. He gasped when he looked through the door entryway. There were two crumpled bodies slouched across chairs behind 2 large desks, sandwiches forgotten on the carpet. "Did you kill them?" Matthew cried, fearing the worst. "Of course not." Kevin scoffed. "Only the SIA do that. I just shot them with my dart gun. Figured it would be easier than punching them. Sorry I pushed you." Kevin added apologetically. "Where's the next room?" Still stunned, Matthew absentmindedly led him to the next closest room, letting Kevin do the honors of opening the door this time. He had no desire to get shoved out of the way again. This time, there was no one inside. Instead, it looked like a cheery break lounge, with couches and bright sunlight coming through the window. "Wrong again." Kevin huffed, shutting the door. "Next." The next two rooms were also a bust, one being an indoor garden, and the other being a room covered in detailed maps with tacks clumped in particular cities or valleys. Matthew memorized as many as he could while Kevin took pictures with a bulked-up phone. "Why is almost no one up here?" Matthew asked, slightly worried. "I would've thought there would be more guards up here, since it has the most valuable SIA stuff, right?" Kevin nodded. "The shortage of guards *is* weird. There's usually many more than what we've seen here. In any case, it's a blessing I'll take." "It just doesn't feel right." Matthew persisted. Kevin sighed. "I'll check in with the NIB when this is over and see if they have an explanation, but they probably all got restationed downstairs to handle the crowd. Okay?" "I guess." Matthew reluctantly conceded. "Can we please find that office now?" The next room wasn't far away, so Matthew was able to speed up his pace and bring them to a door that was very different from all of the others. Rather than wood, it was made from steel, and had a complicated key code locking the door. "Do your NIB friends happen to have the code?" Matthew asked Kevin. Kevin scowled at him. "No. Do you?" "We could kick it." Matthew suggested, ignoring Kevin's jibe. "Annika did that all the time when she was doing laser training." Kevin shook his head. "I was thinking we could use the plasma torch to fry its circuits." Matthew shrugged. "That works too." He agreed, deciding it didn't matter how they broke into the office, just that they *did* break into the office. Kevin pulled the plasma torch out of his bag again and flicked it on, aiming at the lock. Almost instantly it began to melt around the edges, but it took another three minutes just to break through the metal's thick shell. Watching it, Matthew was suddenly glad he hadn't tried to kick it as he'd suggested. He likely would have come home with a shattered ankle. Suddenly, sparks erupted from the panel, and the door clicked open. Matthew slid the heavy door open, and stepped inside. An alarm rang out, blaring and wailing the second Matthew crossed the threshold. Kevin gave him a panicked look. "What did you do?" He yelled at Matthew over the sirens. "Nothing!" Matthew yelled back. Over the sound of the alarm, footsteps could be heard pounding up nearby stairs. Kevin quickly removed the flashdrive from his backpack and pressed them both into Matthew's hands. "Go hack that computer and get the files we need. I'll hold the guards off. When you have the file, use something in the bag to help us escape out the window; but **let me know** before you leave, so I can follow. Okay?" Kevin yelled the instructions. Wide eyed, all Matthew could do was nod. Kevin thrust his hand back into his backpack and pulled out another dart gun, then pushed Matthew farther into the room and partially shut the door so Matthew would be out of sight, and out of the line of fire. Kevin steadied his weapons and waited for the guards. As the first one rounded the corner, down he went, a dart protruding from his shoulder. Several more followed, but Kevin knew he didn't have enough darts to take them all down. He could only hope Matthew was as good as he needed to be.

Matthew's eyes went straight to the computer sitting on a thin aluminum desk. He seated himself at the large, overstuffed chair behind the desk and inserted the flashdrive into the USB hole on the side of the computer. Almost instantly, the algorithm Matthew had created smashed through the first two layers of the computer's systems, and the screen began to flash, belatedly trying to fight it back out; but it was too late. Matthew was in. His hands flew over the keyboard, finding access points invisible to anyone else. He slipped through layer after layer, easily dismantling all the security and passwords he normally would have needed. He felt oddly powerful, hacking into the head of the SIA's computer with almost no help or work. He quickly pulled up the files he needed and downloaded them onto the extra space on his flashdrive. He couldn't believe how easy it was. When the files finished downloading onto his flashdrive, he quickly took it out and slipped it into the inside pocket in his sweater. With the most important part taken care of, he rifled through Kevin's backpack, pushing past sharp, spare darts, a spray bottle filled with a misty gas, their grappling hooks, the plasma torch, and a box labeled "Fragile: Do Not Open." Normally something like that would've tempted him, but after seeing Kevin in action, he decided it would be wiser to heed the warning than to satisfy his curiosity. Matthew pulled out a square, book sized case with gold letters engraved on it. **Auto inflating air bag- use only in extreme circumstances**.

Matthew was pretty sure this counted as "extreme circumstances," so he unzipped the case and removed a small pillow-like object, and a paper sheet of instructions.

- *Smack pillow on wall*
- *Quickly throw it out the window onto the ground below*
- *Wait 20 seconds, then jump out the window. Pillow will deflate gradually over time. Don't dawdle.*

Matthew stared at the simple instructions with disbelief. They were going to jump out the window? They were at least 130 feet off the ground! Still, he could hear grunting and shouting from outside the room, so he dashed to the window, threw it open, and looked down. It was unbelievable how much he could see from that height. Suddenly, he was happy Ivy hadn't come with them to the fifth floor. Seeing as she had a hard time climbing the rope, he wasn't sure she would have been able to jump. She seemed scared from 40 feet in the air; this was *so* much worse. Matthew squared his shoulders, and smacked the pillow against the wall as hard as he could. It immediately began swelling, and Matthew wrestled it to the window and threw it out. It grew bigger as it fell, until it finally hit the bottom. After zipping up the backpack, so nothing would fall out during the long descent, he ran over to the door, yelling to Kevin, "Let's go!" Sweaty and looking strained, not to mention holding his side in pain, Kevin ran in, shoving the door closed behind him. "What's our escape?" "An inflatable pillow-thingy." Matthew told him. Kevin looked relieved. "Good thinking. Has it been 20 seconds?" "Huh? Oh, yeah, it has." Matthew confirmed. "Then what are you waiting for?" Kevin cried. "It's deflating already!" He pushed Matthew towards the window, and removed a round, shell-shaped, see-through container from a hidden pocket in his sweater. Inside, a cloudy blue liquid sloshed around. "What's that?" Matthew asked in alarm. "A serum to wipe short term memories. That's why I need you to jump first." Matthew's jaw dropped. "I have to go first?" "GO!" Kevin insisted. Handing the backpack to him, Matthew put one leg on the sill and hesitated; he must be crazy, about to jump 130 feet onto a deflating air mat! "Jump, or I push you." Kevin's tone was dangerously low. "I'm going!" Matthew yelped, and without a final thought, he pushed off the ground with his leg and toppled over the sill into midair. For a split second, Matthew wondered why he had to pick a deflating pillow instead of a rope. Even though Matthew was well aware the mat beneath him would stop his fall, he panicked, his scream being lost in the rush of air surrounding him as he descended. Above him, Kevin pushed backwards off the sill, squeezing the shell thing into the air as he fell. Matthew hit the mat, and it wrapped around him, taking all potential fall damage away. He lay there for a moment, stunned he hadn't gotten hurt. Suddenly, he realized Kevin had already jumped and was falling towards him. Matthew's eyes widened and he panicked, trying to get free of the mat and roll off before Kevin landed. He was almost off when Kevin crashed onto the mat besides him, sending Matthew flying sideways. He skidded across the grass for several yards before coming to a stop with a groan. He picked himself off the grass and glared at Kevin, who was preoccupied making sure the stuff in his backpack wasn't damaged. Matthew almost would've believed Kevin hadn't meant to send him flying if he hadn't right then looked up and smirked in Matthew's direction. Matthew jogged back over to him, but before he could get on Kevin for doing that, Kevin shuddered, and said, "I hate doing that. Last time one of these emergency crash mats was used, the agent ended up paralyzed for the rest of her life." "What!" Matthew cried, completely forgetting what Kevin had just done. "Are you serious?" "Yes." Kevin answered. "What happened to 'not potentially endangering us' and, 'promised to protect you'?" Matthew protested. Kevin rolled his eyes. "I'm not the one who chose to use the 'extreme circumstances' air bag. That's on you." Their argument was interrupted when Dan came tearing across the courtyard. He looked astonished, then angry, to see Kevin and Matthew on the ground- *without* Ivy. "Where's Ivy?" He demanded. As an afterthought, he added, "And why did you just fall out of a window? You were supposed to come out through the door!" Kevin and Matthew looked at each other, neither wanting to be the one to explain it to Dan. Kevin sighed, forfeiting the staring contest he and Matthew had entered. "She, uh, got caught. She'll be coming out the entrance soon. As for the window," Kevin sucked in a breath. "We got cornered. I told Matthew to get us a quick escape, so he did." Dan looked bewildered. "Caught?" Then his eyes widened. "Cornered? You make it sound like the mission failed!" "NO, no, we succeeded. Matthew has the files." Kevin interrupted hastily. He spun on his heel to face Matthew. "Right?" Matthew nodded. Kevin blew out a relieved breath. "Can we go? I *really* don't want to stay here any longer, and we need to go get Ivy." By then, the crash mat had fully deflated, so Kevin wrapped it around itself and put it in his backpack. "It's a one-use item." Kevin told Matthew when he saw the confused look on his face. The trio jogged back to the iron fence and slipped through. There was no relocking it, so Dan placed a large rock behind the gate to keep it from swinging open. They quickly walked back to the car and piled in. In a tense silence not unlike the one they had arrived in, Dan drove the Cybertruck to the front of the building as the crowd inside began to spill out onto the parking lot. It was Matthew who spotted Ivy first, bright-eyed and beaming, yet also walking with a slight limp. He waved to her as the car pulled up beside her, and she climbed in. "Did you get it?" She asked instantly. He nodded. "I knew you could do it!" She smiled. "How's your foot?" Matthew asked. She waved his concern away. "Just a minor sprain. It'll go away in a day or two." She answered cheerfully. Then she crinkled her nose. "How was your trip back through the basement?" Matthew shook his head. "We didn't go back through the basement. We jumped out of a window." She was shocked. "What?" "We jumped out a fifth story window onto a crash mat below." He repeated, purposefully neglecting to mention Kevin's comment on the last person's injury upon using it. "How long were you falling?" Matthew shrugged. "Like, two seconds." She looked impressed. "I don't think I would've had the courage to jump out a window that high. You're brave." Matthew smiled, slightly embarrassed with her compliment. He certainly hadn't felt brave. As Dan drove them away from the mansion, Ivy told her part of the story after she left them. "The guards took me to the main room again, bandaged my foot with a splint, and put me in another tour group. You wouldn't believe what I saw! There were live animals, like alligators, two lion cubs, a poisonous-" Ivy cut herself off, peering distractedly out the window. "Where are we going?" She asked Dan. "My house. It'll be the safest place to view those files." He answered shortly. Matthew gave the older man a look, noticing the white-knuckled hands gripping the steering wheel, and the rigidness in his shoulders. Matthew wondered what he had been thinking about while he waited for them to come back. His wife? His daughters? How difficult it would be to rescue his wife, perhaps? It must have been torture, being stuck out there, alone, worrying about them, wondering if they would be able to pull off this heist. But now, they had it and were all safe. Why then, was Mr. Helmcott still so nervous? At last, they pulled to a stop in front of his home, a large, 2 story black house, with a pretty balcony wrapping around the front of the second floor, covered with winding ivy and irises. A rocking chair sat on it, looking empty and abandoned. Through the black tinted glass behind it, Matthew could vaguely see the interior of Annika's bedroom. They piled out of the car, and Dan led them to the front door. He removed his shoe, pulled a key out from under the liner, and fitted it into the lock, turning it until a click was heard. He replaced the key, picked up his shoe, and walked inside. The others quickly followed. The house was extremely warm, a sharp contrast to Matthew's last visit. The air seemed stale and stagnant, apparently evident to Dan as well, for he opened a window to let a light breeze in. Kevin relocked the door, and turned to Dan. "Where do you want to view it?" He didn't hesitate. "Down here." Dan led them into the kitchen, and crouched down by the kitchen island. He put his hand under the bottom of it and clicked a button; a second later, a small door swung open, revealing a hollow space with a ladder extending into the darkness below. It was not unlike the one they had found in the ventilation shaft. Ivy swallowed hard, feeling fear despite her awe at finding Mr. Helmcott had a secret room. "How far down does it go?" She asked quietly. "17 feet." Dan answered, crawling inside. He flipped a switch on the ceiling, and rows of LED lights lit up, lighting the way down. He began his descent, moving at a steady pace, trying to fight away the memories that resurfaced. Louisa had been dragged up this ladder the last time it was used, and he'd never thought to come back down. But, the files ought to be viewed in secrecy, and this was the best place for that. Even Annika didn't know this was here! When his feet hit the bottom, Dan flicked another switch on the wall, and the strong LEDs on the walls and ceilings lit up the cavernous bunker. There wasn't a lot in the main area; just some desks with computers resting on the dusty surfaces. Beyond this area was the storm shelter they'd used only twice, both times before their daughters had been born. His heart twinged with pain, seeing the scuffed footprints frozen in time in the dust coating the smooth, glittery black floor of the bunker. Up ahead, he noticed the door to the storm shelter lay on the ground in a twisted pile of metal. It was evident Louisa had been hiding in there. It seemed even the poor door couldn't withstand the hatred those evil men had for her. Beside him, Kevin, Ivy, and Matthew stared around the room, taking in everything. Dan supposed it was exciting for them to see this place for the first time, and wished the place didn't look so abandoned. Ivy's sharp gasp a moment later told him she'd noticed the door and footprints. Kevin's face was grim, but a small smile appeared on his face when he saw a small scrap of fabric, identical to the suits the SIA agents wore, covered with dried blood. Louisa had definitely put up a fight. Dan walked over to a computer on one of the desks and turned it on, brushing dust off the cover and screen while he waited. As soon as it flickered on, he entered a complex passcode, and had it read his fingerprint with a sensor on the keyboard. Then, he held out his hand for the flashdrive. Matthew fished it out of his sweater and handed it over. Dan inserted the flashdrive into the computer. Since it was already unlocked, Matthew's program did nothing to his computer, and he was able to access the files. The others gathered closely around the computer as a list of names appeared on the screen. There were two columns; one heading said "Alive" and the other said "Deceased." Dan's and Kevin's eyes scanned each column frantically, searching for Louisa's name. At last, near the bottom, in the "Alive" column, was the name **Louisa A. Helmcott**. Dan looked about to cry with relief, and Ivy hugged Matthew tightly. Kevin kept scanning, trying to locate all the names of NIB agents that had been captured in the line of duty. Finally, he stepped back from the screen. Out of the 95 who had been captured, only 68 of them were still alive, and a lot of their best agents were on the "Deceased" list. It made him feel sick. He opened the files containing the labor camp locations and scanned through them. The camps were located *everywhere*. Argentina, Mexico, India, Indiana, Sweden... He opened the sub file in the labor camp locations and found a list of who was in each camp, and all the names of guards stationed there. "I've got good news and bad news. Which do you want to hear first?" Kevin asked, turning away from the screen to face the others. "The good news." Ivy answered instantly. "Louisa is in Mexico, not too far from here." "What's the bad news?" Dan asked, bracing for the worst. "There's about 75 guards stationed in the camp she's in." He told them. Ivy sucked in a breath. "That's a lot." Kevin nodded. "What's our next step?" He asked Dan. Dan didn't hesitate. "Rescuing her, of course." "How?" Matthew queried. The three of them looked at Kevin expectantly, who was deep in thought. "Maybe it's time for you all to meet the director of the NIB." Kevin suggested. "Now that we know where Louisa is, it might be best if we were all on the same page, rather than having me be a messenger." "Wait." Ivy said suddenly. "Shouldn't Annika know about this? It *is* her mother we're talking about." Matthew's face grew concerned. "Shouldn't Annika and Rachel be back by now? Mom said yesterday that the Ravenstone twins dropped off the recording. I thought contestants were supposed to be home *before* the episode aired. Right?" He asked, his tone worried. Kevin glanced at Dan. "He's right. Where's your daughter?" Dan, with worry blossoming in his gut, snatched his phone out of his back pocket and quickly dialed the *Survival Race!* studio. A cheery woman picked up the phone almost instantly. Dan, trying to keep the concern out of his voice, asked about his daughter. "Annika? Yes, she left almost a week ago! She climbed into a Cybertruck with Rachel. I haven't seen them since. Why, have you not seen them recently?" The woman asked. "They probably just went to stay with a friend. Thanks anyway." Dan answered, and abruptly hung up, his hand shaking slightly. "They've been gone for almost a week." He told them. Matthew's jaw dropped. "Then where are they?" Ivy asked, receiving no response.

CHAPTER 9

Rachel wasn't having a great day. Yes, her parents had sent her a bucketful of sweets, and her sisters each wrote hilarious letters complaining about the amount of chores they had to do in her absence, but Jane had disrupted their text-catch up. To make things worse, they were all brought out to the racetrack and challenged to a "first to run 6 laps" race. Seeing as each lap was a mile long, Rachel had collapsed to the ground after the first lap and a half. To no one's surprise, Annika won the race, Jane a close second. After that, they had a race on the woodsy track. Rachel had actually been in the lead for part of it, but then she tripped over a large stone, reigniting the pain in her big toe that had subsided a while ago. Annika won again. For the rest of the day, Rachel stayed in the exercise room, lifting weights and trying to ignore the stabbing pains in her foot. When evening fell and the pain had only intensified, Rachel finally decided it was time to swallow her pride and check in to the doctor on campus. It seemed to take forever, but finally she found a simple door with a gold-colored plaque that read, "Dr. Leonard Crossing." She had found it. Swallowing a groan of pain as her toe throbbed again, she pushed the door open and stumbled into the room. It was a bright room with a white walled interior. Shelves and pictures hung on the walls, bringing cheerful color to the otherwise dull room. A desk sat near the back, with a laptop open on its surface. Several thin, cushioned beds were scattered along the walls. Next to them were small metal push trays lined with tools Rachel often saw in the doctor's office back home. From a door near the back, a man emerged, his eyes large and focused behind the circular glasses he wore. He was seemingly typing in the air. He looked up briefly and noticed her, but continued typing for a moment longer. Finally, he removed the glasses, set them on a nearby desk, and hurried over to her. His black hair was in tight curls, and his dark skin contrasted sharply with the white room. "Welcome! What can I do for you?" He asked cheerfully. Rachel was still in the doorway, becoming convinced this guy was crazy. "Why were you typing in the air?" She asked skeptically. Dr. Crossing laughed. "I was using the glasses to wirelessly connect with my computer, and putting notes in with the virtual keyboard that popped up." He explained. Rachel had heard technology like that existed, but she had never seen it in action. Convinced he maybe wasn't crazy after all, Rachel hobbled in farther and closed the door firmly behind her. "My toe hurts." She answered vaguely. "All right." Dr. Crossing motioned to the beds along the wall. "Hop up, and I'll take a look." She did as he asked, hoisting herself up onto one of the beds and removing her sock and shoe. She winced at the sight. The flesh had become swollen and red, and was crookedly pushing into her other toes. Tiny parts of it had turned black from circulation loss, and it stunk like crazy. Dr. Crossing was unable to hide his look of disgust and dismay. "What happened?" He demanded, hurriedly pulling on gloves and grabbing a small, sharp blade and a thin needle. "My toe got jammed under a door." Rachel answered quietly. "When?" He asked in surprise. Rachel shrugged. "Over a week ago." The doctor looked shocked. "You're joking, right?" Rachel bit her lip and shook her head. Dr. Crossing inserted the needle into the top of her foot, injecting her with a numbing agent. "You do realize," He said a minute later, bringing the blade down to carve away a bit of the infected flesh, making Rachel look away. "That had you waited much longer you would have walked out of this room missing a toe?" "Seriously?" Rachel whispered anxiously. He nodded, then asked. "How did your toe get jammed under a door if you were wearing tennis shoes?" Rachel winced as the blade carved deeper. "I wasn't wearing tennis shoes. I was wearing sandals." He glanced up in surprise. "What? Why? The letter sent to all contestants always includes a 'wear close-toed shoes' note. This place is way too dangerous to have open-toed shoes." "Oh." Was all Rachel could think to say. When he had gotten most of the infected and excess flesh off her foot, he spread an antibacterial salve on it and wrapped it tightly with a bandage. Then, he stood up and walked to a closet she hadn't noticed earlier, and pulled out a pair of large white shoes with holes the size of beads scattered along it. He brought them over to her. "You'll be wearing these until your toe has gone back to normal." He instructed. "And no socks. That'll suffocate it." Rachel nodded, and put them on. Sheepishly, she said, "Thanks." "No problem. Next time, come to me first, okay?" She nodded. The doctor cleaned up the mess on the ground and walked over to the computer on the desk and turned it on. The screen opened to a detailed map of a building, and Rachel stared at it in fascination. There were tiny moving dots on the screen! On closer look, Rachel realized they were people. Dr. Crossing quickly changed the screen to some medical thing, and began typing an entry. He didn't seem to realize she'd seen the moving map. She took that as her excuse to leave, so she crossed to the door and pulled the door open, colliding with Annika. "Rachel! What are you doing here?" Annika didn't wait for an answer. "Wait for me outside?" She asked, though it sounded more like an order than a request. Rachel nodded miserably. This was what she *hadn't* wanted, for anyone to find out about her injury. She sighed and slid to the ground outside the doctor's infirmary and waited for Annika. A few minutes later, Annika came back out. "Hey Rachel. Thanks for waiting." Rachel smiled thinly. "No problem. What were you in there for?" Annika held up her wrist, which was bandaged. "Smacked my wrist on the side of the pool trying to climb out. What were you doing in there?" She asked. "Stubbed my toe." Rachel answered. Annika gave her a look. "Seriously?" Rachel looked down and didn't answer, so Annika slid to the floor next to her and gently asked, "What happened?" "My toe got jammed under a door on our first day here. Dr. Crossing said if I had waited much longer to go in, he would have had to amputate my toe." She admitted. Annika looked shocked. "Oh, wow." Without looking at Rachel, Annika took a deep breath before quickly blurting, "Um, listen, I need to tell you something." "What?" Rachel asked suspiciously. Annika never acted this way. It was almost like she was nervous, but that wasn't possible. Annika *never* got nervous. "Er," Now Rachel was curious. "What?" She asked again. Annika stood up and began pacing, still avoiding

Rachel's eyes. "You're not going to like this." She warned. Rachel rolled her eyes. "I don't like the suspense." She informed Annika. Annika nodded, but said nothing, continuing her relentless pacing. "Annika!" Rachel cried, exasperated. "Just say whatever it is you have to say!" Annika turned to face her, and said in a rush, "Cathy didn't mean to invite you on to *Survival Race!* The invitation was supposed to go to your cousin, Rebecca, but that doesn't matter because you're doing awesome here anyway. They weren't going to tell you, but after Ivy's comment in the group chat today I felt really bad, and I'm really sorry I didn't tell you sooner, but I was afraid you would hate me, or do something rash, and then I forgot. Will you please forgive me?" Rachel almost didn't register everything Annika said after 'Cathy didn't mean to invite you on to *Survival Race!*', her mind was spinning so fast. No wonder she was so outranked by Annika and Bethany and Eliza. She didn't belong here! Of course *Rebecca* did. She was always doing stuff like climbing mountains in faraway places, and doing crazy-dangerous stunts. And *they* weren't going to tell her? "Do Eliza and Bethany know?" She asked quietly, dearly hoping Annika had kept this to herself. Annika hesitated, then nodded. "I don't suppose they forgot too?" Rachel pressed, feeling suddenly angry. Annika shook her head again. "They decided to stay out of it." Her expression turned pleading. "Don't you see, this is why they advised me not to tell you. You're getting all worked up!" Rachel's jaw dropped. "They advised- getting worked up? Of course I'm getting worked up! You would too, had you just found out *you-*" Rachel furiously cut herself off, and abruptly stood up. "I'm leaving." "What?" Annika said, looking panicked. "Where are you going?" Rachel stomped down the corridor. "I don't know! Just leave me alone." She yelled over her shoulder, and disappeared around the corner. Annika stared after her helplessly. Perhaps Eliza and Bethany had been right... But that wasn't fair to Rachel. Of course she would react angrily. Annika knew she would have responded the same way had it been her in Rachel's position. She could only hope Rachel didn't leave the studio, or the *Survival Race!* property. If she did, she could get in a lot of trouble. It was already very dark, so Annika made her way back to their room. Inside, Bethany and

Eliza were playing a game of chess on the carpet, and whispering urgently to each other. They broke off when Annika entered. Eliza glanced up, took one look at the doleful expression on Annika's face, and asked, "I'm assuming you told her?" Annika nodded with a sigh, and plopped down on the couch. "She didn't take it very well." Eliza nodded understandingly, and moved one of her rooks on the board. "That's to be expected. Check." Bethany looked up too. "What are you guys talking about? Who didn't take what very well?" Eliza gave her a look. "Rachel? Accidental invite to the show?" She prompted. "Oh yeah." Bethany absentmindedly moved her pawn. "Where is she now?" Annika shrugged sadly. "Who knows? She just stomped off, said she wanted to be left alone. Hey, weren't you in check?" Annika added, pointing at the board. Bethany looked absolutely baffled as she tried to process what Annika was telling her, and play the game at the same time. "She's out there? Alone? Wait, you're right, I am in check. Rachel doesn't know her way around this place yet!" She reminded Annika while moving her pawn back into its place and moving her bishop to protect her king. Annika sighed again, partially in frustration, partially with irritation at the horrible move Bethany had just done. "I know. I was just trying to respect her wishes." "Checkmate." Eliza cried triumphantly. Bethany turned her attention back to the board. "Wait, how did that happen? Oh. Darn." She sighed. Eliza stood up and walked to the kitchen. "Let's start dinner, so it will be ready when Rachel comes back." She called over her shoulder, leaving Bethany to put their game away.

Rachel hadn't come back after dinner was done. Annika had called her, but it went to voicemail. Rachel wasn't back by dessert either; Annika didn't see her until the next morning, when she found Rachel walking bleary-eyed through the halls, covered in grass stains. She ignored Annika's attempts at conversation, seemingly still mad from the night before. When Annika went outside for a morning jog on the racetrack, she discovered a large, human-shaped imprint on the flattened grass. Rachel barely spoke to her for the next week, constantly leaving the room whenever Annika, Bethany, or Eliza entered. Several days before the big race, Cathy and Jane took the four of them out to the tents on the grounds and were showing them some of the things that would be in their backpacks. "Already Made Meals, or AMM's, have a lot of variety. You all will get to choose some of your favorites to put in your bag." Cathy said, opening a large bin and showing them the freeze-dried bags resting inside. "And over here, we have energy snacks, like nuts, dried fruit, and granola bars-" Cathy broke off and stared into the **Granola Bars** bin for a moment before pulling out a pair of thick gloves. "Who keeps doing this?" She asked furiously. "This is the fourth time this week I've found things in the wrong bin!" Annika looked around her. Jane, who was standing behind Cathy, was trying very hard not to laugh. Bethany and Eliza looked confused. Rachel, however, looked extremely relieved, and exchanged a smile with Jane. Was there something Rachel knew that she hadn't told anyone about? Annika wished Rachel was still speaking to her. "Anyway," Cathy said, annoyed, as she switched them back to their regular spots. "This is the food you will be eating. It is not advised that you eat anything you find on the course. We have no way of perfectly scrounging the race grounds, so you could find anything there." She moved on, switching to the topic of first aid and resting.

Annika tried to talk to Rachel that night, but she just rolled over and ignored her. It seemed Annika would never find out what had happened between her friend and Jane. It wasn't until a few days before the show race that they were all on speaking terms again. Rachel seemed to have forgiven them, but none of them ever brought the subject up again. Annika was relieved; had Rachel still been holding the grudge when the race started, neither of them would have been able to concentrate. The morning of the big race dawned on a sunny, yet chilly, morning. Jane came to rouse them at six in the morning, bright-eyed and jumpy. She seemed as excited as they were nervous, and after they had had their last breakfast together, she brought them back to the entrance of the studio they had been in their first day there. Cathy was there, as were many other grey-jumpsuit clad workers. "Are you girls ready?" Cathy asked them, smiling kindly. The contestants nodded immediately, though she noticed Rebecca- no, *Rachel*, seemed a bit more hesitant. That was understandable. The girl didn't belong on a prestigious game show like this. But still, Jane had reported remarkable feats and improvement from all of them. If Rachel did well, maybe they could look into options like inviting other non-hardcore survivalists on. "If you will please follow me?" Cathy asked, turning away and leading them through a door to the room Jane had interviewed them in over three weeks ago. The room was familiar, and Annika again found herself wondering what was behind the dark pane of glass. It seemed they were going to find out, as Cathy pulled a heavy key ring out from under her sweater, and fit a smooth gold key into the lock. It turned easily, and she led them into a small square room. Annika realized with surprise that now, on this side, she could see through the pane, into the room she had been interviewed in. Several chairs sat behind the glass, providing a viewing area to watch the interviews without being seen. Cathy opened another door, this one solid steel, and walked onto a smooth stretch of grass at the borderline of the forest. Annika felt her heart speed up as she followed Eliza onto the grass. They were standing on *Survival Race!* territory! A steel wall followed the studio its whole length, and moved past far beyond her vision. Annika recalled Jane telling them it extended 90 miles long. At the very edge of her vision traveling across the grass to her left, she could faintly see another tall steel wall. A moment later, a loud roaring sound made them all jump and turn to see Jane driving an oversized hover cart. "Hop in!" She called. Annika raised her eyebrows and smiled at Rachel, who gave a nervous chuckle. The five of them piled into the cart with Jane, who began driving away from the studio, towards a huge helicopter hangar 30 yards away. The doors had been rolled wide open, with several grey-clad workers bustling around the opening, and readying a bright-red helicopter for launch. As soon as Jane pulled the cart to a stop, the contestants jumped out and raced over to the hangar, Jane and Cathy following close behind. Bethany looked positively thrilled, and was stroking the side of the chopper and talking to the workers preparing it for flight. Eliza grinned at the sight, but didn't seem as enthralled as Bethany. "My cousin told me all about this."

She whispered to Rachel. "Get this- they have free snacks in there!" Rachel stared at Eliza incredulously. "How can you think about food at a time like this?" Eliza rolled her eyes. "Not for now, of course. But you could stick some in your pockets, then put them in your bag when you get on the course!" She suggested hopefully. "We don't have pockets." Rachel reminded her. Eliza looked crestfallen. "Oh yeah." She sighed. "Are you girls coming or not?" Annika called from the doorway of the helicopter. They hurried over to the helicopter, and Annika helped them in. Jane took the pilots seat, and in moments they had lifted off the ground and were gliding out of the hangar. She took them higher, lifting them to heights so great all the people on the ground became tiny pinpricks of grey on the smooth green land beneath them. Annika grasped firmly to one of the handles near the opening of the chopper, and leaned out into the thin air to get a better view. Besides her, Bethany did the same. Rachel chose to sit firmly on the cushioned bench in the back of the helicopter, with the seat belt firmly in place. She most definitely did *not* want to fall out. To her right, Eliza was peering into a small refrigerator affixed to the wall. She noticed Rachel watching her, and gave a wink. Rachel shook her head in disbelief but did not say anything, for at that moment Cathy emerged from the co-pilots seat to talk to them. She was carrying 4 large, heavy-duty backpacks, red in color, with the *Survival Race!* logo emblazoned onto them. Annika, Bethany, and Eliza quickly sat down and accepted the backpacks handed to them. "There are four lanes. All are equally challenging, but you need to decide which lane you want so Jane can drop you off in front of it." Cathy shouted to be heard over the noise of the chopper's blades. "I'll take the far-left lane." Eliza decided first. "Then I'll take the far-right." Bethany said, grinning at Eliza. Annika looked at Rachel to see if she had a preference. Rachel shrugged, and said, "I guess I'll take the one next to Eliza." "So, Annika is in the one next to Bethany?" Cathy double-checked. Annika nodded. "Perfect-" She was cut off as a loud message blared through the speakers hidden in the helicopter. It was Jane. "Chopper number 2, do you read?" Rachel was confused. "Chopper number 2?" Bethany stood up and walked over to the open doorway to see outside. "There's another helicopter following us." She reported. After a moments pause, she added, "And we're descending." She was right. The helicopter swooped down and settled onto the turf. As soon as the blades had stopped rotating, Cathy turned to Eliza, who was back at the minifridge, stuffing fruit bars into her backpack. Cathy chose to ignore this, and told her, "Off you go. Your camera people will let you know when to start. Wait for their signal." She instructed. Eliza nodded, zipped her bag up, and hopped off the helicopter, landed gently on the grass, and jogged over to a second helicopter that had landed several yards behind them. Two of the workers they had seen in the hangar got off, carrying a large high-tech camera between them. They led Eliza over to a huge red X in the ground, and began setting the camera up on another large X. Then, their helicopter lifted again, and Jane turned it around and began flying it the direction they had come from. Minutes later, it was Rachel disembarking, clutching her backpack tightly as she trailed another two helpers to more red X's. Finally, it was Annika's turn. She waved goodbye to Bethany, who was still in the helicopter, and marched over to Chopper number 2, where another two people were climbing down. "Hello! You ready?" One of them asked with a smile. Annika nodded confidently. "Let's go." Annika followed behind them, obeying when they instructed her to stand on the red X. They bustled about the camera for several nerve-racking minutes before finally getting it set up in a position that clearly captured her face. A second later, they both put their hand to their ears; when they put their hands back down, Annika noticed they wore red ear communicators. One of them quietly addressed Annika. "Get ready." Annika shifted on her feet and focused on the best path through the brush that started the forest in front of her. "On your mark." The camera person whispered. Annika gave her a quick glance, and realized her hand was to her ear. She was repeating whatever she was hearing through the earpiece. Annika crouched slightly, readying herself for a sprint into the trees. "Get set." Annika swallowed and tightened her grip on the straps of her backpack. "GO!" The woman hissed suddenly. Annika took off, veering to the right into a break in the trees. The transition from grassland to forest was instantaneous. She was surrounded by trees, the chirps of birds, and the rustle of animals hiding. When she slowed, she could no longer see the grass she had left behind. Moving quickly, she pulled her backpack off and dropped it to the ground so she could rummage through it, taking stock of the meager supplies she had. Annika withdrew a compass, and held it forward in front of her. She was facing East, and it would be East she was traveling to. She slipped the compasses strap over her wrist and rezipped the backpack, slinging it over her shoulder in one quick motion and heading off for the thicker parts of the forest in front of her, quickly coming to the foot of a steep mountain. She had to average about 12 miles per day if she was to make it. That wouldn't be too hard, if she traveled for 12 hours a day, slept for 8, and spent the last 4 making camp and resting. She smirked. This would be too easy.

Four hours of switching between walking and jogging up the steep hills passed in an agonizingly long time. Annika collapsed to the ground, and removed her water bottle to again take another long drink from the bottle. Her backpack had become alarmingly lighter, with how much water she kept drinking to keep her energy up. It had to last 7 days, or at least until she got to a clean stream so she could use a filter and get more water. Biting back a groan, Annika heaved herself back up to a standing position, checked her compass to make sure she was still heading East, and started the long trek forwards again.

It was nearing dark when Annika finally stopped for the night. Her mile counter that she found in her backpack said she covered a grueling 10 miles, so when she finally stumbled upon a glade where she could set up camp, she gladly took the excuse to rest. Trying to squash the disappointed feeling in her gut of not reaching her goal, she pulled off her backpack to get a fire started. It wasn't her fault she'd come short of her goal. Well, maybe it was. That made the feeling intensify, so she busied herself getting firewood. Judging by the remains of a very old campfire, she could guess it wasn't the first time someone had found this place. It took only moments to get a fire going, and she was eating an AMM soon after. When at last she collapsed onto her bedroll, she was asleep in an instant. Annika awoke the next morning well-rested, but freezing. After quickly consuming an energy bar, she packed up camp and set forth with a renewed determination. She'd come two miles short yesterday, and would have to make up for it today. Annika crashed through the undergrowth, shoving aside branches, tall ferns, and the baby chipmunk that jumped on her wrist. She could run 5 ½ minute miles. Surely she could use that same speed here. At first, it was working. Then, three painful miles later, she was reduced to walking speed for the rest of the day. On Annika's third day, she came across a raging stream, with the water crashing down its banks with so much force she was sure that trying to swim it would be fruitless. Instead, she removed the thickest rope from her backpack and lassoed it onto a strong branch on the other side. After giving it a firm tug, Annika backed up, took a running start, and leaped into the air, holding tightly to the rope. Her momentum carried her far across the stream; but she delayed in jumping off at the end. When at last she let go, she plummeted, straight into the stream. She landed near the end, where the water was only waist-high. She scrambled out, fearful for the contents inside the bag. Dripping water, she carefully opened the bag and peered inside. Her blanket, resting on the bottom, was slightly damp, but everything else was dry, except for the shoes she was wearing. For some odd reason, Annika felt like crying. What was wrong with her? She sunk to the ground and buried her face in her hands. Her original assumption at the beginning of the race had been that this would be extremely easy. Her first thoughts upon arriving at the studio were that she could beat them all even without training! Yet, for some reason, it was the most difficult challenge she had ever faced. Trial after trial got in her way, and exhaustion hampered her thinking. This was nothing like a simple puzzle she could beat, as it was in laser training or gymnastics. This was no marathon she could beat in a few hours. This was *days*, and it drained her in a way she'd never felt. For the first time in her life, she felt homesick, and not for the first time in her life, she missed her mom. She missed the support and encouragement she always got from her father and friends, something Annika had never realized she depended on so much. Here, alone, she felt defeated. And yet, she knew the only way she could see them again was to get out of here, and to never return. This forest was sucking all her confidence away, all her hope for winning. The only way to defeat that would be to escape this wretched prison of unending woods. Slowly, Annika could tell her strength was coming back. The only way to ensure she saw her father again was to push forward, pushing her physical and mental capacities past their limits. She was Annika. Annika could do anything. And this was no different. She stood, filled her water bottle, emptied the water from her shoes, and replaced them before checking her compass again. She had four days to get out of here. She could get out of here. She just had to believe it. Filled with a renewed sense of optimism, Annika became unstoppable. By day, she was scaling obstacles, darting through the trees at top speeds, and wading through knee-deep creeks. By night, she was sleeping soundly, waking rested and ready for another long day. On the morning of her seventh day, Annika could tell she was nearing the end. The brush and woods were becoming thinner, and at least twice she was positive she caught a glimpse of glinting grass. But it seemed like there was something else glinting along with the grass. There was a shimmer in the air just on the edge of her vision, and she couldn't figure out what was causing it. Curious to find out what it was, she increased her speed, knowing she *had* to be close. Suddenly, she stopped in confusion. A wall? In a forest? She cautiously touched it. Indeed, it was a wall, the wall separating hers and Bethany's tracks. She hadn't realized she'd been going so far to the right. With a shrug, she tripled her speed, using the wall as her guiding line as she trampled the underbrush beneath her feet. At last, the grass was fully in sight. She burst from the trees, across a thick white line, and screamed in surprise. Bethany emerged right next to her from the other side of the wall. They stared at each other in shock. "What are you doing here?" They blurted at the same time. Turning away from her friend, Annika looked around the grass. It wasn't as big as the grass they had started on, and when she backed up several yards, she could clearly see all four lanes. That was odd. You could hardly see the walls from the other side. Why had they gotten so narrow? Perhaps, Annika realized, it was to save space. Bethany was flopped on the grass, looking breathless. Her backpack was missing. "Where's your bag?" Annika asked curiously. "I lost it in one of the rivers." Bethany answered with a nonchalant tone. "I don't suppose you have something I can eat?" As an answer, Annika tossed her bag to Bethany, who gratefully rummaged through it before removing several energy bars and quickly scarfing them up. 15 minutes later, the sound of a helicopter's blades tore through the veil of silence the girls had fallen into. A bright red helicopter touched down several feet away from them, and from it Jane and Cathy hopped out. The helicopter lifted again and headed off to the farthest right track. Jane ran over to them and hugged them tightly. "It's so good to see you again!" She cried happily. Bethany looked startled. "How did you get here so fast? It should have taken at least two hours!" She reasoned. "We've been hovering over the area for over an hour, waiting for you girls to finish. And now you're here!" Jane answered cheerfully. Bethany smiled tolerantly, but was more focused on the helicopter that had abandoned them. "Where's it going?" She asked. "To go get Eliza and Rachel." Cathy answered as she drew nearer. "You two did so well. I'll admit I'm surprised you both emerged at the same time." "Who won?" Annika asked, hiding her worry. Jane shrugged. "We'll check the cameras when we get back. In my eyes, you're both champions." She smiled encouragingly. They waited patiently for the helicopter to return, and when it did, Rachel hopped out immediately and ran over to them. She stood in front of Annika, eyes glowing with pride and happiness. "I made it over 4/5 of the way before they got me!" She announced. Annika grinned. "Good job!" Obviously she had more fun than me, Annika thought wryly. "Did you win?" Rachel asked expectantly. Annika shrugged. "We both came out at the same time." Her jaw dropped. "A tie?" Cathy shook her head. "We'll check the cameras to find out who was first back at the studio." Rachel's eyes widened. From the helicopter, Dr. Crossing was waving them over. To Annika's surprise, Eliza lay across the seats, her ankle twisted at an odd angle. Her face was deathly pale. Bethany emitted a sharp gasp. "What happened to her?" She cried, rushing into the helicopter to kneel by her friend. It was Dr. Crossing who answered. "She broke her ankle a few hours ago, near the end of the course." "And you didn't go get her?" Bethany cried accusingly. "She didn't want us to get her. She said she could take care of it herself, and only to fetch her after someone won." Jane responded sadly. "Were there any painkillers in the medical kit in the bag?" Annika asked, averting her eyes from Eliza's still form. Cathy bit her lip and shook her head. "But that's changing." Jane quickly assured them. "From now on, every med kit will have an emergency painkiller." "Then again, if you had let me pull Eliza out immediately, I wouldn't have had to sedate her until I can reset the bone." Dr. Crossing added angrily. Cathy sighed, her hazel eyes looking troubled. "I try to respect the contestants wishes." She answered. He glared at her. "And now that you've respected her wishes, it's gonna take a lot longer for her ankle to heal properly, if it ever does!" "I believe in you." Cathy answered simply, and got on the helicopter. Wide-eyed, Rachel and Annika followed, and the helicopter lifted off to take them back to the studio. It was a long ride they mostly spent sleeping, and two hours later they landed inside the hangar. Dr. Crossing quickly loaded Eliza into one of the hover carts with a workers help, and they took off for the studio. Cathy, Jane, Bethany, Annika, and Rachel hopped into a second, and Jane drove them back, the wind fluttering her curls into her face, slowing their pace as she kept brushing them away. When at last they arrived at the studio, Dr. Crossing's cart was empty, and the door to the studio was wide open. As soon as Jane parked beside it, Cathy jumped out and hurried inside, crossing to the very end of the room where she had sat on their first day there, and slid open a door behind the chairs and disappeared inside. Jane was quick to follow. The girls were left there, shifting awkwardly in the middle of the room as they waited for them to come back out. To pass the time, Rachel wandered over to the wall where all the pictures hung, and stared at them. Hundreds of smiling faces stared back at her, and she silently read the nameplates beneath them. There were so many, each with a number besides their names. The biggest number was 1453. And now, Annika or Bethany would become number 1454. She hoped it was Annika. Still, she would be happy for Bethany if it turned out to be her instead. She deserved it too! She still hoped it was Annika. Jane leaned out of the doorway and waved them forward. They crossed the room and entered the darkened room where Cathy was watching a clip on a monitor. When they had gathered around her, she reset the clip, set in slow motion, so they could watch. It was a clear view of both Annika's and Bethany's race tracks. They watched the forestry scene, and finally Annika caught a glimpse of something red coming through the trees. It was Bethany, running in slow motion towards the camera. A second later, Annika saw herself, running slowly towards the camera too. She watched their feet as they neared the white line, hoping desperately it would be her foot that crossed the line first. Instead, Bethany was half a leg over by the time Annika's toe crossed the finish line. In the recording, they were staring at each other in shock, but Annika couldn't focus anymore. She hadn't won. Bethany had! A quiet, dry laugh escaped her. She'd been so sure she would win. And yet, for the first time in her life, she had been beaten by someone equally as good as her. Looking for Bethany's reaction, she looked startled, like she too had been expecting to see Annika cross the line first. Identical to their duplicates on the screen, they stared at each other for a moment; then Annika extended her hand for a shake. Bethany took the silent congratulations, a smile spreading over her face as they shook hands. "Well, Bethany. It looks like you're the next *Survival Race!* champion." Cathy unnecessarily informed her. "If you will follow me?" They all trailed her back out of the room, and she took them into a simple, black room with a large, sturdy camera set up facing a wall. Cathy pulled a solid gold medal from atop a shelf, and handed it to Bethany, who almost dropped it in surprise. "Is this real?" She asked, eyes wide. Cathy chuckled and nodded. "Of course. Now please, stand over here?" She motioned to the wall, and Jane lined the hovering camera up. "Smile!" Click! A moment later, two full color pictures of a beaming Bethany slid out from a wide slot. Jane handed one to Bethany, and put the other in a wooden frame. Cathy, who had disappeared into yet another secret room, emerged with a gold-colored nameplate bearing Bethany's name, and the number 1454 beneath it. Jane took it and carried it out to the wall where the rest were, and carefully hung it up.

Bethany couldn't stop grinning, though she looked slightly guilty whenever she cast a look in Annika's direction. After Jane, Rachel, and Cathy had gone to check on Eliza, she drew Annika aside. "I'm sorry." Annika was surprised. "Why?" "It feels like it should have been you who won." She answered, seeming slightly embarrassed. Annika shook her head. "You deserved the win. We worked equally hard. In the end, the best one won. I've accepted it wasn't me." Bethany studied her for a moment. "Are you going to be... alright?" Annika understood what she meant. "I don't know if I'll ever not wonder if the outcome would have been different had I not delayed in a certain place, or, uh," She cut herself off as she remembered how close she had come to crying. Annika chose a different approach. "I might always feel like beating myself up. All I can do is remember I tried my best, and practically tied with the champion. What more could I want? Besides, winning wouldn't have helped my ego." She admitted with a sheepish smile. Bethany returned it, looking relieved, and started to head away. "Hey." Annika called after her. Bethany turned expectantly. "What are you going to do with the medal? I heard some winners melt it down to sell." Bethany shook her head exuberantly. "No way! I'm keeping it forever." Annika grinned. "I would've done the same." Bethany held her gaze for a moment, then turned away and walked over to two whispering workers who were staring at her. She talked quietly to them, then shook their hands and walked away looking extremely satisfied. Annika watched them curiously, but was distracted by the sounds of arguing coming from the double doors that led back to where they had lived and trained for the past month. She and Bethany hurried over to the doors to find out what the commotion was. A short way down the hall, Eliza was leaning on crutches, talking loudly to Cathy. Jane hovered behind her, and Rachel looked extremely embarrassed as she watched Eliza. Exchanging confused looks, Bethany and Annika hurried closer. "Why did you say you were surprised Rachel got so far?" Eliza demanded. Cathy didn't answer. "I heard you talking to Dr. Crossing when Rachel was in the bathroom. You couldn't believe that 'someone so average' had gotten farther than expected." She waited for a response, and when she didn't get one, her pretty features twisted into an angry expression. "I know that you didn't mean to invite Rachel onto *Survival Race!* It was an accident." She told Cathy, who finally gave a reaction, though slight. Her eyes widened in surprise. Behind her, Jane's jaw dropped; whether from surprise at the news or surprise that Eliza knew, Annika wasn't sure. Rachel took a sudden interest in the floor, staring at it intently. "You know what else I noticed?" Eliza asked, hardly waiting for a response. "Our letters arrived the day before we were supposed to be here. My cousin had a four-day warning!" Cathy bit her lip, but didn't deny it. Suddenly, Eliza's expression grew thoughtful. "That's why you seemed confused when Rachel introduced herself. You expected a Rebecca Ravenstone, but got the wrong person. You never would have made a mistake like that, unless..." She gasped. "That's why! You were getting stressed you couldn't find another eligible candidate for the show. Our letters were late because you chose Rebecca at the last minute. You were shocked Rachel did so well because you thought no ordinary person could ever even slightly measure up to the people who had been training all their life. You messed up, and it turned out so much better than you expected!" She cried triumphantly, jabbing a finger at Cathy, who flinched. "And you know what? She beat me!" Eliza insisted. "She did better than I did!" Cathy finally found her voice. "Only because you broke your ankle!" She argued. By this point, people had been sticking their heads out of doorways to see what the source of the noise was. They had gathered into a circle around Eliza and Cathy, silently watching the fight. Even Dr. Crossing had opened the door to the infirmary and was leaning in the doorway with his arms crossed, intently watching Cathy with an amused expression. Annika heard him mumble something under his breath, and it sounded a lot like, "Always knew her words would come back to bite her someday." She suppressed a smile and glanced at Rachel, who looked extremely uncomfortable. "And whose fault was that?" Eliza asked in response to the broken ankle comment. "Mine! *I* wasn't looking where I was going. *I* tripped. That's all on me!" Cathy glowered at her, but evidently agreed, for she stayed quiet. "So." Eliza asked pointedly, seeming to enjoy her crowd. "What are you going to do about it?" "About what?" Cathy asked tartly. "Your mistake! Don't you see? Rachel's success solved your problem! Maybe, instead of only inviting the elite, the top of the top, you could have a system where people who want to be on the game show can enter their name or something. Then, instead of having to search for four people every month for every studio you have set up, you could draw four names, and voila! Instant new competitors." Eliza suggested. Cathy, though still scowling at Eliza, looked grudgingly impressed. "It might work." She admitted quietly, bringing excited smiles from the *Survival Race!* crew. Eliza smiled too, happy with herself. "Good. Now. *I'm* going to take a nap. She thumped off in the direction of their room, and after a moment, her friends followed, the crowd parting to let them through.

CHAPTER 10

Annika woke up to insistent text pings the next morning. Groggily, she rolled over and grabbed her phone, staring blearily at the screen for several moments. Suddenly her eyes widened, and all sleepiness fled instantly as she comprehended the message. She scrambled down the ladder, forgetting to stay quiet, and began packing her bag. She would have to get out of here as soon as possible! Her rummaging woke the others, to their great annoyance. "Someone's anxious to get out of here." Bethany mumbled sleepily. Eliza yawned too. "We're not allowed back in the training rooms anymore." She reminded Annika, who smiled brightly. "I've got to go." She told them, throwing the last of her souvenirs into her bag and starting for the bathroom. "Where?" Rachel asked in confusion. Annika poked her head out from the bathroom. "To Paris!" "What?" The other three cried out at the same time. "What about me?" Rachel asked, toppling onto the floor in her hurry to get out of bed. Annika shook her head. "The SIA has a new mission for me. Dad's Cybertruck will take you home." Behind her, Bethany and Eliza shared a look of horror. "No way. I'm coming with you." Rachel declared, pulling her bag from the wardrobe and hurriedly packing it. Annika gave her a look. "Don't you want to go home? See your parents and sisters and... Matthew?" A slight blush colored Rachel's cheeks, but she simply said, "And miss Paris? No thanks. Besides, I've lived there before. I speak French! You'll definitely need me, so you can tell that to your SIA boss." Rachel quickly slipped into the bathroom to get changed. Annika sighed and sent a quick text to her boss. *I'm bringing my best friend too. She'll be helpful.* After a moment, she received an affirmative text. "Ok." She announced, slipping her phone into her bag, noting its low percentage. "We gotta go. They said my dad already approved it, and he's sending his Cybertruck to take us to the airport." "What about breakfast?" Bethany asked, fully alert. Annika didn't hear her, and a cheery door slam meant she- and Rachel- had just left the room. Eliza's face paled. "What's in Paris that the SIA would want her to take care of?" Bethany swallowed hard. "Elle." She answered grimly. "You've got to stop her!" Eliza cried. Bethany nodded and darted out of the room, just to return seconds later and dash into the bathroom to get dressed first.

Annika and Rachel met up with Jane in the hallways as they headed towards the main room this adventure had started in. "You girls ready to go?" She asked, hurrying alongside them as Annika strode to the double doors. Rachel nodded. "Annika's dad sent his car, so we're in a hurry." Annika slowed at the doors and glanced through the glass to outside. Sure enough, a gleaming silver Cybertruck waited patiently outside. Annika turned suddenly towards Jane and embraced her, whispered a "Thank you," and stepped back. Jane smiled at her, handed them two small breakfast bags, and watched them climb into the car and drive away, mistily wishing they didn't have to go. Behind her, Bethany came rushing out, looking disheveled and not at all ready to go. "Where's Annika?" She implored, looking panicked. "She just left." Jane answered in confusion. "Did she forget something?" Bethany bit her lip, shook her head, and dashed out of the building. Through the glass, Jane watched her run down the road a bit, before finally coming back inside. Jane was concerned. "What's wrong?" Bethany swallowed hard. "Nothing." She answered quietly, and disappeared back through the double doors.

Annika glanced at the car's dashboard and saw it had a new destination, set for the nearest airport. "We have a three-hour drive ahead of us." She quickly texted her dad a "Thanks!" and pulled up a movie on Rachel's phone so she and Rachel could watch it. Her battery died with only 10 minutes of the drive left, so they settled to playing card games, eating the breakfasts Jane packed for them, and eating chocolate, now that Rachel had two full jugs worth. At last, the car pulled into a busy airport and the girls got out. Once they were standing safely on the sidewalk right outside it, the Cybertruck pulled away, no doubt heading back to her dad's house. Annika walked up to one of the gates of a plane headed to Paris, and said she and her friend already had pre-booked tickets. Minutes later, she and Rachel were being seated on a lush private plane, having been hurried right to the front of the line. It was a ten hour flight, so they flipped on the TV screen in front of them and spent the entire flight bingeing episodes of Star Trek, which nowadays were almost impossible to come by. Go figure an expensive plane would have old shows like that. Finally, the plane touched down onto a beautiful airport in Paris just as the sun was starting to set, and the girls rushed out. Stretching, Annika breathed in the wonderful scents coming from nearby pastry shops, and listened to the locals speaking in a language she didn't know. Rachel, however, was pleased to find she understood every word that was said. Annika's phone came out, and she typed a message to her boss. "*We're here. Where do we go?*" A moment later, she received the address for a secluded business 14 miles away. Rachel hailed a taxi, and repeated to the driver in French where they needed to go. She turned sheepishly to Annika. "Do you have money?" Annika nodded and withdrew two gold coins stamped with 20's on them. Rachel took one and talked animatedly with the driver, who took it and gave back two dollar coins, and a 26-cent coin. Annika dropped them back into her bag, and turned to look at Rachel. "I guess I'm lucky you came along." She grinned. Rachel laughed. "Told you! You know, it's so handy having a worldwide currency. I learned in school last year that before the War, almost every place in the world had a different currency, and that some of the old money was paper! Nowadays, everything is coins. I can bet it's much easier." Annika laughed. "No kidding. Could you imagine believing a slip of paper was worth the same as a 100-dollar gold coin? There's some stuff back in the old days that's just unbelievable." Rachel gazed out the window for a moment. "Oh, look! Lavenders! It's been years since I last saw French Lavender." Annika was curious. "When did you last go to Paris?" "We moved here when I turned 6 as a birthday present, and moved back to Idaho when I was 9. The twins were actually born here!" "That's cool." Annika told her. "Do they remember it?" She asked. Rachel shook her head. "Not really. They have fragmented memories, but they were only 2 when we moved back." Annika nodded. "That's a long birthday present." Rachel grinned. "And if we hadn't moved, I never would've met you!" She informed her happily. Annika was perplexed. "What? Why?" "We used to live in White Bird, Idaho. When we moved back, my parents found a new home in Grangeville. If I hadn't wanted to go to Paris, we would still be living there, and I'd never have met you!" Annika laughed. "Wow. Guess fate meant for us to be together, huh?" Rachel smiled. "Guess so." She agreed. "Guess so." At last, the taxi pulled to a stop outside a simple white brick building with blue shutters sealed shut over the windows. Several tall hedges cut it off from the also-plain businesses on either side of it. It looked like an overall pleasant place to be, and Annika was excited to go inside. She had never seen the inside of this SIA base before. How proud her mom would have been, knowing her youngest was following in her footsteps to make the world a better place. Rachel exited beside her, calling a quick, "*Merci!*" after their driver. Annika approached the building, scanning the streets before reaching the front door and rapping on it. Several long moments later, the door swung open and a black-suited man stood there before them, his hand resting easily on his hand gun in a holster attached to his hip. "I'm Annika Helmcott, SIA agent." She introduced herself. He studied her curiously for several long moments, and didn't respond. Finally, he stepped back and beckoned her forward- but stopped Rachel. "She's with me. Makrus already cleared it." Annika clarified quickly. The man looked annoyed, spun on his heel, and marched away. Annika followed closely, and after a moment's hesitation, so did Rachel. He led them through black-carpeted halls to a large office, where a husky, muscular man sat comfortably in a sturdy leather chair. Annika had met him only twice before, and it was quite an honor to once again be in the presence of the greatest man on the planet, with the exception of her father. The guard who had escorted them to the room bowed deeply and walked out, leaving the three of them alone. Rachel gazed around the room, enjoying the sunset visible through the large window that overlooked the city, and taking in the 'trophies' of animal heads on the wall. She realized with alarm that the chair the SIA director was sitting in was made of rhino hide- a near extinct species. He seemed pleasant enough, with his dark spiky hair and dark eyes that crinkled at the corners when he smiled. Still, there was something strangely ominous about him, something in his stance when he stood that unnerved her. "Welcome. I'm grateful you were able to get here so fast." He greeted them. "You said there was an urgent mission that needs my attention?" Annika prompted. He nodded. "Indeed. But first- this is your friend you said would be valuable?" He asked curiously, regarding Rachel with an interested look that for some reason made her uncomfortable. Annika nodded. "Well." He extended his hand to shake. "My name is Leo Makrus. I am the director of the Secret Intelligence Agency." He introduced. Rachel gave him a nervous smile. "Rachel Ravenstone." "Pleasure to make your acquaintance." He said thoughtfully. Then, he sat back down and shuffled through some papers on his desk before pulling one out of the tall stack and laying it down on the desk so the girls could see it clearly. It was a file on a girl, with a full color picture and a detailed description about her. The picture was of a white-haired teen who looked to be about 18. The picture was from a side shot, with her hair partially covering her face, indicating she hadn't been aware there was a picture being taken of her. The description detailed a young woman who was developing a dangerous new technology. "Her name is Elle Thompson. We know she's creating a technology that will cause a lot of harm. Problem is, we can't legally arrest her until we know for sure what the specifics of that technology is." Makrus told them. "What type of technology?" Annika asked, looking puzzled. "And why would she be developing something dangerous? That's illegal." "We know." Makrus agreed. "We have reason to believe she is creating a dematerializer." Annika gave him a perplexed look. "A *what?*" "It vaporizes people." He explained. Rachel's jaw dropped. Annika was disturbed. "If you know it, uh, does that, why haven't you arrested her?" "Because we need more physical proof. None of our agents have been able to get close enough to her to affirm it." "But she's older than me. Why would she open up to us?" To Rachel, Annika looked slightly panicked, like she was trying to get out of

THE HELMCOTT CHRONICLES | 127

it. This certainly wasn't what she had been imagining when she imagined a mission in Paris. "You are the closest in age we have. Besides, I believe in you." He told her with a firm tone. "Oh. I have something for you." He added, and reached into a drawer in his desk and removed a simple metal bangle, decoratively twisted, with several pretty runes carved into it. He handed it over to her. "I had it made especially for you." He told her with an air of lightness. She turned it over in her hands. Especially for her? Too bad she wasn't a jewelry fan. "Thank you." Annika smiled and dropped it into her bag. He looked disappointed. "You're not going to put it on?" He asked. "Uh, not right now. I was going to exercise tonight, and I don't want it bothering me. I'll put it on afterwards." He nodded and stood up abruptly, fishing a heavy looking velvet bag out of his pocket and handing it to her. "Use this for a hotel and food while you stay here." He instructed. "Oh, may I have your phones please?" He asked, holding his hand out expectantly. They dutifully handed them over, and he glanced at them in surprise. "Both dead?" He asked incredulously. Annika sheepishly nodded. "No matter. I'll charge them for you." He offered, slipping them into the same pocket the bag of coins had come out of. "There's no need." Annika protested, holding her hand out to get them back. "I can charge them myself." He didn't give them back. "I'll do it." He repeated. "You'll find Ms. Thompson in La Petite Chateau tonight. It's a French restaurant she often goes to. I would suggest dressing fancily." Then he gestured to the door. "Have a good day. And," He added as they turned obediently towards the door. "I expect you to report back in five days." Annika swallowed and nodded, then led the way back to the entry and let herself out. When they got to the street, they began walking towards town. Only when they were out of sight of the building did she stop and look at Rachel. "We need to make a game plan." She announced. "We're supposed to befriend a girl older than us who is creating a device that kills people, and somehow get her secrets so we can capture her!" Rachel cried, slightly hysterically. "What if she tests it on us?" Annika shrugged. "I didn't take martial art lessons for nothing. If we stick together, we'll be fine." "This is crazy." Rachel complained, trailing Annika over to another taxi. "Why don't we just go home?" Annika glared at her. "You didn't act this way when we took down the arsonists organization." She pointed out. "That's because they weren't creating technology that vaporizes people. She is!" "That's why we have to stop her." Annika reasoned, climbing into the cab. "Can you get him to drive us to the nearest town?" She asked. Rachel rolled her eyes, but addressed the driver in French, and pulled a 15-dollar coin out of the velvet bag Mr. Makrus had given them and handed it to him. "Where are we even going?" Rachel conceded grumpily, handing Annika the bag. "To a clothing store. We can't just walk into an expensive restaurant like this." Annika gestured to their clothes, which hadn't been worn or washed in over a month. Rachel grimaced. Annika laughed and nudged her friend. "Cheer up. We get to dress up! That's like, your favorite thing ever!" Less than thirty minutes later, they were walking out of a fancy French boutique, carrying large bags. To Annika's relief, Rachel had found a gorgeous dark blue dress almost immediately after entering. It hadn't taken her long to convince Annika that the four-hundred-dollar dress was worth the price. After choosing a slim silver dress, Annika got them a room at a nearby hotel. As dusk fell, they entered La Petite Chateau, which Rachel told Annika translated into The Little Castle. Immediately upon entering, Annika could see that her boss had been accurate. This seemed to be where the rich dined, and all around them sat couples and families dressed just as elaborately as they were. "Look." Annika whispered, gesturing slightly to a table near the back. A young woman with pure white hair sat by herself, typing on her phone. "Think that's her?" Rachel whispered back. Annika nodded. "Who else has hair like that?" A waitress came over to them instantly, and it took Rachel only a few seconds to secure them a table near the back in French. Moments later, they were seated at a table near the girl. Annika took one glance at the menu and placed it right back down. "I envy your French abilities." She groaned to Rachel, who laughed in response. "What about all the languages you speak? Didn't it total to 8, or something?" She asked, amused. "Nine. Unfortunately, that never included French. It was always too difficult for me." Annika admitted with a wry smile. Using her peripheral vision, she noticed the girl- Elle- turn her head in their direction. That was odd. She didn't recall the description page including she spoke English. Perhaps she was listening to someone else? Wanting to test her theory, she asked Rachel, "Have you played the new Beat Saber version on the Air Quest 1600?" "What?" Rachel was caught off guard. "The new virtual reality game that came out last year. Have you played it?" Rachel gave her an odd look. "Of course. Ivy got it for her birthday last year. You knew that. You were-" Annika hushed her and turned to the girl. "Can I help you?" She asked politely. The girl immediately looked embarrassed. "I'm sorry, I didn't mean to eavesdrop. I heard you talking about the Air quest 1600. Beat Saber is my favorite game on it." She apologized in a sweet, lilting voice. She had a slight French accent, but it was hardly detectable. Annika smiled. "Mine too! I'm Annika Helmcott. What's your name?" "Elle Thompson." She answered, smiling. "I love your hair." Annika told her. "Is it dyed?" "No." Elle answered, fingering the long strands. "I was born with it. It's extremely rare. My mother always said it was how she knew I was destined for great things." "That's cool." Rachel chimed in. Elle jumped, like she had forgotten she was there. "I'm Rachel." She added with a sheepish grin. Elle smiled. "It is a pleasure to meet you. Your French is excellent, by the way." "Thank you!" Rachel beamed. "I didn't realize people here in France spoke English." Annika noted curiously. Elle shrugged. "Some do, most don't bother. Since the War, not many are interested in traveling. It's quite sad, because they are missing out on seeing the wonders and beauties of Paris." Rachel nodded. "I haven't been here for years. I forgot how pretty night is here." Elle seemed surprised. "You have been here before?" She asked. Rachel nodded. "Years ago, when I was 9." Elle nodded in understanding. "Not much has changed in the past decade or so. I think you will find Paris just as beautiful as you remember." "Do you own an Air Quest 1600?" Annika interrupted, feeling slightly left out. "Yes, but I haven't played it in a while. I've been busy." "Oh?" Annika prompted, feigning interest. "With what?" Inwardly, she thought, *probably making human 'dematerializers.'* "I've been building something." Elle answered vaguely. "It will improve a lot of lives when it is finished." Annika bit the inside of her cheek to stop herself from blurting, "Killing people will help them?" Rachel's acting skills were much better. She leaned forward conspiratorially. "When you say it will help a lot of people, what exactly do you mean by that? Are you talking about a type of new technology or something?" Elle hesitated, looking extremely uncomfortable. "Well," She paused. "Kind of." Another pause. "It's... confidential right now." Annika rearranged her expression into one of hurt, as if she couldn't believe her new friend didn't trust her. The guilt card worked, for Elle said, "I'm sorry. It's not you, it's just..." She broke off and turned away. "I gotta go. It was nice to meet you two." She stood up abruptly and started walking away. In a flash, Annika darted in front of her. "No, I'm sorry. I shouldn't have been so pushy. It's totally not my business. Please, come join us at our table?" She apologized, feeling slightly bad. She hadn't meant to scare her away! If she did, she would never find out what type of technology Elle was creating. Reluctantly, Elle joined them, and they spent the rest of the evening creating small talk. When they finally parted ways, Elle looked considerably more cheerful, and they had plans to meet at a bakery for breakfast the next morning. When Annika and Rachel got back to their hotel, they collapsed onto the white couches. "Well, at least we've got progress!" Annika pointed out tiredly. "I'm not so sure she's creating a technology that kills people. She's too nice!" Rachel objected. She already wasn't sure she trusted that Makrus guy. He just gave off weird vibes. From Elle, she was sensing sincerity, like she never intended any harm to anyone. Annika brushed her concerns away. "Nonsense. She's making a device that vaporizes people, Rachel. You can't seriously say you trust her!" Rachel shook her head. "I think his information was wrong." She insisted, locking eyes with Annika, who was angry. "I'm going to bed. Tomorrow's going to be another long day of playing friends with the enemy." She yawned and strode away. Rachel sighed. Elle was innocent. How could she prove that to her stubborn friend? She curled up to sleep on the plush couch and fell asleep instantly, tired from the long day. In her dreams, Elle was standing in front of a tall silver control panel, frantically pushing buttons and telling Rachel, "It won't stop vaporizing people!" Rachel woke up in a cold sweat and shivered, wondering if her dream was trying to tell her Elle was guilty- or innocent. The next morning, Rachel awoke to bright sunlight streaming in through the window that looked over the Paris gardens. Annika was gone; a note rested on the coffee table, stating Annika had left to go to breakfast with Elle. That woke her right up. "You left without me?" She cried, enraged, to no one in particular. What time even was it? A quick glance at the clock showed it to be 3 in the afternoon. She hadn't realized she had slept in so long. No wonder Annika had left her. Maddie loved telling Rachel how impossible she was to wake up, though Rachel secretly suspected she also used that as her excuse for eating all the cupcakes in the mornings before Rachel woke up. Her rage subsiding, Rachel grabbed a 300-dollar coin from the velvet bag and set out into town. She was determined to at least get some souvenirs to give to her family back home. When she arrived back at the hotel that night, Annika was waiting in the living room, reading a book. When Rachel entered, her arms laden with heavy bags, Annika jumped up and tossed the book to the side, wobbling slightly when she stood. "Where were you?" She accused. "I've been waiting for you for hours!" Rachel shrugged nonchalantly. "You didn't wake me up to go to breakfast with Elle, so I went shopping." She dropped a 7-dollar coin on the table and walked over to the bedroom. Annika stared down at it. "What's this?" "All that's left of my shopping spree." Rachel answered cheerfully. Annika stared at the mounds of bags Rachel had dumped on the couch. "How much did you take?" She asked incredulously. "300." Rachel watched carefully for Annika's reaction, and for a moment it looked like she would get mad. Then, she shrugged and began digging through the bags. "Did you get anything for me?" She asked, rifling through a bag full of new clothing and trinkets. Rachel swatted her hand away. "Stop peeking! Your birthday present is in there." Annika laughed, then stopped. "You're serious? My birthday is over a month away!" "Who cares?" Rachel retorted, scooping up the bags and staggering over to the kitchen to get them out of Annika's sight. "It's not like we're going to be in Paris next month. I had to take advantage of the opportunity!"

She plopped onto the couch beside Annika. "So, did you find out what the technology Elle's making is?" Annika shook her head regretfully. "No, we mostly talked about Beat Saber. She's apparently one of the top five Beat Saber players in France." Rachel laughed. "Did you tell her you're number 1 in the USA?" Annika shook her head, looking mischievous. "She'll find out tomorrow." "Tomorrow?" "Oh, we're going over to her place to hang out at 2 p.m. tomorrow." Annika said, bending to retrieve her book. "Why?" "So we can find out what the technology is. I bought something to aid us." Annika replied, placing her book on the table. "It's a type of berry called Rozenberries. It makes the consumer a little more loose in their conversation." Rachel raised an eyebrow. "So it's going to make her drunk?" Annika shook her head. "No, not really. It's more like it makes the consumer talk about things they normally wouldn't talk about. There's only one side effect, and it wears off in an hour or so." She explained. Rachel gave her a skeptical look. "They work! I tested them." Annika insisted. "There's something you're not telling me." Rachel guessed, looking at the sheepish face Annika was trying to hide. "What do you mean?" Annika protested, but it was too late. "What did it make you do?" Rachel asked, a smile spreading over her face. Without removing her face from the pillow it was now squished in, Annika pointed to the painting hanging on one of the walls. Rachel stared at it quizzically. It was a simple portrait of a gingerhaired woman posing in a garden. There was absolutely nothing special about it. "What?" She asked, confused. "I spent the first 40 minutes after eating the berries convinced I was talking to my mother, and another 20 after that crying." Annika admitted, her voice muffled. Rachel fought not to laugh, fearing her friend would take it the wrong way. The painting looked nothing like Mrs. Helmcott! Then again, if a few berries could make *Annika* act that irrationally... "Are you sure they're safe to consume?" Rachel asked, her smile fading into a frown. "If they're that powerful... Things shouldn't mess with people's minds like that." Then her curiosity won over. "How did you think it was your mom?" Annika shrugged and lifted her head from the pillow, seemingly convinced her friend wasn't going to mock or laugh at her. "I don't know."

Annika said. "It just... started to look like her, and then it spoke to me." "Annika, paintings don't talk." "I know that." She answered sadly, gazing at the painting. "But it did. Well, my mind made me *think* it did. It didn't really." She paused. "I don't think it did." She seemed bewildered, like she could no longer differentiate reality from fantasy. Rachel was concerned. "Annika, I don't think they're safe to eat. Berries aren't supposed to make people hallucinate." Annika groaned and rubbed her forehead. "I know. I just... I need to sleep. I was waiting for you to get back." She stood up and walked over to the bedroom and shut the door behind her. Rachel watched her go, worry for her friend filling her mind. Obviously, the berries had lasted longer than an hour. If only she knew what time Annika had eaten them, and how many she had eaten. Annika was an extremely cautious person. She must be desperate to resort to these "Rozenberries" to solve her problems. And where had she gotten them? Rachel had been wandering the city for hours and never saw anyplace selling berries, let alone berries that altered minds so badly the person who ate them started believing paintings could talk. Rachel stood up and walked over to the painting and stared at it. From what she could remember of Mrs. Helmcott, this painting held little similarities. Annika's mother shared her daughters bright red hair, not the faded ginger in the picture. Besides, Annika's mother would be around the age of 40 by now, and this woman looked mid-thirties. Still, Rachel reasoned, the last time Annika saw her mom, she was in her mid-thirties too. It could make sense for an addled brain to confuse this woman for another. And yet, that just proved how powerful the Rozenberries could be. Shaking her head, Rachel retrieved the bags from the kitchen and put them back on the couch so she could sort through the stuff she had bought. She would have to ask Annika about the amount of berries she ate when she woke up.

The next morning, Rachel was eating a chocolate croissant when Annika came out of her room, looking considerably better than she had the night before. "What time is it?" She asked, glancing out the window at the sun, which was past the noon position. "Check your watch." Rachel answered, her mouth full. Annika had forgotten it was there, and lifted her wrist to glance at it. "It's lunchtime?" Rachel nodded. "Why didn't you wake me up?" Annika asked, frowning slightly. "The same reason you didn't wake me up yesterday. I couldn't." Rachel responded, trying not to sound sassy. Annika rolled her eyes, grabbed the bag of Rozenberries, snatched a croissant from Rachel's plate, and walked over to the door and pulled it open. "That was mine!" Rachel protested. "Sorry." Annika tossed over her shoulder as she walked out the door, clearly not sorry at all. Rachel jumped up as Annika disappeared into the hallway, grabbed an extra croissant to take with her, and chased after Annika, catching up to her near the lobby stairs. "Where are we going?" Rachel asked, panting slightly as she tried to match Annika's brisk pace. "Elle's house." She answered, darting through the closing hotel doors into the street beyond. "Aren't we too early?" "Not if we want to get there on time." Annika replied, hailing a cab and quickly relaying a long address to the driver. He gave her a baffled look, so Rachel quickly repeated the message in French. The driver nodded and veered into the traffic, heading west. "She lives on the far edge of Paris." Annika explained between bites of her stolen breakfast. "I hardly made it there on foot yesterday, and that was from the rooftops. I didn't think you'd be comfortable doing that, so we're taking the long way." Rachel glanced out the window to the building roofs far above. "You could have died." She observed. To Annika, she sounded frustrated. "No, I actually couldn't have." She responded causally. Rachel turned towards her, both upset and angry. "It's like you don't care if you die doing that!" Annika raised an eyebrow in surprise, which just seemed to anger her friend more. "You act like you're invincible, but you're not! I don't want to find your body-" She broke off. "Rachel." Annika said gently, touched by the sudden burst of concern. "I do value my life. I just have more faith in my abilities to succeed than my fear of falling. I'm sorry that worries you." Rachel shook her head, staring out the window again. "And when you don't make it?" "It won't come to that." Annika promised. Why was Rachel talking like that? She would be fine. They sat in an uncomfortable silence for the rest of the ride, until the cab driver pulled to a stop outside a forest-green house with white lilies planted along the sides. The girls climbed out of the car and approached the door. The small bag of Rozenberries dangled from Annika's left hand. After checking her watch, she knocked on the door, the sound ringing throughout the quiet neighborhood. A moment later, Elle's face appeared in the window. She waved at them, then quickly unlocked the door and ushered them inside, locking the door behind them. "Hi! I'm so glad you're here. It's been ages since I've had friends over." The interior of her home was gorgeous, with light blue ribbons of flowers painted over the white walls, and simple furniture arranged around a large television- an old one, Annika noted- that had the Beat Saber loaded on it. Elle's Air Quest 1600 lenses sat on the couch nearest them. Annika handed Elle the bag, who set it on the table, removed the container the berries were in, and placed it on the table. "What are these?" She asked, interested. "Berries. I thought we could snack on them while we play." Annika explained. "Sounds good." Elle approved happily, popping one into her mouth. "I've got some snacks too. So, who's going to go first on the Beat Saber?" Elle asked, turning towards the TV. "How about Annika?" Rachel suggested. "Sure." Annika agreed, picking up a pair of contact lenses and securing them. They were specially designed for this version of the game. Instantly, the technology interfaced with her nervous system, and as Annika lifted her hands, a pair of digital hands appeared on the TV screen, allowing her to manipulate the settings of the game when she gestured at the screen. Elle's phone chimed, so she turned away from them and picked it up. "Go ahead and pick a song." She called from the kitchen. "I'll be right out." Annika flipped through the songs and chose the most difficult one, then put it onto the hardest setting there was. "Oh, that one's really hard." Elle commented without looking. "Maybe you should start with an easier one." "I'm good. I really want to try this one." Annika called back, grinning at Rachel, who laughed. Annika hit play and the music started. Her wrists flicked at superspeed, her digital light sabers hitting every block that came her way. It was good to see she hadn't lost her touch. When Elle emerged from the kitchen, carrying a platter of cheese and crackers, her jaw dropped in surprise. Speechless, she stared the screen, watching Annika's blurred sabers slice every block in half. When it ended, Annika deactivated the contacts. Her score was well above Elle's high score on that level. "You tricked me." Elle said, torn between confusion and astonishment. Then she shook her head and laughed. "I have never seen anyone move like that. Good job!" She complimented. Turning to Rachel, she asked, "Are you that good too?" Rachel was quick to say, "Definitely not. Annika's one of a kind." Elle laughed again, and said, "Let me have a turn." They played for hours, and the container of Rozenberries slowly diminished. Rachel stayed far away from the berries, deciding that at least one of them needed to keep their head, though it was mostly Elle indulging in them. Late in the evening, when Rachel was in the bathroom, Annika turned to Elle. "You've mentioned you were creating something important. Can you tell me more about it?" Annika asked carefully, sensing this was the time. Elle perked up instantly. "Yeah, why not?" She answered enthusiastically. "You'll love it." Elle led her over to the kitchen pantry, fiddled with something at the back of one of the shelves, and slid the back of the pantry open, revealing a hidden staircase descending into the darkness. A slight crackling sound came from the darkness, chasing away some of the clouds starting to fog Annika's mind. *This must be where she is keeping the vaporizer*, Annika thought with a shudder. Elle started down the stairs and led Annika though a long tunnel until they came to a well-lit laboratory space. There were tables set up everywhere, all of them covered with pieces of metal, detailed drawings and schematics, and piles of electronic parts. Over in the far corner was a tall silver cylinder, with a sliding door wide open revealing a compartment large enough to fit two people. Attached to its side was a keypad of sorts. Annika felt a chill run through her. Surely this was all the evidence Makrus would need to make an arrest now. "This is my lab." Elle told her, waving her arm around the space. "I've been creating a technology that will entirely change life as we know it." "How so?" Annika asked quietly, trying to look impressed. Elle walked over to the silver cylinder, swiping a teddy bear off a nearby table and bringing it with her. "It's a transporter." She explained, setting the bear inside the tube. "It's supposed to move this bear from here to over there." She gestured to another cylinder, sitting six yards away. Its door was firmly sealed. "It works by dematerializing the occupants inside, sending a signal to another transporter, and rematerializing them inside the other tube." She entered a complicated code on the keypad, and clicked a green button. Annika watched as the door slid shut, and a humming started from the transporter. Then, the door on the *other* transporter opened, and a pile of stuffing and shredded bear cloth lay on the ground inside it. "Only one transporter will have open doors at a time." Elle explained, typing another complicated code into the panel. "That way, the signals can't mix. If they did, the occupants in both tubes would be lost forever." The code she entered caused the first door to open, and the one with the shredded bear to close. There was nothing inside the first cylinder. "So it vaporizes people?" Annika asked, needing to be sure. Elle looked bewildered and shrugged. "I guess you could technically say that. But really, it just moves people and objects from one location to another. I haven't actually tested it on anything living, since I don't want to clean up animal remains from the inside of my transporter. Once I get the last few quirks figured out though, I want to test it on small animals, and then on myself before I reveal it to the world." She walked over to the second transporter and forced it open, then scooped the bear remains out of it and carried it over to a towering pile of similarly shredded toy bears. Beside it was an equally tall pile of full, brand-new bears. "But *no one* can find out about this. If they did, I could get arrested. It obviously isn't dangerous… Well, it technically *could* be dangerous, but it's not. Problem is, until I can get it to stop shredding my bears in the transport, it's legally considered dangerous, and I could get imprisoned for life. Then anyone would have their hands on my work, and who knows what they would use it for!" Annika nodded in understanding. Elle seemed like she was only going to use it for good… Elle shut off the transporters, and ushered Annika back up the stairs. "You're one of the very few people who know about it. You won't tell anyone?" It wasn't so much a request as a demand. "Of course not." Annika lied, her mind elsewhere. Looking relieved, Elle locked the secret entrance to her lab and shut the pantry door. Rachel was playing another Beat Saber round. After Elle excused herself to go to the bathroom, Rachel abandoned her game and rounded on Annika. "Where were you?" She hissed. "Elle showed me her invention." Annika replied, plopping down onto the couch. Rachel sat next to her. "That's great! Now we can tell the SIA, and go home." "Yeah." Annika agreed. "Well?" Rachel prompted. "What's she making?" "Uh." Annika froze, thinking. "I don't think I should tell you." She answered, avoiding Rachel's hurt gaze. "Why not?" Her friend demanded. "I'm in this just as much as you are!" "I know." Annika amended. "But I think it would be safer if you didn't know. That way you won't accidentally tell anyone." Rachel gave her a weird look. "But you're telling the SIA anyway. So why can't I know? The thing is going to get destroyed anyway." "Well, yeah, but I just don't think you should know." She apologized. Before Rachel could make a retort, Elle's horrified voice interrupted them. "The SIA? Oh my go- Annika, you can't! You promised! They'll kill me! They'll take it for themselves and use it to control and threaten people!" She stood behind them, looking like she was about to cry. The peaceful look on her face had been replaced with one of pure betrayal. Annika knew instantly that the berries had no more control over her. "The first time I trust someone, and this is how they repay me." Elle had started talking to herself, her face contorted in anger and pain. "This is why I've been friendless the past 3 years of my life. This is why I didn't trust anyone. I'm ruined!" That last part she aimed at Annika. "Annika, the SIA are evil! I never thought you were one of *them*!" "They're not evil!" Annika protested. "They were afraid you were killing people!" Elle looked shocked. "But you know I'm not. I would never hurt anyone! You can't tell them, Annika, you just can't." Annika looked torn, and looked to Rachel for help. Rachel was suddenly glad Annika had refused to tell her what it was that Elle was making. She shook her head slightly. "Of..." Annika faltered, then said, "Of course I won't tell." "You mean that this time?" Elle demanded, remembering Annika's last promise. "Yes. I won't tell them." Elle's eyes filled with tears again. "Thank you, I guess. All I can do is take your word for that. But we all know how much *that* is worth now." She spat. Elle didn't seem to know what else to say, so she walked her guests to the door. "Good night." She shut the door on them and locked it, leaving them standing on her front porch in the still night. Shaken, Annika started walking, not really caring where she ended up. Rachel kept pace besides her, finally breaking the silence to ask, "What are you going to tell the SIA?" "I don't know." Annika answered sharply, not in the mood to talk. "Why do you think Elle said the SIA was evil?" "I don't know." Annika said through gritted teeth. Rachel paused, but after a moment she asked, "How are you going to explain this to the SIA?" "I *don't know*, Rachel!" Annika exploded angrily. "What can I tell them?" "Maybe just tell them you couldn't get close to her, and that you didn't find out what it was." Rachel suggested. Annika shrugged wearily. "I guess." Rachel gave her a sympathetic smile. "I'm sorry I got mad at you for not telling me what she's making. I realize now I don't want to know. I'll never doubt your judgement again." She promised loyally. Annika shook her head, a dry chuckle escaping her lips. "If you follow me blindly, you'll fall too when I supposedly fall off a roof." She reminded her. Rachel exhaled deeply and bit her lip. "Yeah. Um, sorry about that. I don't really think you'll fall." She apologized. "Then why did you say it?" Annika asked pointedly. "To remind you we're not indestructible. It's too easy to get injured in random everyday activities." Annika frowned. "I think I know that. My mom *did* die in a car accident." She instantly regretted saying it the second she did, but it was too late. Rachel was equally aware it was the first time Annika had acknowledged in front of her friend that her mom hadn't been around for almost five years. "Sorry." Rachel whispered, her voice so quiet it was almost completely drowned out by the zephyr drifting over their faces. Annika didn't respond. She never wanted her friends' sympathy, or their guilt every time they talked about something they did with their mothers. She didn't want them to think it bothered her, because it really didn't. Jessica Ravenstone and Cristine Taryn were like mothers to her. If she couldn't have her own, at least her friends were generous enough to share theirs. She never really saw Matthew's mom though, because she was always working. And, her dad was a fantastic parent. He definitely made up for Mom being gone, as much as he could. They arrived at the hotel late that night, and went to sleep immediately.

CHAPTER 11

The next day dawned just as bright and warm as the day before. Yet, as Annika pulled her shoes on, she had a bad feeling today wasn't going to go the way she hoped it would. If all went well, her boss would believe her, and let her go home. If he didn't, well, she wasn't sure what would happen. They took another taxi to the SIA headquarters, and Annika took a deep breath before arranging her features into a look of regret and knocking on the door. They had left their bags in the taxi, but Annika had her main bag with her, not wanting to take the chance that the taxi driver would go rifling through her bag and steal the bag of money Makrus had given her. Hopefully, she and Rachel would be able to leave here and go directly to the airport once they were done talking to Makrus. The door swung open, and once again the guard stared out at them suspiciously. "I need to speak to Makrus." Annika informed him. He laughed suddenly. "Follow me." He ordered. There was a small spring in his step as he stalked down the hallway to Makrus's office. "Annika." Rachel whispered suddenly, tugging on the sleeve of Annika's sweater. "I don't like this." Annika turned, confusion etched onto her face. "Like what?" Rachel shrugged helplessly. "Something doesn't feel right." Annika studied her friend for a moment, then said, "Alright. Wait for me outside. I'll be right out." "Okay." Rachel agreed. She turned to go, and almost screamed. A man stepped out of the shadows in front of her, blocking her way. "I'm sorry, but Makrus wants to speak with both of you." He gently spun her back around towards Annika, who looked in confusion down the hall where the first guard was standing. What was going on? He gestured her forward. Giving Rachel a shrug, Annika continued forward, keeping her calm façade. It would be the only way she would trick the director of the SIA. She entered Makrus's office, Rachel and the guards close behind. He was seated once again behind his desk, and motioned his guards to close the door. Annika heard a tell-tale *click*, and knew they were locked in. But why? "Ms. Helmcott." He greeted, beckoning her forward. She approached his desk, stopping a few feet away from it. "I notice you aren't wearing the bracelet I gave you?" "I forgot about it." She admitted, realizing it was the first time she'd thought about it in days. "May I see your bag?" He asked, holding his hand out. Annika shrugged and handed it over. He rummaged through her bag and pulled out the bracelet and his bag of money. He placed the coins on his desk, then came around the desk so he was next to her. Makrus turned the bracelet over in his hands and opened it, studying it carefully. "Here." Annika watched in confusion as he snapped it closed around her wrist. "Why did you do that?" She asked in bewilderment, tugging gently at the clasp. It didn't budge. "I assume, since you are here, that you were able to get the information we desire?" He asked politely, ignoring her. Annika shook her head regretfully, and pulled at the tight-fitting metal band. She couldn't even slip it off of her wrist. It was too snug. "I messed up. She didn't trust me. She kicked me out of her house and forbid me from ever entering again. I'm sorry." She made sure to look him straight in the eyes, and kept an embarrassed expression on her face. It didn't matter what he thought of her after this 'failure.' He studied her, and the smile vanished from his face. "You're lying to me." *How did he know?* "Sir." She protested. "I would never-" "Save it." He dismissed her, and turned to Rachel. "Did she find out what Ms. Thompson was creating?" He demanded angrily. Her eyes widened in fright. "I-I don't know!" He at least seemed convinced with her, so Makrus returned his attention to Annika. "Ms. Helmcott. I am generous enough to give you one more chance. Tell me what Ms. Thompson is creating, and I will let you walk out of here right now. If you refuse again and try to convince me you don't have the information, mark my word you won't be leaving this building for a *long* time." Refusing to show her fear, Annika repeated. "I can't give you what you want." Makrus looked disappointed, and his face hardened into a cold, unreadable expression. "Very well." He murmured. "We'll do things the hard way." Addressing his guards, he ordered, "Seize them." The guards obeyed instantly, grabbing Rachel and Annika tightly by the wrists and forcing them behind them. Annika struggled against him, but he kicked the backs of her knees, causing her to collapse slightly. Makrus pulled open one of his drawers, and hit a button hidden inside. The sound of grinding gears filled the room, and Annika watched in shock as the floor to their right began shrinking into the wall. When it had finished retracting, a gleaming metal staircase could be seen descending beneath them. Annika couldn't believe she hadn't suspected anything was there. Did every building in Paris have secret rooms? It wasn't like there were any in America. That she knew of, anyway. "Let's go." Makrus said, starting down the staircase. "Why are you doing this?" Annika protested, trying to break free with no success. "You are my agent, Annika. Refusing to tell me the very information I sent you out to get isn't allowed." The guards pushed the girls towards the stairs. As she stumbled forward, Annika took a longing glance out the window, to the bright sun beyond. Who knew when the next time she would see sunlight would be? Rachel was close behind her, and Annika could feel her shaking as they climbed down the stairs. Annika felt so bad for her. Rachel had sensed something wrong from the beginning. She shouldn't even be here! Coming to a stop, Annika spoke loudly to Makrus, refusing to be pushed further down the stairs. "Let Rachel go. She doesn't know anything." She demanded. He turned around to face her curiously. "Doesn't know anything about what?" He asked. "She doesn't know anything about what Elle is creating! I didn't tell her!" Annika burst out angrily. Watching a smile spread across his face, Annika realized she'd made a fatal error. "So you're admitting you *do* know what Ms. Thompson is creating? That's good to know, but I'm afraid I still can't let Ms. Ravenstone go until you specify what it is that Ms. Thompson is creating." He told her with an insincere look of regret. "I couldn't risk her revealing your whereabouts to anyone. But you can still end it right here. All you have to do is-" "Forget it." She answered coldly, trying to ignore the strangled cries coming from behind her. Yes, she felt awful condemning Rachel to the same fate as her, but Elle's secret mattered more. In time, someone would have to rescue them.

Besides, it was illegal for this organization to hold someone for more than three days just for questioning. They couldn't accuse her of anything else. She could hold out for three days. She only hoped Rachel would feel the same way. She swallowed hard, steeling her nerves as the floor above them began sliding back into place, leaving them trapped in utter darkness. A moment later a light switch flicked on, flooding the hallway in a blinding artificial light. They had reached the bottom of the stairs. The guards followed Makrus down a hallway that slanted down before finally opening up to a vast cavern. Down here, it was a busy complex; the main room they were standing in was as big as a football field. They had entered the heart of the SIA. There were people everywhere, hurrying in and out of doors and rooms scattered everywhere. Many people stopped when they noticed the director of the SIA, and everyone cleared out of their way as he led his prisoners across the room to a locked metal door with a heavy-duty keypad. It looked so tough that Annika was sure if she tried to kick it, she would break her ankle. He pressed his finger to the scanner, and the door slid open. From inside the blank white halls, sobs and moans could be heard, and there was a stench unlike anything Annika had ever smelled. People stared after them as they disappeared through the door, and as the door swooshed shut behind them, Annika could hear murmurs as the other agents wondered what those two girls could have done to get into *there*.

Makrus gestured to the guard holding Rachel, and he shoved her unceremoniously into a cell-like room, with a steel door and grimy bars acting as windows. She stared after Annika with a panicked expression. Hadn't Elle warned them of this? The SIA didn't have to do this, and yet they were. Rachel wasn't exactly sure what all constituted as evil, but surely their actions fit that. Annika's helpless glance was the last Rachel saw of her friend as the guard forced her down the hallway after Makrus. Annika expected to be put in a similar cell, but Makrus had other plans. They walked through endless halls before finally coming to yet another sealed door that required the SIA director's fingerprint. The guards silently followed Makrus into a black room, well-lit with bright strips of lights above their head. To one side, there was another cell, this one with a sliding door made of thick bars. The front wall of the cell was designed the same way. The other three walls were made of concrete, though Annika suspected they were likely reinforced with something else as well. Across from the cell, a desk and chair sat facing it. To Annika's right, there was another doored off room. She watched as he walked over to a wall and removed a pair of handcuffs. Sliding them open, he motioned for Annika to hold out her hands. She stared at them for a moment, then raised her arms and allowed him to lock the cuffs into place. If she didn't resist, maybe she wouldn't be harmed. She allowed herself to be ushered into the cell, and stood there stoically staring at a wall. Seemingly satisfied she wasn't going to go anywhere, Makrus clicked a button on his desk, locking her cell. He sat behind the desk, and motioned for the guards to leave. The first one spun on his heel and marched out the door, but the second one followed more slowly, shooting Annika a concerned expression. She glared back at him coldly, and he quickly retreated, shutting the door behind him. There was a soft click, and then the room turned silent. Rather than looking at her boss, Annika studied her cell. The floor was steel reinforced concrete, and there was absolutely nothing inside but her. With a sigh, she dropped to the ground and tucked her knees into her chest, placing her cuffed hands around them. Why was her boss locking her up like this? She'd been loyal for almost three years now. She'd done so much to help the SIA. Surely she didn't deserve to be treated like this! Then her thoughts wandered back to Rachel, and her panicked expression as Makrus led Annika away. If only Rachel hadn't insisted on coming to Paris. Then she wouldn't be locked up underground too. Rachel wasn't even an agent for the SIA. It was only because she was Annika's friend that she was here. Annika sat quietly for hours, doing her best to ignore the intense stares coming from her boss. At last, just as she was starting to feel hunger pains, he spoke. "Ms. Helmcott. Are you hungry?" Annika raised her head and looked him square in the eyes. Was this a trick question? "I'm not telling you what you want to know." She warned, inwardly shushing the tiny growl that emitted from her stomach. "Very well." He held down a button on his desk and spoke quietly into it. After a moment, Annika realized he was speaking in French. *Why* did that have to be the one language she couldn't understand? Minutes later a knock sounded on the door, and an agent entered, carrying a plate laden with sweet-smelling food, and two cups, one of them large, and the other the size of a shot glass. After the agent had left, leaving the tray and cups on the desk, Makrus proceeded to eat in front of her, never looking at her, but eating with gusto. Annika knew he was trying to get her to break, but she wouldn't. Going hungry for one day wasn't going to kill her. When at last he had finished his meal, he offered her the tiny cup, pushing it through the bars towards her. He laughed when she stared at it suspiciously. "It's just water." He promised. Still, Annika couldn't help but wonder if it was laced with something else, like Rozenberry juice. She placed it to her side and resumed her silent brooding. Hours later, he finally left the room, leaving Annika free to fidget with the metal bracelet Makrus had clamped around her wrist. It was obviously more than just a piece of jewelry; she just had to figure out what it was designed to do. It was locked at a specific point near the center of the band. That was probably its weak spot. Annika dug her nail into the slit, trying to see if there was some way she could loosen it or disable the lock. Suddenly she jolted, flinging her wrist back in pain and shock as a ripple of electricity zapped her wrist. She bit her tongue to stop from crying out, and gaped down at it. This was a shock bracelet? Makrus couldn't be serious! Cautiously, Annika touched the band with her other hand, wondering if it would zap her again. When it didn't, she moved her hand back down to the slit and tried to fit her nail into the gap again. Once again, the bracelet sent a wave of painful electricity shooting down her wrist, this time slightly more intense than before. Was he trying to kill her? All she had to do was disrupt the locking mechanism and be touching one of the bars and it would electrocute her so bad all her insides would fry. Seriously spooked, Annika lay down on the cold concrete floor to try to get some sleep. If he was willing to go so far as to lock a shock bracelet onto a young teen's wrist, who knew what else he would be willing to try to get her to talk?

Annika didn't know how long she had slept, but it felt like less than an hour before Makrus stalked into the room, slid her cell door open with a slam, and reached inside, hauling her to her feet. In her bewildered state, Annika accidentally knocked over her cup, spilling the liquid onto the concrete floor. Both she and Makrus watched it seep into microscopic cracks in the floor before he finally said, "It really was just water." He forced her out of the cell, pushing her in front of him to the other door inside the room. He unlocked it with his fingerprint, then pushed her inside, shutting the door behind them. The room was white, with thousands of flecks of something dark red scattered upon them. Annika sat, crumpled in a corner, positive her wrists would be bruising soon from the amount of pressure the cuffs had been putting on her skin. For a moment, Annika considered trying to fight him. One on one wouldn't be too hard. Yes, he was considerably taller, stronger, more muscled, and more rested than her, but that didn't mean she couldn't try. The second she started to move, his hand moved to his pocket, and he withdrew a small black remote with two red buttons side by side. "I wouldn't move, if I were you." He informed her. "This controls-" He pointed to her bracelet. "*That.*" Her eyes widened slightly. How could she have ever thought this man was one of the greatest? He was insane! "I was hoping I wouldn't have to use it, but if you make one move against me, I guarantee I will." Makrus promised. He sat down on a stool, the only furniture in the room, and said, "Now. Why don't you tell me what Ms. Thompson is creating?" Ignoring him, Annika asked, "Have you hurt Rachel?" "Ms. Ravenstone is fine." He assured her, before adding, "For now." "You'd better not hurt her." Annika threatened. "If you do, I swear I'll-" "You'll what?" Makrus interrupted coldly. "Beat me up? Turn me in to the NIB? Kill me? You can't hurt me, Helmcott. No one can. So I would save your threats." Though Annika was shaken by his proclamation, she was more fixed on what he had said. "Turn you in to the NIB? For what?" He gave her a look. "You're so naïve." "I am not!" She protested hotly. Makrus took a deep breath, and his voice turned kinder. "Annika, I know you just want to go home. Why spend days here when you can end it right now?" He asked. "No." She corrected. "*You* can end it right now. I've served you for years. Why can't you just accept this is something you can't know and just let me and Rachel go?" He growled, frustrated at her words. "Annika, Elle is vaporizing people! She can't just go free!" He insisted. "No, she's not!" Annika cried, feeling near tears. She was hungry, tired, thirsty, and confused. Did she mention she was hungry? "She hasn't vaporized anyone! She's just de-" Annika cut herself off, her eyes wide with fury. "You're evil!" She spat, realizing she'd almost told Makrus what she intended to keep secret. He gave a sharp laugh. "I was wondering when you would notice. Honestly, I was starting to think maybe you were dimmer than you seemed." He muttered. Makrus grabbed her by the arms and hauled her to a standing position before unlocking the door and bringing her back into her cell. He withdrew a key from his pocket and unlocked her cuffs, taking them with him. He slid the door shut with a *bang!* and locked it before leaving his office. Annika was left slumped on the freezing concrete of her cell, wondering if Elle's secret was worth all this. She wasn't left alone for very long. In intervals, guards entered the room, sitting behind the desk and keeping an eye on her. It was forever until she was finally fed. The same guard who had given her a look of concern however long ago was here again, carrying a small bowl and cup for her. He sat on the floor in front of the desk, and pushed her food through the bars. Annika accepted them without complaint, though after gagging on her first bite of the lumpy porridge, which tasted like what she'd imagined crab guts would taste like, she set it aside and- without caring if it did contain some sort of truth serum- drained her cup in one go, relishing the sweet liquid that chased her dry throat away. The guard watched her, and asked, "How's your food?" In an attempt to be polite. Annika scowled at him, and replied, "Maybe you should try it. Wanna trade?" She gestured to his sandwich he had not yet taken a bite of. The agent scrunched his nose. "Not really." Annika rolled her eyes, trying to act tougher than she felt, and turned away from him. Seconds later she heard a rustling sound behind her, then a choking sound. Turning around, she saw the guard spit out a bite of her food, and downed it with water. "This is literally the worst thing I have ever put in my mouth." He gasped. He stood up and quickly left the room, carrying her bowl with him. On the floor next to her sat his untouched sandwich. With a shrug and a silent thanks to the agent's generosity, she attacked it, scarfing the sandwich down so fast she was surprised she didn't choke. When it was completely gone, she lay down on the floor again and tried to sleep. He was obviously trying to make her so tired she'd slip and tell him what he wanted to know. It was important she stayed on her guard until she could get out of here. But, when she tried to sleep, her mind kept wandering back to their conversation, and wondered what he meant when he'd said he was evil. She hadn't really meant it. Yeah, he was being ruthless, but he was the director of the SIA, and one of his agents wasn't doing as she was supposed to. That didn't necessarily mean he had to threaten her with a shock bracelet, but she believed he was well within his right to try to get Elle's secret out of her. It was the NIB that was corrupt, going for world domination and total control just like before World War III. Why did he agree to what she was saying? It didn't make sense. Had she missed something? Annika thought back to all her previous missions with the SIA. They had always involved capturing enemy agents, ruining their bases, or breaking their secret codes so more experienced agents could catch the NIB by surprise. They were protecting the world from the NIB. How could that make Makrus classify himself as evil? Annika finally fell into a fitful sleep, waking every so often to tiny jolts coming from the bracelet. It seemed Makrus wasn't going to let her sleep.

Makrus was in his favorite office, the one he had first met Rachel in. He was drinking coffee and reading over reports as the sun set, casting a pretty glow into the room. His peace was interrupted when one of his top agents, Lennon McAulay, burst into the room without knocking. "McAulay!" Makrus growled, startled. "What are you doing?" "Sorry, sir!" McAulay panted. "But the art has been switched." Makrus brightened. The reason he had allowed his home to be toured earlier today was so his agents could switch several valuable pieces of art with fakes. Makrus had tried to get the owner to part with them, but she refused. He had an open house of sorts to lure her away from her home. Then his agents could take the art from her house that they needed without her being there. "The items are in transit to our base in-" McAulay was interrupted when the door flew open again and another agent rushed in. "Sir!" He gasped. "Your home has been compromised!" "What?" Makrus cried in anger. Turning to McAulay, he ordered, "Leave us." The agent promptly left the room, though Makrus could tell he wished he could find out what was going on. "Sir, we just received word that your mansion was broken into. Over two dozen guards were lying unconscious on the floor with darts in their necks, and those who have woken have no memories of today at all." He informed Makrus. "Which floor?" Makrus asked, fully alert. "The fifth." His agent admitted. Makrus stiffened. "My office?" The agent looked uncomfortable, but took a deep breath before delivering the bad news. "It was broken into. Your computer was glitching, trying to shut out a code that hacked straight into it. Several files have disappeared from its memory, but we don't know which ones." "The NIB." Makrus hissed quietly. "It looks that way." His agent agreed. "The darts are NIB style, and our scientists tested the air on the fifth floor. It was filled with a memory wiping gas." "What about the cameras?" Makrus ordered. How had the NIB done this without being noticed? "Most of them were offline, since we were trying to replace them with the better ones we received a week ago." "Why weren't they installed a week ago?" Makrus demanded angrily. The agent shrugged. "What's your name?" Makrus asked instead. He looked surprised, but answered, "Russ Baur, sir." "Listen to me very carefully, Agent Baur, because I'm only going to say this once." The agent nodded. "I want every single guard at my mansion that was on duty today relocated to the prison in Argentina. Then, I want the footage from the cameras facing the front parking lot. Also, tell Agent McAulay to have the agents at my place sweep the grounds and check the gates. I want to know how they got in. Is that clear?" Makrus asked. Baur nodded. "Good. Now go." Baur nodded and hurriedly left the room. Makrus couldn't believe it was the second time this month he'd had to relocate his incompetent guards. There were already less guards than he would've wanted at his home today, since the replacements were still in transit from another posting. He couldn't wait for one of his undercover agents to finish the androids he was currently making. Once Makrus had those added to his staff, the SIA would be unbeatable, and they could finally crush the NIB once and for all. Makrus waited until Baur closed the door, then closed the blinds over his window. Pushing the girls' confiscated phones aside, he pulled a computer from his desk drawer and placed it in front of him. He glanced at the third phone sitting in the drawer. He had used it to infiltrate and block Annika's text thread with her dad. She probably still didn't realize her dad never got her text. Shutting the drawer and opening the laptop, he unlocked it and accessed the secret camera in his mansion office. He rewound it to the time his home became open to the public, and watched it carefully. Finally, he heard whispers, then a sizzling noise. Moments later, his door slid open, and his alarm went off. There were panicked, incomprehensible shouts; then, a boy with white-blonde hair entered his office and sat down in the chair. After inserting something into the computer, his hands moved like lightning over the keyboard. Makrus guessed instantly that this boy must be a professional hacker, as no amateur could ever break past his firewalls that fast. Then, the boy smiled, withdrew the object from the computer, and pulled something out of a bag. He smacked it against the wall, and threw it out the window. Makrus got a clear picture of his face, and gasped. Was it possible? He quickly used his own computer to take a picture of the boy's face, then watched the rest of the recording. A man, not too much older than the boy, dashed in, his jagged brown bangs hanging in front of his emerald eyes. They had a short conversation; then the boy jumped out the window, quickly followed by the older one. His face was perfectly clear as he jumped backwards out the window and sprayed a small container of a gaseous-looking liquid into the air before disappearing. Makrus took a quick picture of his face too, before opening his files of agents- both SIA and NIB- and trying to match his new pictures to old ones. He had been right- one of his undercover agents had had contact with the boy. His name was Matthew Carimella, and he had been inquiring about Louisa Helmcott. What was he doing with the NIB? Had they seriously started letting *teenagers* join? Yeah, he did, but the NIB was different. Or so he thought. The other one matched up to a Kevin- Makrus slammed the lid of his laptop closed as Agent Baur rushed back into the room, carrying a laptop under his arm. "Don't you people ever *knock*?" He snarled. Baur froze. "Sorry, sir! I just thought you might want to know I accessed the front cameras, and the results were really interesting! Also, all the guards that were on duty are in transit to the Argentina prison, though there was some confusion. Some of them thought they were actually being sent to be *prisoners* in the camp, but I assured them you just wanted them repositioned to work there." He smiled proudly, and Makrus decided it wasn't worth wasting his breath telling Baur he actually *had* intended for all the guards on duty there to become prisoners. "Let me see the camera footage." He said instead. Baur nodded and set the laptop he was carrying down on the desk. It was open to a live view of the cameras in the parking lot, and Makrus was happy to see there were several agents scouring the gates. Agent Baur quickly accessed the recordings the cameras had made earlier that day, and they watched the cars pull up, park, and crowds of people start converging on his front porch. When everyone had gone inside, Baur stopped the cameras so they could get a good look at all the cars. "I was really surprised to see so many of them were Cybertrucks!" He said enthusiastically. Makrus raised an eyebrow. "And that means what?" Baur looked confused. "Well, nothing, really. I just found it interesting how popular they've gotten since the War. I mean, the first Cybertruck was just released only a year before World War III began. They didn't have all that many advanced features, but they could drive themselves, had bulletproof glass, and could also drive on water for short distances. That was over fifty years ago! Nowadays, the newest models of Cybertrucks can fully function underwater like a submarine, and there's some rumors that the next Cybertruck model will be able to hover, like much of our technology nowadays can, and will even be able to fly! There's other features too, of course, and the interior of the Cybertruck has changed over the years, but only slightly." Agent Baur babbled excitedly. Makrus raised his hand to get him to stop talking. "Is there any way to tell which car belonged to the intruders?" He asked, trying to get his agent back on the subject he was supposed to be thinking about. To his great frustration, the agent shrugged. "I mean, most of the NIB are using Cybertrucks as their standard vehicles." He offered. "I don't know which model, though. I thought it was the Model 7 or 8, but I could be wrong." Makrus scowled, then asked, "Is there any way you can identify which of these are Models 7 or 8 just by looking at the cameras?" Baur considered that, then shook his head. "No. The best way for me to identify them would be to see the interior of the cars, and the cameras couldn't see any of that." "What if-" Makrus's suggestion was cut off by his office door once again banging open, and McAulay's face appeared. He paused midstride, realized his boss was shooting him a death glare, and meekly backed out, shutting the door in front of him. A moment later, a knock came on the door. Makrus sighed in annoyance. "Enter." He growled. McAulay reentered the room sheepishly. "Sir." He announced. "We just received word from the agents searching the mansion grounds. They found the gate on the back side of your property, where the courtyard is, unlocked, with a large stone holding it in place." "How was it unlocked?" Makrus asked, confused. "The wires keeping the locking mechanism in place had been pulled out and rearranged, releasing the lock." McAulay answered. Despite his anger, Makrus felt a grudging respect for the person that unlocked that gate. He- or she- was obviously very talented, and Makrus made a mental note to offer a pardon to the person if he ever got the chance. The catch, of course, being that they served him, putting their skill to a *much* better use. "That doesn't tell me how they got into the building." Makrus reminded McAulay. The agent nodded. "From what we can tell, they must have gone into the basement door, but the door was still locked. There *is* a large imprint on the grass beneath your office window, so they might have climbed straight up to your office." "That doesn't make sense." Agent Baur objected. "That window only opens from the inside, and all the guards were unconscious on the fifth floor. Besides, the office door had been forced open. That's what activated the alarms. They couldn't have come in through the window." He told the older agent confidently. McAulay scowled, not liking the fact that both Baur was correct, and that he was making him look bad in front of their boss. "Fine. Then you tell us how they got in." He challenged, crossing his arms defiantly. Baur shrugged cheerfully. "I don't know. Have you checked how the locking mechanism actually works? I mean, if I'm not mistaken, that courtyard did use to hold prisoners decades ago. What good would it do if they could unlock the gate, and keep it unlocked?" He suggested. McAulay scoffed. "That's foolish." "Actually." Makrus interrupted. "He's right." Both agents turned to look at him. "That door relocks itself. The best way to confirm if they went in through that door is to check the basement for footprints, or other signs of disturbance." He told them. "So get on it!" He ordered, when they just stared at him. Agent Baur was first to go, turning and quickly marching out the door. McAulay was slower, scowling at Baur's back. After they had gone, Makrus opened his computer again. If that Carimella kid had been asking about Louisa Helmcott five weeks before he broke into Makrus's mansion, it was likely he had helped steal the files containing Louisa's whereabouts, and at the very least knew she was alive. He hadn't thought the boy's curiosity could ever be a threat. Should he have Louisa moved to a different camp? But what had made the NIB go after her now, almost 5 years later? Makrus shook his head, shoving his questions to the back of his mind. Right now, he had Annika to worry about. She was still down there, holding an extremely dangerous secret he needed to know. Minutes later he was standing in front of her again, watching her pace around the cell. She turned to face him when he entered. "Can I go now?" She asked immediately. "No." He answered, watching her carefully. She didn't look too bad. Her eyes were bright again, and she looked well-rested. She almost seemed to be emitting an aura of confidence. What had happened to her in the 24 hours he'd been gone? His eyes turned to her bracelet, which was sending out tiny bursts of electricity to her wrist. She didn't seem to notice them. Dropping his hand down to his pocket, he realized he had accidentally left the remote in his office. Hiding a tiny twinge of guilt at leaving the bracelet on, he ordered, "Let's go." "Where?"

She asked casually. Rather than answering, he unlocked her cell and walked her into the other room, with the red-flecked walls. Rather than sitting, she stood, facing him confidently. It made him uneasy. What had happened to restore her spirit? "What is Ms. Thompson creating?" He asked, hiding his discomfort. Annika crossed her arms defiantly and didn't answer. Makrus realized he would never get to her this way. "You Helmcott girls are so stubborn. Why can't you guys just give up immediately?" He complained. Her causal demeanor dropped instantly, and her eyes filled with confusion, though there was a hint of pride as well. "What do you mean *Helmcott girls*?" She asked. A slow smile crept onto Makrus's face. He had her. "Exactly what I said. They just don't tell you what you want to know." He continued. "What did you do to my sister?" Annika demanded angrily. Why hadn't she thought to check in on Amelia recently? "I haven't touched your sister." Makrus answered. "Then what Helmcott girls are you talking about? It's just me and my sister. Unless you count Aunt Brittany." She added, mostly to herself. Makrus shook his head. "I'm talking about your *mother*. She still thinks she'll be escaping any day now, even though it's been almost five years." He told her, carefully weighing how much to tell her. Annika's brows furrowed. "Escaping? What? She died in a car accident." Annika protested, though she could tell something was wrong. Why was he smiling? "Of course you would think that." He agreed with a cruel smile. Annika's eyes widened in understanding. "What did you do to her?" She demanded. "What is Ms. Thompson creating?" He asked again, dodging her question. He watched her conflicted emotions flash across her face. She seemed to be fighting herself on whether she should tell him what he wanted to know in exchange for the information she wanted, but finally, she raised her fists towards him. He watched them, amused. "You don't seriously plan to fight me." It was more of a statement than a question. "Why not?" Annika asked, stepping forward a half-step. "You will end up with many painful injuries if you choose to fight me." He promised. "We'll see about that." She said, and launched herself at him. Makrus found one of her fists aimed for his face, another for his stomach, and her knee bent to hit him in a very sensitive place. In one smooth motion, his arm swung to meet hers, knocking her fists away from him. Then, he elbowed her in the stomach, shoving her away from him. Annika slammed into the wall with an *oof*, her hands clasped over her gut. "Are you done yet?" Makrus asked. Annika scowled, and dove at him again, launching into a side flip. She then swung her leg low, tripping him. He fell to the floor with a surprised thud, then quickly scrambled back up. He lashed out with his leg, striking her hard in the shin. Annika's startled scream was as loud as the crack that echoed throughout the room. She crumpled to the ground in pain, clutching her leg, which was twisted at an odd angle. Makrus stared down at her for a moment, surprised at himself for the foul deed he had done. Since when had he started hurting children? "Get up." He told her. Annika was already trying, gritting her teeth as she tried to stand on her mangled leg, but fell down. Blood had started to drip out of the gash created from Makrus's boot tearing into her skin, leaving crimson drops shining on the floor. Annika watched them for a moment, then stared at the other dark red spots adorning the walls and floor, and her pained expression turned to one of horror as she tried again to scramble up off the floor. Makrus helped her up, and watched as she tried to put her weight on her leg. She grimaced and shoved him away, just to collapse again a second later. He helped her up again, and this time she didn't object when he led her out of the room and back into her cell. He made another call in French, repeatedly glancing at Annika, who was hyperventilating and about ready to pass out from the excruciating pain. Ten minutes later, a tall man with dark hair and a scruffy beard rushed in, a medical bag swinging at his side. He looked at Makrus, then into Annika's cell where she lay half propped against the corner. The doctor stared in surprise for only an instant before slapping a button on Makrus's desk that released the lock on Annika's cell. Rushing in, he dropped to his knees in front of Annika, and hurriedly opened his kit. He removed a small electronic square and turned it on, placing it on Annika's leg near the swelling. He then pulled out a long metal circlet and fitted it around her head. Moments later, Annika lost consciousness, her head slumping to her chest. Her breathing deepened, and to Makrus she didn't look like she was in pain anymore. The doctor seemed to agree, for he stood up and backed out of the cell before whirling on Makrus, his anger obvious. "What did you *do* to her?" He demanded savagely. "Mind your place, doctor." Makrus snapped. The doctor didn't seem to care. "Her fibula bone has a nice clean break, her leg is swelling, and she's bleeding out of a huge gash in her leg!" He exclaimed. "She thought it would be a good idea to fight me. I was only protecting myself." Makrus told him, his mind flashing briefly to when Annika had succeeded in knocking him off his feet. "I need to set the bone." The doctor grunted in annoyance. "I'll take her to the nearest hospital-" "You'll do no such thing." Makrus interrupted. "You can treat her in the medical ward here." "Fine." The doctor agreed with a sigh. "I just want to get back to dinner." "How did you get to France so fast?" Makrus asked, suddenly realizing there was an oddity in the timeline. "You usually work in Idaho, right?" "Yes." The doctor agreed, scooping up Annika's limp body and heading for the door. "But I was visiting my niece for the week. She just had a baby." "Ah." Makrus said. "Congratulations." "Thanks." The doctor snorted. He shifted Annika so he could open the door, then disappeared down the hall. The door banged shut behind him.

Annika cracked her eyes open to find herself still in her cell. For a moment, she wondered if her broken leg had been a dream- then she tried to move it and clamped back a groan. Groggily, she sat up and felt it. Her leg had been set and bandaged, and a pair of crutches had been left beside her in her cell. There was no one else in the room. Annika tried to think back on what Makrus had told her. What did he mean, her mother had been trying to escape for the last five years? And the, 'Of course you would think that.' Was he saying *he* had caused Mom's accident? It was just that, an accident. That's what Dad had told her, anyway. Did Makrus somehow have Mom locked up, and Dad thought the whole crash was real? Or maybe- Annika's rush of thoughts paused to let one through. What if her dad had known all along, and gone along with it? As quickly as it had come, Annika shooed it away. Her dad would never do that. He would never go along with something like that. Ever. The door flung open, and Makrus stormed in, looking furious. He stopped right in front of her cell and glowered at her for a moment. Annika met his gaze readily, and glared back. After what seemed like ages, but was probably only seconds, Makrus told her, "I've informed your father he has three days to locate you and get you. If he fails, you stay in my custody forever." Annika raised an eyebrow in alarm. "What do you mean, in your custody forever?" "It means," Makrus growled. "That if he fails to come get you, as a SIA right I can keep you here forever." As if that wasn't a scary enough thought, another of his words came to her mind. "What do you mean, *locate* me?" "It means I don't have to tell him where you are." "Then how is he supposed to find me?" Annika cried. Makrus shrugged. "Good question. I guess we'll see, hmm?" Then he spun and stalked back out. Annika banged angrily on the bars of her cell with her non-braceleted hand, then collapsed awkwardly onto the floor. She wasn't an animal! She couldn't live the rest of her life cooped up. She'd go crazy. It was horrible enough, having no way of knowing how long she'd been gone, or even how Rachel was doing. But to be trapped like this, in this horrible cell with a horrible man controlling her, for infinity until she died? It was too much. Annika wasn't a religious person, but in that moment she decided to pray, not caring who in the heavens might hear her. As long as she and Rachel got out of here safely, she would never again scoff in her mind whenever people talked about their faiths. If a miracle happened to get her out of here, they could say whatever they wanted and Annika would probably agree with them.

CHAPTER 12

Kevin was the first to snap into action. He pulled the flashdrive out of the computer and sprinted for the ladder that led back up to the kitchen. Matthew stared after him for a moment, then dashed across the bunker floor to catch up to him. Kevin scaled the ladder at an impossible speed and crawled out of the hole, Matthew right behind him. "Where are you- *we* going?" Matthew asked, breathing hard as he stumbled after Kevin. Behind him, he could hear frantic movement as Dan and Ivy tried to follow them. Once outside, Kevin whipped his phone out of his pocket and quickly made a call, speaking so fast Matthew hardly caught the words; it sounded like Kevin was calling in a helicopter. As soon as Dan and Ivy emerged from the house, Kevin ordered, "Get in." He opened the door to the Cybertruck and climbed in. Dan was quick to obey, locking the door to his house and climbing into the driver's seat. Ivy looked scared as she and Matthew slipped back into the seats they had vacated less than half an hour ago. "How could she have been gone for so long without anyone noticing?" She whispered to him. Matthew shrugged, wishing he had an answer. "It's not just Annika that's missing. It's Rachel too." He reminded her. "Do you think they were kidnapped?" Ivy asked, her face ashen. "Out of a Cybertruck?" Matthew countered skeptically. His eyes met hers, which were shimmering with worry. "What if something's happened to them?" "Then we'll rescue them." Matthew promised. "Where are we going?" Dan asked Kevin briskly. He realized he was putting a lot of trust in this young man, but if Kevin was his only hope of rescuing his daughter and wife, he'd take it. "South. The NIB are sending a helicopter to meet us halfway. Then they'll take us to the NIB Headquarters." Kevin told him, leaning down to dig through his backpack. Dan nodded and set the car on autopilot. Suddenly, Matthew realized what he had just said. "Mr. Helmcott." "What?" Dan asked, turning in his seat to look at Matthew. "When you were on the phone with the *Survival Race!* place, did the person you talked to tell you how Annika and Rachel left?" Dan nodded. "Yes, she said they left in a Cybertruck." He answered. Kevin's attention turned from his backpack to Dan as he asked, "Did you send your Cybertruck for them?" Dan's eyes widened. "No. Annika said she'd text me when she needed me to send it." He answered, pulling his phone out of his pocket and quickly opening his messages. He opened Annika's text thread and scrolled through the messages. The most recent was almost seven weeks ago. "She never texted me." He reported. "Annika wouldn't have forgotten." Matthew reasoned. "Maybe she just had bad cell service?" Ivy suggested. Kevin shook his head. "In a place where they film TV? Not likely." "Then where are they?" Ivy asked, sounding desperate. Dan started texting, his fingers flying over the digital keyboard. "Are you texting Annika?" Matthew asked curiously. Dan shook his head. "It's possible she doesn't have her phone, and I don't want to risk alerting whoever has it that we know she's gone." Kevin gave Dan an admiring glance. Not only could this guy disable heavy-duty SIA locks, he had enough sense in a horrible situation not to contact the one person he wanted to. "Then who are you texting?" Ivy called from the back. "Cole and Jessica Ravenstone. I want to know if they've also been wondering where their daughter is." Their answer came almost immediately. The phone rang, and Jessica Ravenstone's worried voice came through the speaker. "Dan! I'm so glad you called. The twins just mentioned yesterday that Rachel should have been home by now, and I was starting to get worried. Do you know where she is?" "No, Annika hasn't come home either. I was wondering if you had heard anything from them." Dan answered. "We haven't!" Isabelle's voice chirped through the phone. "Rachel promised she would text us, and she hasn't." To Matthew, the young girl sounded worried too. Kevin bit his lip with frustration. How could they have been trying to find one Helmcott girl and lose another? "Where are you?" Jessica asked. "We're in the car, heading for the NIB Headquarters." Dan answered, after receiving a quick nod from Kevin. "The NIB!" Jessica cried, her voice turning shrilly. "It surely can't be that serious, is it? Maybe they just, lost track of time?" "I don't know." Dan said gravely. "I hope you're right, but when I contacted the studio they were at, I was told they left about a week ago. I have a friend with me, and hopefully he will be able to help locate them." The sound of whirring blades cut off whatever Jessica had been trying to say next. Kevin craned his neck out the window, spotting a large black helicopter in the sky nearing them. "Huh. They got here faster than I expected." He observed. Dan wrenched the wheel in a sudden motion, skidding to the side of the road and screeching to a stop. The phone flew out of his hand and hit Kevin, who ended the call and gave it back before flinging the car door open and getting out. The choppers' downwash hit him immediately; strong gusts pushed against him, knocking his long bangs into his eyes and pushing him against the car. The helicopter touched down several yards away from him, and Kevin had to put his hand up to shield his face from the extra wind. He waited for the helicopter blades to stop moving, then brushed his bangs out of his eyes and grabbed ahold of a handle on the outside and quickly climbed aboard. Dan hastily followed suit, pulling himself into the helicopter with ease. Matthew and Ivy scrambled out of the car and raced over, Ivy slightly limping on her sprained ankle. Dan stopped Matthew from climbing on. "No, I need you to go back to your homes." He ordered, having to shout over the wind. Matthew's jaw dropped in shock. Ivy was just as speechless. "But Mr. Helmcott! We've been in this together from the start. You can't just send us home now!" She cried, offended. "I know. But right now, your parents are expecting you at home. I don't know how long I'll be gone searching for Annika and Rachel. It could be days." Angered, Matthew felt his pockets for his phone, and when he found it, he yanked it out and sent a quick text to his parents. A triumphant moment later, he held the screen up for Dan to see. "Mom's working really late tonight, and Dad left this morning for a conference in Montana. They told me I was to stay with you while they were gone." He shouted up to Dan. Dan read the text with a scowl. "They didn't intend for that to be away from your home." He argued. Matthew shrugged. "My parents told me to stay with you. Why would I disobey them?" Dan groaned good-naturedly. "Why are you so good at circumventing rules?" Then he rolled his eyes and extended a hand to help Matthew up. Ivy tried to follow next, but that was where Dan was drawing the line. "Sorry, Ivy, but you definitely don't have any excuses to come with me anymore. I'll have the Cybertruck take you home." "But-" She tried, but Dan was adamant. "Get in the car." "If she can't come, I'm not coming." Matthew declared boldly. Dan didn't even blink. "I don't care whether you come or not. Right now, all I care about is finding my daughter. So if you don't want to come, get out!" He yelled over the wind. Matthew glanced hopelessly to Ivy. She shook her head, mouthed the word *stay*, and turned back towards the car. Matthew watched her climb into the Cybertruck, feeling ambivalent. How was this fair to Ivy? She had been just as valuable as the rest of them. When Kevin and Dan went into the cockpit to talk to the pilot, Matthew pulled his phone out again and video-called Ivy. She picked up almost instantly. "Hey Matthew." She glanced to the side of her phone, and Matthew knew she was trying to find the helicopter. Ivy looked back at him, brow furrowed. "Is something wrong?" She asked, her confusion evident. "It wasn't fair for Mr. Helmcott to send you away, so I came up with a way for you to kind-of be here, without really being here." He explained. Matthew flipped the camera so she was seeing out the back of the phone, then slipped it into the front pocket of his pants, so the camera was just peeking out. "Will that work?" He asked quietly, popping the wireless earbud he kept with him into his ear. "Yeah! I mean, it's hard to see from down here, but it will be better than nothing." Ivy's excitement lifted Matthew's spirits a bit. He was glad he had been able to do something to close the distance between them. "I won't be able to talk to you with the others around, but I have my earbud in, so I will be able to hear anything you say. Just in case, I think you should mostly try to stay quiet." He warned. "Ok." She agreed, going silent. A moment later, Kevin and Dan came out of the cockpit. "Matthew." Kevin said, glancing at him. "Yeah?" "Can you close that door?" He asked, pointing to the side of the helicopter. Matthew hadn't realized the sides closed. "Sure." He carefully stepped over to the opening and pulled the door closed, sealing them inside the helicopter. "The pilot has to take evasive measures to get back to Headquarters against the wind, and we don't want to fall out." Kevin explained, pulling the other door shut. Matthew sat on the floor of the chopper, and listened to Kevin and Dan- and Ivy- talking. "Where do we even start our search for them?" Dan asked, his voice strained. "They could be anywhere." "We'll start by searching nearby airports and hotels." Kevin said. Dan's eyebrows flew up so fast Matthew was slightly surprised they didn't fly off his head. "You think they're out of country?" "It's always a possibility." Kevin reasoned. "We could also try asking the other *Survival Race!* contestants if they know where Annika went." "Do they think Annika and Rachel split up?" Ivy asked Matthew quietly. "Do you think they split up?" Matthew asked Dan, to answer Ivy's question. Dan shook his head. "No." "Unless force was used." Kevin added slowly. Dan squeezed his eyes shut, as if the thought itself hurt. "Who would want to hurt my daughter?" He asked. In Matthew's ear, Ivy suddenly gasped. "What if the SIA have Annika and Rachel?" She asked urgently. "I thought Annika worked for the SIA. Maybe she's with them!" A shudder ran through Matthew. "The SIA?" He asked her, wanting to confirm. Kevin heard him and turned to look at him. "What makes you say that?" Caught off guard, Matthew said, "Well, Iv-" "Matthew!" Ivy hissed in his ear. "Don't mention me!" "Uh, I've been thinking; maybe she's with the SIA, doing something for them." Matthew rephrased, trying to cover his mistake. Kevin's eyes darted to Dan. "Or maybe," He suggested, a look of cold fury shadowing his face, "Maybe the SIA know what we did today and captured her as a revenge." It was Matthew's turn to interject. "That's not possible, unless they're psychic. Annika has been gone for days. They might have taken her *before* our break-in, but not after." "True." Ivy and Dan muttered at the same time. Matthew suppressed a smile. Everyone had run out of hypotheses, so the only noises Matthew heard for the next half hour were the chopper blades rotating, and the eerie howl of the wind as it rushed past the helicopter in waves. Its haunting, lonesome call made it seem as if it were in distress, or as if it carried all the sorrows of the world. At last, Matthew felt the helicopter land. Were they finally here? It seemed they were, for Kevin pulled a door open and dropped to the grass. Dan and Matthew jumped down behind him. Matthew's eyes widened in astonishment. The NIB headquarters were a towering complex of white cylindrical towers. Stretching 18 stories high and scintillating in the sunshine, they were surrounded by large buildings dispersed randomly around them. Tinted glass windows lined the sides of the towers in rings. Above them, glass enclosed skybridges connected the towers, giving the agents shortcuts for getting around the place. Matthew could see agents hurrying back and forth inside them. The wind had died down, but Matthew noticed agents chasing after scattered papers aways away. Kevin walked straight for one of the buildings on the right, and as he approached, several agents opened the door for him in greeting, though they gave Matthew and Dan curious stares. Instinctively, Matthew dropped his hand to his pants pocket to hide the lens. "Hey!" Ivy objected, annoyed. Matthew didn't answer her; he didn't want one of the NIB agents to catch him and send him back home. They went through the glass double doors into a lobby-like room. Ivy could see the polished wooden floors, the start of a gleaming gold staircase, far too many feet for one room, and several large black desks obstructing her limited view. For Matthew, the sight was incredible. It wasn't at all what he'd expected; from the gilded spiral staircase to the glass doors, and the elegant desks scattered around, everything glittered in the sunlight. This seemed more fit for a king than a base that held dangerous secrets. The agents surprised him also. Like Kevin, they were all dressed in casual clothes; sweaters, t-shirts, and pants were the most common, though Matthew did see a few people in lab coats. A girl with long black hair secured in a ponytail grabbed his attention. She was wearing a tight jumpsuit with a belt holster. A dart gun and dark green chakram were nestled inside the holster. She caught him staring at her, and scowled back, fingering the bladed circle as if she would love to stab him with it. He nervously turned away, realizing with a pang how much she looked like Annika in that moment. Would he ever see his friend again? "Matthew, you're getting too far behind." Ivy warned him, snapping him out of his thoughts. Ahead of him, Kevin and Dan were pushing through the people and jogging up the stairs. Matthew rushed up after them. Kevin glanced back. "Don't lag." He warned. "If you're with me, the other agents won't touch you, but if they catch you alone, you'll likely be treated like an SIA spy." Matthew nodded, but as he took another step, the building shook with a *boom!* and the sound of shattering glass echoed throughout the complex. The blast knocked Matthew off his feet. Dan wobbled, but Kevin didn't even flinch. "Are we under attack?" Matthew asked, his eyes darting around. "No." Kevin answered calmly. "It's just our scientists testing our new lasers against shatterproof glass. It sounds like the test was successful." Looking about him, Matthew was embarrassed to see he was the only one who fell. All the rest of the agents were talking and walking, not seeming to notice or care that the building had just shook like an earthquake had hit it. Kevin headed for an escalator, and Dan helped Matthew up, murmuring into his ear, "Don't feel bad you fell." "How come you didn't?" Matthew complained, readjusting the phone in his pocket to make sure Ivy could still see clearly. Dan laughed. "I'm an old man. It's not the first time I've been in a shaking building." In Matthew's ear, Ivy snorted with laughter. "Did we just get permission to call him old?" She asked him hopefully. Trying not to smile at Ivy's comment, Matthew muttered to Dan, "Still." They caught up to Kevin, who was climbing up the escalator. Dan rushed to join him, and after a moment Matthew started up too. "Wait." Ivy said, her confused voice filling Matthew's ear. "Aren't escalators supposed to go up?" Matthew stopped climbing to consider that, and realized he was indeed descending again. "MATTHEW!" Kevin hollered. He and Dan were already waiting by the doors of an elevator. Matthew dashed up the escalator, arriving just as the elevator doors slid open. Kevin was tapping his foot impatiently, waiting for Matthew to arrive, and asked, "Why are you moving so slow?" Matthew followed them into the elevator, and countered, "Why does your escalator go down?" Kevin hit the button for the top floor, and said, "What type of agents would we be if we had our stairs carry us places instead of our legs?" Matthew raised his eyebrow. "Smart agents?" Dan laughed, and Kevin seemed to relax too, a natural smile spreading across his face as he led them out of the elevator and down a carpeted hallway. He knocked on the third door on his left, then twisted it open, calling, "It's me." As he entered, a middle-aged woman with short, greying hair turned to face him, and she set down the sheathe of papers she had been reading. "Welcome. I assume the mission went as planned?" She greeted, beckoning them forward. Kevin nodded, withdrew the flashdrive from his pocket, and handed it to her. "She's alive." The woman let out a relieved sigh, and whispered, "Thank god." She turned it over in her hands before slipping it into her own pocket. "Good job, Agent-" "*Kevin.*" Kevin interrupted, throwing a glance over his shoulder at Dan and Matthew. She rolled her eyes and smiled tolerantly. "Agent *Kevin* is one of the best." She told them. "I'm Casey Edins." "Dan Helmcott." Dan said, reaching over to shake her hand. "Matthew." Matthew added with a small wave. "Ivy." Ivy said automatically in his ear. Then, "Oh, sorry Matthew." "Casey is the director of the NIB." Kevin explained before turning to her. "Ma'am, we didn't just come here to give you the flashdrive." Casey raised an eyebrow. "Oh?" "My daughter, Annika-" Dan faltered at the cold scowl that Casey sent him. "She, uh, went missing several days ago, along with her friend, and, um, I was hoping you could help me locate them." "Miss Helmcott does not deserve *help*." Casey hissed through now-clenched teeth. "She deserves to be *locked up* for all the things she's done." Kevin quickly stepped between them to try to smooth things out. "Casey, we think she may have been kidnapped by the SIA." Her brow crinkled in confusion. "Why would the SIA kidnap their own agent? She's been doing so much for them." The scorn was audible in her voice. "Your daughter does not deserve my help and resources." She added again. "But she's just a child!" Dan protested. Even though Matthew was worried about the way this was going, he couldn't help but think what Annika would have to say about being called a child. "I didn't know Louisa had quit the SIA, or I never would have let Annika join them. Me and Louisa never talked about it. Please. I already lost my wife. I can't lose my daughter too." He begged. Kevin's green eyes flicked back and forth between the man and his boss. He silently resolved that, if

Casey refused to help, he would still help Dan recover Annika- no matter what the cost. "I will help you." She agreed at last. "But only because I know how I would feel if my own daughters were to go missing." Dan dipped his head in relief and whispered, "Thank you." With a curt nod, Casey opened a beefy computer on her desk and began typing. "You said you think they may be with the SIA?" She asked, her demeanor more business-like. Kevin nodded. "It's also possible they're out of country." He added, relieved Casey was willing to help. "Of their own free will?" Casey asked, not looking up from her screen. "It looks that way." Dan admitted. "What's her friends name?" She asked. "Rachel Ravenstone." Matthew said, trying to be helpful. A few minutes later, she closed the laptop to look at them. "I have my agents stationed at all nearby airports searching the flight logs for the names Annika Helmcott and Rachel Ravenstone." "So now what?" Matthew asked. Casey sighed. "Now we wait. I'll have Kevin show you to a place where you can rest until we receive word." Noticing the aggrieved expression Dan was giving her, she sent him a sympathetic smile. "We're doing all we can to find your daughter. For now, you have to be ready to rescue her when we do find her." She assured him. She gestured to Kevin, who nodded and turned for the door, exiting as quickly as he had entered. Dan and Matthew followed him closely as he led them back into the hallway, through some turns, into a statue-lined hallway with doors at the far ends. He opened one into a dark room painted grey, with sunlight filtering in through the windows lining the wall. A lone couch sat in the small living room area. Kevin found a light switch on the wall and flicked it on. It was quite quaint, really, to have to turn your lights on by yourself, and when Matthew mentioned it to Kevin, he agreed with a laugh. "Thing is, right now our sensor grid is offline while we're testing the lasers. We had these installed so it wasn't completely dark every time we ran tests. Before we had them, the glass shards flying everywhere during an experiment had a tendency to mix up the motion light sensors, which got unsafe. The one time we made that mistake, every scientist in that room got lacerated with the exploding glass because the light sensors kept shutting off." Upon hearing that, Matthew wondered how hard it would be to get instated as an NIB agent. He was almost fully convinced it would be the best future for him, even if there was a chance he could get paralyzed jumping out of a window onto a deflating air mat, or having his skin shredded by glass shards. "There's a bedroom over there if you want to sleep, and a small kitchen on the right." Kevin explained. "I'll come get you when we get news about the girls." "Where are you going?" Matthew asked in alarm. "I've got some work I need to finish." Kevin answered, giving Matthew a wink. "But it's good to see you miss me already." He laughed and left the room as Matthew indignantly glared at him. As soon as Kevin left, Dan took to pacing in front of the couch, frequently staring out the window to the large grounds beyond. Matthew, realizing he hadn't eaten since breakfast, wandered over to the kitchen, grabbed a small bowl of grapes and a bag of chips and sat on the couch to eat. As time passed, and the sun set, Matthew started to get annoyed at Dan's constant pacing. The room was completely silent, save for the sound of crunching chips. Matthew was startled when Ivy's voice came through his earpiece. He had forgotten she was still there. "Can we talk?" She asked. Matthew stood up, and said to Dan, "I'm going to go take a nap." Dan barely acknowledged him, just gave a brief nod and resumed his relentless pacing. Matthew carefully closed the door to the bedroom and sat on the bed, pulling the phone out of his pocket so he could look at Ivy. She was no longer in the car, but sitting in her bedroom with her own snack resting on her bed beside her. "Hey." "Hi." She responded with a tired smile. "When did you get back?" He asked. "A few hours ago. I've been on mute for a while, since my siblings were screaming until my neighbor came to bring them to the beach." "I didn't notice." Matthew admitted. "Because you forgot about me?" She asked, her tone light but sad. Matthew dropped his head and didn't answer. He had, in fact, forgotten she was there. "Sorry." He apologized, meeting her eyes. "You were so quiet for so long, and I got caught up in my thoughts." Ivy shrugged and gave a small laugh. "I didn't want to disturb you, in case you were coming up with some way to rescue Rachel and Annika." "All I could mostly think about was how irritating it was to watch Mr. Helmcott pacing for hours straight. I swear he's worn a hole through the carpet all the way to the floor." "I know." Ivy agreed. "I was watching." That simple realization made Matthew feel even worse. "I just keep messing up, don't I? It's so easy to forget you're a human too, with your own thoughts and feelings, when you're so much like an angel. You give and give, and all I do is keep taking without ever giving back." He confessed. Her features softened, and she smiled. "Aw, Matthew, that's really sweet of you. But it's not true. You give in your own way- you risked being kicked out, just so I wouldn't have to be alone here, wondering and wishing I knew what was going on. That means a lot to me." Matthew sighed. "How do you do it?" He asked. "Do what?" "Be so kind, and smart, and understanding, and forgiving, and sweet, and a good listener all the time? Don't you ever get sad, or frustrated, or angry?" "Oh, Matthew. Of course I do." She answered gently. "I just think, is there anything I can do to make whatever I'm not happy with better? And if I can't, then I just ignore it, and let it pass. Most of the time, it's not worth my frustration. Why waste time being unhappy when I can forgive, forget, and be happy again? You think I like cleaning up my sibling's messes? I don't. At all. But then I think, is it worth trying to get them to do it themselves, or can I just put them to bed and do it myself with less time and stress being spent? I made the decision to do it myself, and now, whenever I look back on that day, I don't get mad at my siblings for making me clean up after them again. I'm happy, because I got to spend time with my friend that day. I had more fun with you than I would've had had I tried to get my siblings to do the dirty work themselves, just because I didn't want to have to pick up their mess again. It really comes down to perspective, and once you make a choice, you have to stick with it and make the best out of it. That's why I always seem happy. It's because I made the decision not to be bothered by my surroundings or circumstances, but to do everything in my power to make them better." "You are one of a kind, Ivy Taryn." Matthew whispered. She laughed, but her next words were cut off when the sound of a phone ringing broke through the silence. Their eyes widened simultaneously. "It's not on my end." Ivy whispered. The ringing stopped, and Dan's voice came through the wall. "Hello?

Amelia! Are you okay? That's great, sweetie. Oh, Annika will love that. Yeah... I don't know if she even has her phone. We think... she's been kidnapped." Matthew and Ivy, who had been listening as best they could to this one side of the conversation, were surprised when a shrilly voice exclaimed, "**What? What do you mean, kidnapped?**" "She's been on that survival show, but I called today and they said she's been gone for almost a week." Dan explained. "**Annika?**" "And her friend, Rachel." Dan added. "**And you don't have any idea where they are?**" Amelia asked, sounding panicked. "No. The NIB are looking into it though, trying to find out where they might be." Now she just sounded bewildered. "**The NIB?**" "Yeah." Dan said again. "Is he going to say anything about Mrs. Helmcott?" Ivy whispered to Matthew, who shrugged. "Mmhmm. Ok, bye." Dan hung up. Matthew gave Ivy a confused glance. "I think we missed part of the conversation." She whispered. Suddenly her eyes widened. "Uh oh." "What?" Matthew asked. "I gotta go. Bye!" "Bye?" Matthew said back, but she had already hung up. Feeling more confused than he had before, Matthew repocketed his phone and left the bedroom to find Dan staring out of the window at the glittering, starry sky beyond. "Who was that?" He asked, coming to stand by him. "My daughter. Amelia." Dan answered dismissively. He sounded distracted and tired. "I don't think I've met her." Matthew commented quietly. He'd definitely heard mention of her, but he had no visual picture of another Helmcott girl stored in his mind. "Probably not." Dan agreed. "She was always more of an indoors person." "Why did she call?" When Matthew didn't get an answer, he nudged the man. "Mr. Helmcott?" "Hmm?" Dan said, startled. "Why did she call?" "Oh. Um, she wanted to tell me she's coming to stay for Annika's birthday." "That's nice." Matthew noted. Side-eyeing Dan, he added, "Why didn't you tell her about Mrs. Helmcott?" Dan shrugged, shifting to avoid Matthew's gaze. "She was already worried about her sister. Why add the possibility her mom might be alive to her already overflowing plate?" It took Matthew a moment to catch the meaning behind the older man's words. "You think she might not be alive after all?" Dan's jaw clenched, and when he turned to face Matthew, there were small tears in the corners of his eyes. "Matthew, I don't know what to think! We have no way of knowing how updated those files are, or if the information on them is accurate. All I know is that ever since Louisa joined the SIA, they've been surreptitiously tearing my family apart, and now I don't even know if half my family is dead or not!" A shudder ran through Matthew. Did Mr. Helmcott think Annika was... dead? That was impossible. Annika couldn't... How could Mr. Helmcott even consider that? Dan's phone chimed with a text, but he didn't move to answer it. Matthew stepped towards it and picked it up, reading the text with increasing surprise. "Mr. Helmcott! It's about Annika!" Dan reacted immediately, snatching the phone out of Matthew's hands and reading it. "Do you remember the directions to Casey Edin's office?" He demanded. "Uh, yeah, it was right, er, no, left-" "Matthew!" "I remember! It was left, left, straight past two hallways, right, left, third door on the left." Matthew recalled, though his brain was scrambling to compensate for Dan's hasty departure as he tore out of the room, racing down the hall out of sight. Matthew was left standing there, bewildered, his mind repeating the text message over and over, until he realized he needed to catch up to Mr. Helmcott, and dashed out of the room after him, but Dan was nowhere in sight along the hall. Matthew ran, following the instructions he had given Dan, and crashed straight into Kevin, who was coming down the hallway towards him. Kevin stumbled, catching Matthew's arms to stop him from falling to the floor, and hauled him back into a standing position. "Whoa, hey, where you going?" Kevin asked. The weird look he was giving Matthew was enough to remind him he was panting, so he quickly stopped, and explained, "Mr. Helmcott got a text, about Annika! He's gone to tell Mrs. Edins." "*Director* Edins." Kevin corrected, looking slightly offended. Despite his curiosity about the message, he glanced at Matthew's pocket, and said, "I see you aren't in your video call with Ivy anymore." Matthew froze. There was no way he knew... "What are you talking about?" Matthew asked nervously. Kevin flashed him a knowing smile. "I can't expect she got much of a view from down there, but I'm sure it was enough to feel included." Dropping all pretenses, Matthew asked, "How did you know?" No, wait.

That sounded lame. "Why didn't you tell?" Matthew could tell his second question was much more satisfactory to Kevin. "Because bros don't snitch on each other." He answered, holding out his hand for a fist bump. "You're awesome." Matthew told him, completing the fist bump. Kevin grinned. "I try." He agreed. "Come on." "Where are we going?" Matthew asked, as Kevin walked over to a door and flung it open. "Back to Casey's office. This is a shortcut." "You're joking!" Matthew gaped. "We could have taken this the entire time?" When Kevin nodded his confirmation, Matthew cried, "Then why didn't we take it the first time?" "Cause good agents never take the same path twice in the same week, to avoid being followed." He answered indignantly, walking through the doorway into a narrow stretch of hallway. "That is so lame." Matthew muttered, following him. They emerged right next to Dan, who was coming from the right. He stared at them in disbelief. "You're joking. That doorway was there the entire time?" "That's what I said!" Matthew agreed, throwing his hands up for emphasis. "You got a message from Annika?" Kevin asked urgently. "Yes. No! It's not from her, even though it's her number." Dan tried to explain as he rapped on Casey's office door. Kevin pushed past him and swung it open, yelling, "Casey, it's me. We got word on Annika." Casey wasn't alone; two people, one guy and one girl, were having a heated discussion with Casey when Kevin, Dan, and Matthew barged in. Matthew was alarmed to notice the girl was the same one he'd seen downstairs, in the jumpsuit. She glared at him as she cut off her conversation. Kevin froze midstep. "Sorry, is this bad timing?" He asked. Casey gave him a wry smile. "Just because you don't knock, Kevin, doesn't mean you shouldn't." "Mr. Helmcott did it for me." He answered dismissively. Glancing at the other two agents, he asked, "What's going on?" "Nothing that concerns you." The girl agent answered in a haughty voice. "Not nice!" Kevin objected angrily. "I'm practically Casey's right hand! I have every right to know what's going on." "Key word in that sentence was 'practically'." The girl snapped. "You're no more special than the rest of us, but you act like you are!" Before Kevin could make an angry retort back, Casey was holding her hands up for them to stop. "That's *quite* enough."

She said severely. Turning to the two agents who had been in here before Kevin had burst in, she calmly said, "I'll be looking into it. You'll receive your orders within 18 hours." The girl nodded curtly, and shoved past Matthew out of the room. Matthew hastily scooted out of the way when the other agent followed, who flashed Matthew an apologetic smile for his comrade's rude behavior. As soon as the door closed behind them, Kevin whirled on Casey. "How dare she talk to me like that? She thinks she's something special-" "Like you do?" Casey asked calmly, interrupting his rage. "She's just jealous." Kevin complained. He looked angrier than Matthew had ever seen him, and it scared him a bit. Was this really the same laughing person from a few minutes ago? "Belle is just upset with the way you act like you run the place. No, don't give me that look. She's quite correct. You do overstep your boundaries sometimes, and while I've been tolerant for the time being, it's making the other agents think I'm favoring you, and that's what leads to a mutiny. Anyway, what we were talking about really wasn't any of your business. You said you got word on Annika?" She asked, signaling the end of their argument. Kevin looked like he was trying to contain his anger and didn't answer, so Dan stepped forwards. "Yes. It's Annika's number, but it says that Annika is being held in custody and that I have three days to come get her, or they reserve the right to hold her forever, like they did with my wife. It's signed by the SIA." "Did they say where she is?" Casey asked hopefully. Dan shook his head despairingly. "How am I supposed to get her if I don't know where they're holding her?" "Well, our search radius has narrowed a bit. My agents positioned at the Benewald Airport reported that five days ago, a girl with long red hair and a girl with long blonde hair had prebought tickets and boarded a private airplane they identified as SIA style." "Where did it go?" Matthew asked, hardly daring to breathe. "Paris, France." Was Casey's response. "They weren't being forced? Or with anybody?" Dan double-checked. Casey shook her head sadly. "They were alone, and boarded of their own will. The good news is we can start sending search patrols right away." "How many?" Kevin asked. He had lost the angry look, and instead looked excited at the thought of getting to raid an SIA base. "Not a lot.

We're not going to seize a base. We're just going to rescue the girls. Hopefully, it will be done peacefully. We can't afford to lose any more agents right now. Besides, soon enough we'll be rescuing all the agents in the labor prisons. No point putting them on their guard now. I'll send out three jets; we'll figure out what to do once you're there. The three leaders of the search parties will be you, Agent Murow, and Agent Ranning." Casey told him. Kevin groaned. "Why does Belle have to come? She hates me!" "Because she is a good agent." Casey responded firmly. "Of course, if you prefer, I could always have another agent go in your place-" "No, that's okay. I'll go." Kevin interrupted hastily. Casey nodded. "The jets are waiting in Hangar 3. I will inform Murow and Ranning of their mission." She waited for them to leave, and as soon as they did, she broadcasted a message over all the speakers. "Agents Murow and Ranning, report to my office for a mission briefing."

Kevin led the way to a heavy steel door with reinforced glass in its windows. He entered a code into the keypad, then swung it open and walked out into thin air. A split second later, Matthew realized Kevin was standing in one of the enclosed glass bridges that connected the buildings. It was dark, with only the stars and the moon lighting the pathways. As soon as Kevin got four feet in, a long row of bright fluorescent lights kicked on. Kevin started across as carelessly as if he was simply walking on the ground. No other agent on any of the bridges looked scared either, and certainly none of them were crossing the way Matthew was, nervously keeping his hand on the wall as he slid his way across, trying not to look down. It was one thing to be climbing a rope forty feet off the ground; it was quite another to be several *hundred* feet off the ground in a glass tube. It must have been annoying Dan, for he leaned down and whispered into Matthew's ear. "I wonder what Ivy would think if she saw you moving this slowly." What did he mean by that? Ivy was terrified of heights. She'd probably refuse, and take the long way just to avoid having to take these bridges. Of course, if that happened, Matthew would kindly volunteer to use his photographic memory to guide her to their destination without using the bridges, effectively keeping him from having to cross them too. Still, Matthew sped up, trying to keep a neutral expression on his face as he followed Kevin. He could have collapsed with relief when Kevin opened the door at the end of the bridge. Once Dan was inside, Kevin closed the door, and jogged over to the elevator. When the doors slid open, he was greeted with Belle's scowling face. Beside her was the agent she had been with when she was talking to Casey earlier. He offered them a smile as Kevin, Matthew, and Dan squeezed into the elevator with them. Only Matthew returned it; Dan was preoccupied on his phone, and Kevin's taut, angry face had returned, as he jabbed the button for the top floor. They rode in an uncomfortable silence, and Matthew was almost surprised there was no pushing to get out when the doors slid open. Kevin exited first, leading the way to another steel door. Matthew could feel his apprehension growing. Not another bridge! It was another bridge, and Matthew was forced to follow Kevin out onto it, with Belle following so closely behind, it was like she was pushing him forward. "What's the matter?" She hissed. "You're not scared, are you?" "Of course not." Matthew shot back, lying through his teeth. He forced himself to go faster, wishing Belle wasn't behind him. When he emerged back into the NIB headquarters, he whispered to Kevin, "There's no more of those, right?" Kevin laughed. "That was the last one." He promised. He led the way into yet another elevator, and hit the button for the top floor when everyone was inside. "Kevin." The man agent said suddenly. "I don't believe you've introduced us to your friends." Kevin grinned. "Sorry. I forgot. Rich, these are my friends Dan Helmcott and Matthew." Now speaking to Dan and Matthew, he added, "Mr. Helmcott, Matthew, this is Richard Ranning, and Belle Murow." "It's a pleasure to meet you." Rich said cheerfully. Belle merely rolled her eyes and looked away. The elevator doors opened to a noisy rooftop, well-lit with floodlights illuminating a helicopter pad and two jet runways. A third jet hovered in the air, doing its best to maintain its position in the strong wind that had once again picked up. Two other agents were seated in one of the planes on the runway, and Rich dashed over to it and climbed in. Belle sprinted for the jet hovering, her long ponytail swinging behind her as she jumped, grasped the rope they had lowered, and pulled herself inside. It flew away immediately. Kevin, Matthew, and Dan headed for the last remaining jet and boarded quickly. Moments later, they too were in the air and following the other two jets. As it was a long flight to Paris, the trio took the chance to sleep and eat, knowing it might be their last for a while.

The jets finally landed around ten in the morning, dropping them off in an empty field before lifting off again and flying away. Kevin, Matthew, and Dan were left standing with Belle, Rich, and four other agents on the stretch of grass. "We have to find some way to contact the SIA, let them know we're here." Kevin told Dan and Matthew. "We were specifically told not to storm the base, but I don't know how we will convince them to give up Annika and Rachel without a fight." "We should start with talking to Elle." Belle suggested, glancing at Kevin. It seemed, for the time being, they had called a truce, for neither had looks of malice. "Good idea." Kevin agreed. "Not all of us should go." Rich interrupted. "Nine people is too many for one questioning." "How about I go to Elle's house, Kevin can go search the cities hotels to see if they checked in anywhere before they were kidnapped, and Richard can start trying to locate the SIA base. Then, we can meet up tonight to try to piece together what happened to the girls." Belle proposed. Kevin shrugged. "Works for me." When Rich also nodded his confirmation, Belle clapped her hands. "All right then. I'll notify you guys when it's time to meet up." Beckoning to the agents she had arrived with, she walked away, heading towards the central part of Paris. Rich split ways too, and Kevin, Dan, and Matthew were left standing alone in the middle of the field. Dan pulled his phone out immediately. "There's 63 hotels in Paris." He reported. "The nearest one is a six-mile walk." "Then we walk." Kevin said firmly. They trudged along the grass for what seemed like hours, until they finally entered the city of Paris. Kevin hailed a taxi immediately, ordering the driver to go to the nearest hotel, and when they arrived, to wait for them outside. Every time they pulled to a stop, one of them would run in to ask if anyone named Annika Helmcott or Rachel Ravenstone had checked in; after two dozen of these, they started asking if anyone remembered a girl with long, bright red hair checking in. It wasn't until their 40th stop that someone was helpful. A girl at the front counter did happen to remember seeing a young teen with long red hair, who was accompanied by a blonde teen. When she checked the register for them, she found the name Annika H. under the room registration. "When did they check out?" Kevin asked her. "Two days ago." She answered. Kevin secured the room for them, and after running out to tell their driver he could leave now, they settled into the room, with Matthew making dinner while Kevin and Dan searched the room for anything that might have been left by Annika or Rachel. There was nothing, and the room had been spotlessly cleaned by a maid. When dusk fell, Belle and Rich joined them, while the other agents stayed in a different room Belle had secured for them. "Elle said they came to visit her three days ago, but that she met them five days ago." Belle informed them as they ate. "She admitted to showing Annika her invention, then overheard Annika telling Rachel she was going to tell the SIA the next day. She said she got Annika to promise not to tell them, but there's honestly no way of knowing if they know about it or not now." "I'm so sorry." Dan apologized. "I should've done something to prevent this..." "There's nothing we can do now." Belle said briskly, almost kindly. "But that's not the only thing Annika did. I asked Elle why she showed Annika her invention in the first place, and she said it just seemed like a good idea at the time. When I tried to get more details, she said Annika brought some berries to eat while they hung out." Dan's brow furrowed in confusion. "What does that have to do with anything?" He asked. Belle sighed. "The type of berries Annika brought looked like blackberries, but under closer inspection I found out they were actually *Rubus veridicus*. Better known as Rozenberries. In essence, Annika drugged Elle to get the secret out of her." She explained. "Annika would never do that." Matthew objected, feeling sick. Belle gave him a look. "Well, she did. I don't know where she even got them. They're illegal." "That doesn't seem like the Annika I knew before she left for that game show." Dan answered grimly. "But you can bet I'll be asking her when we find her." That seemed to remind everyone of the priority they were supposed to be focusing on. Turning to Rich, Belle asked, "Did you find anything on your search?" He shook his head. "I wasn't really sure what I was supposed to be searching for, to tell the truth. They were obviously well hidden." "Well, we found out they left here two days ago. So, if Elle met them five days ago, and last saw them three days ago, it sounds like the timeline is they left the survival place, came here, checked in, met Elle, hung out with her for a few days, checked out, and never heard from since." Kevin pieced together. "If Mr. Helmcott only got the message from the SIA saying they have Annika and Rachel yesterday, where have they been those other two days?" Matthew asked, finding the irregularity in the timeline. "Don't the SIA have some sort of rule for questioning?" Rich asked. "What do you mean?" Dan asked worriedly. Questioning? Like what they put Louisa through? Rich shrugged. "I don't know. I just thought I remembered hearing something about how if SIA agents only arrest for questioning, they can only hold them for a few days before they have to alert a guardian or friend of the arrested to go get them. It sounds to me like that's what they did to Annika. If they're alerting you now, and it's been three days, there's a possibility Annika hasn't yet told them what they want to know." He theorized. Belle suddenly looked hopeful, as did Kevin. "You think Annika may not have told Makrus what Elle is creating?" Kevin confirmed. "Annika's always been stubborn." Dan agreed. "She certainly might have had the willpower to avoid telling him, if she really intended to keep her promise to Elle." "So what do we do now?" Belle asked. When no one answered, she threw her hands up in irritation. "It just occurred to me that I don't even know what Annika looks like." "I can show you a picture." Matthew offered. When she nodded, he pulled out his phone. Matthew had been intending to show her one of the photos he'd taken on his phone, but instead went to his search bar and typed in the name *Annika Helmcott*. He had hoped to find a picture of Annika jumping between rooftops, but instead found posted pictures from the *Survival Race!* race. "Huh. Look at that." He mused aloud. "People have already started posting pictures from the survival race. Here's some of Annika." He added, turning the phone so Belle could see. It was Annika, moving through the forest, her long red braid flying behind her, her face locked in an intense expression. Belle, however, noticed something different as she looked through all the posted pictures of Annika on the race. "Wait." She said suddenly, plucking the phone out of Matthew's hand in one smooth motion to study the pictures closer. "Hey." He complained, but didn't have a chance to say more. As soon as Belle showed the picture to Kevin, he gasped aloud. "No way! She's wearing a tracker!" "What?" Dan cried, jumping to his feet to look at the screen. "What do you mean?" "See that jeweled hairtie securing her braid?" Belle asked, allowing Dan and Matthew to see. "The NIB special ordered raindrop-shaped sapphire trackers from a company that makes trackers for children so parents won't lose them. We're the only ones to have that style. How on earth did Annika get one?" She asked, staring at the photo. Dan's eyes widened. "I gave it to her!" He blurted. "It used to be Louisa's-" He cut himself off as he realized what he had just said. "It used to be Louisa's." He repeated. "She wore it all the time. I never even considered it was anything more than her good-luck charm." "Do you guys have them too?" Matthew asked curiously. They nodded. Belle wore hers as a small gold pinky ring studded with the sapphire raindrop. Rich wore his imbedded on a stylish watch, and Kevin's was attached to his belt. "Now all we need to do is have Matthew hack into the tracking system, and we'll be able to find Annika!" Kevin cheered excitedly. Matthew found himself smiling too, until he realized the implication of Kevin's words. "Me?" He cried in disbelief. "Of course. You hacked into Makrus's computer. Surely you can hack into this!" Kevin replied. Noticing the look on Matthew's face, he added, "You can do this, can't you?" "Well, I can try." Matthew sighed. Eight minutes later, he had successfully hacked into the hotel's computer, and was viewing all the trackers. "There's 37 million trackers worldwide, but if I don't count all the ones in the NIB headquarters, and all the ones in the company's storage space, we have about 33 million left. Any one of them could be Annika." Matthew said, moving his mouse around the screen. "The good news is, if I change the search to only include trackers in Paris, that gives me... fifteen. No, hold on. I just realized it's not excluding all of yours." With a few clicks of the mouse, almost all the tiny little dots on the screen disappeared, including all the ones in the hotel they now stood in. Only eight trackers remained. "So now we just visit all eight trackers to find which one is Annika?" Rich asked hopefully. "Nope!" Matthew said. "This is showing where they all are now. If I change the time to six days ago exactly, there's only one dot that entered this hotel." "That doesn't entirely signal it's Annika." Belle argued. "Of course not." Matthew agreed. "So here's how I'm gonna check. If I isolate just this tracker, I can move it back in time to the evening of six days ago. It arrived in Benewald Airport. From there, it went to this place..." Matthew trailed off, squinting at the screen. "What is that place?" "It's just a business or office. I walked past it while trying to scan the streets for any sign of SIA interference." Rich piped up helpfully. "Ok, so she went there. Then, she went to a clothing store, and to this hotel, then to a restaurant, and back to the hotel. The next day she left once to go to a bakery, and the day after she went to this house and stayed there all day before finally going back to the hotel with a different route." Matthew continued. "That's Elle's house!" Belle cried excitedly. "Okay." Matthew agreed, though he wished he knew more about this 'Elle' person that everyone seemed fixated on. "The next morning, she went directly back to that office building... and never came back out." Matthew finished proudly. "We found Annika." Kevin whispered. He was too overwhelmed to say much more. "You did it, Matthew!" Dan cheered, excitedly squeezing the boy's shoulders. Turning to face the agents, he added, "Can we leave now?" Kevin shook his head. "We'll go first thing tomorrow morning." "Why not now?" Dan pushed. "If the SIA's front is a business, they'll be 'closed' until tomorrow morning. If we try to visit now, it could alert them to the fact that we know where Annika is, and they might try to move her." "But Matthew knows which tracker is hers." Dan argued. "But if they move her in the middle of the night, and tomorrow is your last day to retrieve her, we could end up missing their deadline, and you'd never see her again. It's better to play it safe." Kevin reasoned. "Fine." Dan agreed, sounding tired. "We'll do it tomorrow." "Me and Belle will go back to Headquarters to inform Director Edins about our progress." Rich said. "You're not coming with us?" Matthew asked in surprise. Belle shook her head. "We were specifically told to find Annika, not to retrieve her. Director Edins doesn't want to give the SIA any impression that we plan to seize the base." "Are you planning to seize the base?" Dan asked. "That's up to the Director." Belle replied, heading for the door. Rich followed, and the two exited, shutting the door behind them. "I claim the couch!" Kevin called, plopping down onto the couch opposite Matthew and pulling a deck of cards from a hidden pocket in his sweater. "You can have the bed, Matthew." Dan said absently. "No thanks, I want the couch." Matthew declared as Kevin delt him a hand so they could play Garbage. Dan rolled his eyes but didn't protest, retreating silently into the bedroom for the rest of the night. Kevin proceeded to cream Matthew in several rounds of Garbage before calling it a night and laying down to sleep. Matthew found he had trouble sleeping, as he stared at the tiny, unmoving dot on the computer screen. Though no one had mentioned it, he hoped Rachel was with Annika. Rachel didn't have a tracker, and if they had split up, it was likely they would never find her. Everyone was assuming they were together, and Matthew dearly hoped they were right...

CHAPTER 13

Matthew was awoken by the sound of eggs frying the next morning. Sitting up blearily, he found Dan in the kitchen, cooking breakfast. Kevin was already awake, and was reading a book on the couch. "Morning, Matthew!" Dan called cheerfully. "We're leaving soon, so make sure you're ready to go." Glancing at the clock, Matthew's eyes widened. "It's only seven in the morning!" He protested sleepily. "And their fake business front opens at eight." Dan replied, bringing two plates over for Kevin and Matthew. Matthew's phone chimed, and he grew more alert with every word he read. "Mr. Helmcott? My parents want to know where I am." "Ignore it." Dan said calmly. "I'll explain everything to them when we get back home." "Everything?" Kevin asked, looking concerned. "Everything." Dan confirmed. "And not just Matthew's parents. Ivy's and Rachel's parents all deserve an explanation as to why their children have been gone for so long, and been acting so strangely." "Doesn't sound like a fun conversation." Kevin commented. "That's why you'll be with me." Dan added pointedly. They locked eyes, and after a moment, Kevin conceded. "Fine. But let's focus on getting Annika back first." "And Rachel." Matthew added, releasing the computer from its hacked state so it could go back to normal. Half an hour later, they were in a taxi, heading for the SIA's base. When they pulled up, a white brick building was there to greet them, looking cheery with its blue shutters, and the hedges growing around it. "This is the place." Matthew confirmed. They climbed out, and Dan approached the door, preparing to give it a solid knock. Kevin and Matthew clustered behind him. Before he did, a teenage girl barreled out of the bushes into Kevin's arms. "Kevin!" She gasped. "I'm so glad you're here!" Her wavy blonde hair fell into her eyes, and she backed up to brush it out of the way.

"Bethany?" Kevin said in surprise. "What are you doing here?" "Trying to find you. I found out Annika was heading to Paris, and I was worried about Elle, so I came here immediately. I've been trying to get ahold of Headquarters for days!" Bethany explained breathlessly, her deep blue eyes twinkling. "Annika's wearing an NIB tracker!" She added. "Yeah, we know. That's how we found her." Kevin replied, overcoming his surprise. "How do you know Annika?" Dan asked curiously. "We were on the *Survival Race!* show together." Bethany explained. "I had to melt down my medal to pay to get here." She added mournfully. "But now you're here. You can help me rescue Annika and Rachel!" Dan nodded, deciding to take this random turn of events in stride, and rapped on the door. It swung open, and a black suited man stared out at them curiously. "I'm here to speak to Makrus." Dan demanded. The man's eyes flitted over the group, and when they landed on Kevin and Bethany, his eyes widened slightly, recognizing them as NIB agents. "Wait here." The man ordered, shutting the door in their faces. A minute later, it opened again. "He is ready to speak with you." The man said, waving them inside. He led them down a hallway, to a door, and swung it open, ushering them inside. A man sat behind a desk, and Kevin recognized him instantly. It was Makrus, and a slight sneer developed when he realized there were NIB agents in his office. "You two are the ones that broke into my office." Makrus observed calmly, speaking to Kevin and Matthew. Kevin's scowl didn't change, but the young boys' eyes widened considerably. His naivety brought a small smile to Makrus's face. The child didn't seriously think he wouldn't know what was happening in his own mansion. Makrus turned to Dan with a sudden realization. "And I suppose it was you who broke through my locks?" Dan didn't answer, but the uncomfortable look on his face was enough to tell Makrus everything he wanted to know. "You're a traitor." He hissed angrily. "Your whole family is a bunch of traitors." Dan's eyes flashed as he struggled to stay calm, but Makrus had already moved on. "And you, young lady. I don't think I know you." He told Bethany, who glared back. "And it's going to stay that way." She replied sassily. For a moment, they all stared at each other menacingly, before Dan finally spoke up. "I want my daughter back." He demanded, stepping forward threateningly. When Matthew elbowed him, he added, "And her friend." Without breaking eye contact, Makrus pressed a button on his desk, and spoke quietly in French. Matthew and Dan didn't know what he said, but a small smile crossed Kevin's face. *Bring the girls into my office.* A few moments later, a section of the floor began sliding away, pulling into the wall. Two guards emerged, each hauling a disheveled girl up the stairs that had been hidden. Annika looked horrible. Her wrists and face were bruised, and a heavy cast was on her leg. Her long hair was matted and greasy, but the sapphire tracker was still secured in her hair, and there was a thin metal bracelet secured on her wrist. The guard holding her pulled out a key and unlocked the bracelet, letting it fall to the floor. Rachel didn't look like she'd been physically harmed, but she too was ragged-looking. When she saw Matthew, she looked so relieved she almost burst into tears. It took Annika longer to realize she was being rescued, but when she finally found the strength to lift her head, she found her father, best friend, a friend she'd never thought she would see again, and a stranger waiting in the room. "Dad!" She rasped. At a jerk of Makrus's head, the guards released the girls and shoved them across the room. Rachel stumbled, falling into Matthew and hugging him tightly. Dan had to dash forward to catch Annika, as she tripped over the cast when she was pushed. He picked her up, ignoring her faint protests, and glared at Makrus with undisguised hatred. "What did you do to my daughter?" "Your daughter is a traitor and will never again be recognized as an SIA agent." Makrus replied. "Be warned. I am not yet done with your family, Helmcott. Now leave." Dan didn't have to be asked twice, and the six of them quickly retreated out of the building, got in their rented Cybertruck, and drove away. "Are you okay?" Matthew asked Rachel as he and Bethany helped her into the car. "I'll be fine." She promised. "They never hurt me, but I never got to see Annika. Is she alright?" Dan was already trying to figure that out. "Oh, Annika." He whispered. "What did he do to you?" Annika ignored him. "Dad, I think mom's alive!" She told him urgently. "I think he captured her!" "I know." Dan assured her. "I know where she is." Annika stared at him, fearing the worst.

Had her dad known all along and gone with it? How else could he know? "We broke into Makrus's mansion and stole the files containing your mom's whereabouts." He told her. "But how did you know she was alive?" Annika demanded. Holding her gaze, Dan said, "I *promise* I will explain everything when we get back home tonight." Satisfied for the time being, Annika turned to Bethany and Matthew. "What are you doing here?" She asked, bewildered. "We came to rescue you." Bethany replied gently. "But-" "I'm with the NIB." Bethany explained. "So is Eliza." "How did I never even suspect that?" Annika asked, looking disappointed with herself. Bethany shrugged, but Matthew had a bigger question. "What happened to your leg?" He asked her as the car left Paris. "Makrus broke it." She answered grimly. "I knocked him off his feet, and he lashed out with his leg. Thankfully, the bone that broke doesn't take long to heal. I'll be fine in a month or so." "Annika." Dan said suddenly, twisting in his seat to make eye contact with her. "Where did you get the berries you gave Elle?" Annika gave him a startled look. "How do you know about that?" "Answer the question." He ordered. "I-I bought them off the street." Annika answered cautiously. "Where?" Rachel asked, her confusion evident. "I explored the entire city that day I went shopping. There weren't any Rozenberry vendors." "It was a small cart on the outskirts of the city. The lady who sold them to me said they made people say things without considering the consequences. I thought that was perfect, so I bought a container." She explained. Bethany shook her head with a sigh. "At least she's resourceful." Kevin muttered to her. After that, everyone in the car lapsed into silence, and they stopped only to get food for Annika, Rachel, and Bethany, who hadn't eaten yet. They arrived at Dan's home late that night with the private NIB plane Kevin borrowed, just as the sun was setting, and while Annika and Rachel showered, Matthew and Dan called the Ravenstone's, Taryn's, and Carimella's, telling them to come to the Helmcott Household right away. When they arrived, thankfully without Ivy's younger siblings, they all sat down in the living room, and Dan began explaining. Fourteen people watched him, waiting for the answers to the questions they were all thinking. "Almost five years ago, the SIA burst into my home and dragged Louisa away." Dan began. "She begged me to go along with the story they created that she died. She didn't want anyone, especially Annika, trying to rescue her because she was afraid the SIA would tear apart more families that way. I went along with it to honor her, and in time began to believe it myself. After Annika and Rachel left to the *Survival Race!* studio, Matthew heard some interesting information about Louisa, and became convinced her death was fake. He did a lot of research, and even went to visit a doctor who was on the scene when Louisa's death was faked." At that, Caroline inhaled sharply as she stared at her son. So it had never been about becoming a doctor after all? Dan wasn't finished. "He confided in Ivy, and she advised him to come to me, so he did. He showed me a text he had gotten from a mysterious stranger, offering more information about Louisa. The text told him to bring a trusted adult, and he asked me to come with him. As it happened, there was a meteor shower that night, and that was the excuse he used to escape that night so we could meet with the stranger. That stranger turned out to be Kevin, a man I now trust with my life." Dan gestured to Kevin, who gave a half-smile and a small wave. "He was part of the NIB, and had noticed Matthew's interest concerning Louisa. He wanted to reach out and ask for help in recovering files of Louisa's whereabouts, located in the SIA director's mansion. So, for the next few weeks, I moved temporarily into Matthew's house, under the pretense that I was lonely in my big house by myself. We collaborated secretly with Kevin for a few weeks, disguising our plans to break into the mansion with star charts. Matthew also created a program that could instantly hack into any locked computer. Finally, on the day the mansion was open to the public, we snuck in, with me disabling the locks on the back gate and the lock to the courtyard door. I had to stay there to make sure they could get back out, and Matthew, Kevin, and Ivy went on ahead. Finally, Kevin and Matthew jumped out the fifth-floor window onto a self-inflating air mat Matthew had activated and thrown out the window. Ivy was not with them. Matthew's program had worked and they had the files we needed, but Ivy had been caught by some guards, so she played innocent and met us out by the front gates, and we drove here. We viewed the files, and discovered Louisa is in an SIA labor camp in Mexico. It was then that Ivy brought up the fact that Annika and Rachel should have been home days ago, and when I called the *Survival Race!* studio, a woman informed me they left almost a week ago. Kevin had the NIB send us a helicopter, and he and Matthew accompanied me to the NIB Headquarters. I sent Ivy home, since I knew her parents would be worried about her if she didn't come home." Dan sent Ivy an apologetic look, and she smiled and shrugged, side-eying Matthew with a twinkle in her eye. Dan didn't seem to notice, and he continued with his story. "Kevin introduced us to the NIB director, and she agreed to help me find the girls. Hours later, I received a text from the SIA, from Annika's number, saying they had her and I had three days to get her or they reserved the right to keep her forever, like they did with Louisa. They didn't tell me where she was. By then, the NIB director had discovered Annika and Rachel had entered Benewald Airport and boarded a private SIA plane headed to Paris, of their own will." At that, Rachel blushed. She had been foolish in doing that, when her parents had been trusting her to come straight home. Now they looked at her as if she had deeply betrayed them, and in a way she had. Even Isabelle sniffled a bit, but Maddie looked just as quietly hurt as her parents. Dan still wasn't done. "The director gave us three jets and seven NIB agents, including Kevin, to aid in our search. The next morning, we arrived in Paris and began our search. We found the hotel the girls had stayed at, and one of the NIB agents was able to identify a special tracker I had accidentally given Annika from seeing some recently posted pictures of her during the survival race." Annika's eyes widened in surprise. "I was wearing a tracker?" She whispered to Bethany, who nodded. "It's NIB style. I wear mine as a pendant, and Eliza wears hers as earrings. When we saw you had a tracker on your ponytail, we realized something was up with you, and kept our eye on you while at the *Survival Race!* studio." She whisper-explained. Dan wasn't done explaining, and he shot her a *shh* look before continuing his story. "Matthew hacked into the hotel's computer, and was able to locate Annika. The next morning, we went to the SIA's base, where they had Annika and Rachel, and met up with another NIB agent, who had known Annika from the *Survival Race!* show. We rescued them, and brought them back here. You all deserved an explanation for the deception we all took part in, and I want to apologize for deceiving you. I understand I put Matthew and Ivy in danger, and Annika put Rachel in danger when she allowed her to accompany her to Paris. I took every precaution to keep them safe, and the only person with any lasting damage is Annika, until her leg heals. I know now that I am safe to try to get Louisa back, since Makrus broke his promise to stay away from my family. I will be relentlessly pursuing her until my family is whole again, but I know I could never have gotten this far without Matthew, Kevin, and Ivy's help. If Matthew had never gotten 'bored' this summer, I would never have tried to get Louisa back, and we would have lost Annika and Rachel to the same organization that took my wife. I understand if you decide you want nothing to do with me after this. I have no problem continuing alone." Dan said, both determined and sad. For a moment, everyone in the room stared at each other; then Matthew spoke up. "I'm with you to the end, Mr. Helmcott. We'll get her back, no matter what." He vowed. His mom stared at him in disbelief, but Ben slowly nodded. "I trust you with my son." He told Dan simply. "You have the full support of the NIB." Kevin added. Bethany nodded eagerly in agreement. "Mine too." Ivy added, placing an arm around Annika's shoulders. "I'll never leave you." "We're with you, no matter what happens." Rachel agreed, avoiding her parents conflicted gaze. Ivy's mother was the next to speak. "We'll help you, Dan. However we can." In the fading light, surrounded by the promises from friends, Dan felt overcome with emotion. "Thank you." He choked out. Here were people who truly cared. Why had he ever thought he had to be alone in his sorrow? Surrounded by people who were devoted to helping, Dan felt truly happy. The solemness broke, and some of the adults headed to the kitchen to talk and cook dinner, since no one had had the chance to eat that night. Kevin stayed in the living room, his face growing grim as he watched something on his phone. "Look at this." He sighed, showing Dan the video playing. "This was live in Paris." The video showed the building they had been in, the one housing the SIA complex, disintegrating into dust.

The reporter was talking really fast, describing how the building had just disappeared, vaporized, leaving no rubble. Kevin clicked the phone off. "They don't want the NIB going in and taking it, so they ruined it." He explained. Dan shrugged. "Does it matter to us?" Kevin grinned and shook his head, and the two went to join the others in the kitchen. They were all home, together, and that was what truly mattered.

ACKNOWLEDGEMENTS

First off, all the thanks to my mom and dad. Without their love, support, guidance, research help, and late-night editing by the computer with a snack, this would never have evolved beyond a simple dream, and would have been lost forever in my crazily cluttered mind. They helped shape my idea into a beautiful story that never would have happened had I not been told I had to write a novel for school, and been told I had to learn how to type without looking at my hands. I likely also would have quit had they not been there every step of the way to keep me going forwards.

My family probably also deserves some recognition for dealing with me patiently every time I asked them a random question from out of nowhere about what a character should look like, or what a good, one-time use name would be. Even though most of their answers were, "I don't know." It still helped me get my own ideas into order. Kailey Wood, thanks for suggesting Kevin should have green hair! (Which sparked the idea for Kevin's iconic green eyes.) ☺ Totally made my day.

Grandma Rosanne, thank you so much for bothering to teach me proper grammar and double-spacing years ago. I might have thought it was tiresome then, but it helped my writing not have as many mistakes I had to correct later on, which *seriously* speeds up the editing process.

Michaelbrent Collings, thank you for making your Bestseller Life writing courses. By watching them and applying what I learned there, my novel is so much better than it used to be, which would not have happened had you not taken the time to sit down and make a course to help budding authors along.

Thanks to my girl-squad editors and beta readers: Tonya Parker, Josalyn Mulanax, Brooke Harter, and Elizabeth Scott. Without each of your valued opinions and input, this book would not have been as fantastic as it is, and there would have been a whole lot of weird, random stuff I hadn't fully thought through. I think we all know what I'm talking about...

A huge thank you to my amazing book cover creator, Sheri S. The cover truly is a work of art.

MEET THE AUTHOR

Kanine Parker is a teen author who has been reading and writing as long as she can remember. She loves gymnastics, acting, and anything Star Trek, outer space, or aliens. She lives in Idaho with her family. This is her debut novel.

www.ingramcontent.com/pod-product-compliance
Lightning Source LLC
LaVergne TN
LVHW041709070526
838199LV00045B/1275